"With a host of quirky friends and family members, Abby Collette's new series is a welcome addition to the cozy mystery scene, and life at Crewse Creamery promises plenty of delectable adventures to come. Only one warning: *A Deadly Inside Scoop* causes a deep yearning for scoops of homemade ice cream, no matter the weather."

—Juliet Blackwell, *New York Times* bestselling author of the Haunted Home Renovation series and the Witchcraft Mystery series

"What do you get when you put together a tight-knit, slightly quirky family, a delectable collection of ice cream flavors, and an original mystery? A tasty start to a new cozy series. *A Deadly Inside Scoop* is a cleverly crafted mystery with a relatable main character in Bronwyn Crewse."

—*New York Times* bestselling author Sofie Kelly

"Cozy readers will look forward to the further adventures of Win and friends."   —*Publishers Weekly*

"This cozy mystery will leave you with a pleasant feeling when you read it, as you cannot help but love the characters, [who] will steal your heart."   —Fresh Fiction

"This setting is extremely appealing and the characters introduced are entertaining and memorable. . . . A promising start to a new series that will appeal to fans of foodie fiction."

—Genre Minx Reviews

Praise for Abby Collette's
Ice Cream Parlor Mysteries

"Delightful. . . . Bronwyn is ever more confident about rooting herself in her community. Chagrin Falls turns out to be an entrancing place to spend time."   —*The New York Times*

"Fun! Fresh! Fabulous! Abby Collette has crafted a delicious addition to the cozy mystery world with her superbly written *A Deadly Inside Scoop*. Delightful characters and a puzzler of a plot kept me turning pages until the very end. I can't wait for my next visit to the Crewse Creamery for another decadent taste."

—*New York Times* bestselling author Jenn McKinlay

"A deliciously satisfying new cozy mystery series. It's got humor, a quirky cast of characters, and ice cream. What more could you want?"

—V. M. Burns, Agatha Award–nominated author of the

Mystery Bookshop Mystery Series

"With an endearing cast of characters ranging from [Bronwyn's] close-knit, multigenerational family to her feisty best friends, this intricate mystery plays out with plenty of suspects, tons of motives, and an ending I didn't see coming."

—*New York Times* bestselling author Bailey Cates

Berkley Titles by Abby Collette

❦

THE BOOKS & BISCUITS MYSTERIES

Body and Soul Food

THE ICE CREAM PARLOR MYSTERIES

A Deadly Inside Scoop

A Game of Cones

A Killer Sundae

A Killer Sundae

Abby Collette

Berkley Prime Crime
New York

BERKLEY PRIME CRIME
Published by Berkley
An imprint of Penguin Random House LLC
penguinrandomhouse.com

Library of Congress Cataloging-in-Publication Data

Names: Collette, Abby, author.
Title: A killer sundae / Abby Collette.
Description: First Edition. | New York: Berkley Prime Crime, 2022. |
Series: An ice cream parlor mystery; 3
Identifiers: LCCN 2021035097 (print) | LCCN 2021035098 (ebook) |
ISBN 9780593099704 (trade paperback) | ISBN 9780593099711 (ebook)
Subjects: GSAFD: Mystery fiction.
Classification: LCC PS3603.O4397 K55 2022 (print) |
LCC PS3603.O4397 (ebook) | DDC 813/.6—dc23
LC record available at https://lccn.loc.gov/2021035097
LC ebook record available at https://lccn.loc.gov/2021035098

First Edition: January 2022

Printed in the United States of America
1st Printing

Book design by Alison Cnockaert

To the Village of Chagrin Falls, Ohio,
the Blossom Time Festival and Balloon Glow,
thank you for your inspiration.

A Killer Sundae

chapter

ONE

It was going to be a killer weekend.

The Harvest Time Festival in Chagrin Falls was a favorite event around Northeast Ohio. From the dusk Balloon Glow lighting to the crowning of the Harvest Time Festival Queen during the Labor Day Parade on Monday. Visitors from near and far crowded the streets, enjoying hayrides, the hot-dog-eating contest, and a score of food trucks parked around the center of downtown on the triangle and in Riverside Park. But this year was going to be extra special. It was going to mark the inaugural voyage of my ice cream shop's newly minted food truck.

I'd gotten up extra early to get to Crewse Creamery. I had dozens of frozen delights to make for the shop and now for the truck, too. I knew there were going to be busloads of people coming through.

I made my usual morning meetup with my grandfather, who was already dressed and had a pot of coffee percolating.

"I can't stay long," I said.

"You need me to help?" he asked. "I'm ready if you need me."

I smiled. "I got this."

"Who would have ever thought Crewse Creamery would have a food truck?" He laughed and patted me on my back. "Leave it to you, Win. Carrying on the entrepreneurial spirit we started this business with. Your grandmother would be proud."

It was still dark as I came down Carriage Hill after leaving PopPop, and I saw the soft glow of the lanterns outside the door of my family's shop. A staple on that corner next to the falls' overlook since 1965, the baby blue and yellow awning flapped gently in the early September breeze. My Grandma Kay's wrought iron and wood bench sitting stalwart, giving note that our business had been and would always be about family.

Once inside, I turned the jukebox on even before I pulled one mixing bowl from the shelf. I closed my eyes, humming along to Ben E. King's "Stand by Me," and whirled around on the big checkerboard floor, dancing with my grandmother. Not literally. Grandma Kay had been dead since I was in high school, and no, she wasn't a ghost. She'd always said she'd make sure those pearly gates closed tight behind her. Still, I could always feel her, standing with me, especially when I was surrounded by the walls of Crewse Creamery.

My grandparents, Aloysius and Kaylene Crewse, had worked hard starting a business. The only black-owned one in Chagrin Falls, it had weathered the ups and downs of the twentieth century and with a new face, courtesy of *moi*, was going to make it through the twenty-first. I'd put in new pretty cobalt-blue-covered booths and stools, added a big menu chalkboard on the back wall, which I'd painted to match the seat covers, and put a huge wall of glass at the back that overlooked the falls our village was built around.

Back in the kitchen, standing at the stainless-steel table, Sam Cooke's "Frankie and Johnny" playing in the background, I cut open the dark-skinned purple fruit for the plum sorbet. The juice dripped from my hands as my knife sliced through. I plucked out the pits, exposing the tender yellowish-tinged fruit inside. I placed the halves on a baking sheet, then sprinkled them with light brown sugar. Wiping my hands on the tea towel I took from my shoulder, I slid them into the oven.

It might have been out of place, but the liquor cabinet in the ice cream shop had all kinds of bottles inside, all opened, all tried. My Grandma Kay had been the originator of her own artisanal ice cream recipes, and the little tin box she stored them in was filled with her penciled-in additions of how to use the hard-to-freeze distilled spirits to make ice cream. I had carried on the tradition but only after paying and getting the required licensure. Ohio lawmakers, in 2017, decided ice cream with alcohol needed to be regulated. I could hear my grandmother fussing about the government wanting to put their noses in everything.

I uprooted a bottle of vodka, poured it into a blender along with some lemon juice, water, sugar and the plums after they'd cooled from being in the oven. I hummed along as the commercial mixer pureed the ingredients, then I put them into the cooler to chill. I pulled out the basket of deep blue, plump blueberries and Greek yogurt I'd mix together until smooth and pour into Popsicle molds.

I heard a knock on the side door, the one that led from the kitchen to the alley between our building and the Flower Pot. I glanced up at the clock on the wall. My help was starting to arrive. I usually scheduled my employees and my mother (not an official employee, just part of the "family" in our family business) to come in an hour or two after I'd gotten in. I liked spending time alone in the shop making ice cream, with the quiet of the morning and the memories of my grandmother.

I wiped my hands on my apron and went to unlock the door.

"Morning," I said. It was Candy. Earbuds in ears, she had her phone in hand and pack on her back. One of my two latest hires. Young. Not as enthusiastic as Wilhelmina, my other new hire, but she was always willing to help.

"Hi," she said and let out a yawn.

I closed the door behind her and she stood in the middle of the floor. She had never been in this early, and other than handing me needed ingredients out of the fridge or cooler when passing through the kitchen when I made batches in the evenings, she had never made ice cream.

Wasn't so sure about how excited she was to be doing it now, especially at six in the morning.

"Thanks for helping me out," I said. "With Maisie out, I needed the extra hand."

"Sure," she said, pulling one earbud out. "I don't mind." She pulled her backpack off. "How's Maisie doing?"

"She's good," I said and smiled.

Maisie Solomon, one of my two best friends and my first employee hired outside of family, was home dealing with the chicken pox. "The doctor said she's not contagious anymore, but she's covered in red spots," I said. "She says her body aches and she's itchy all over. Still best for her to stay at home for a few more days."

The last part of my comment seemed to make both of us scratch. My sudden itch was at the elbow and in the ear. Candy's was on her cheek.

"How did she get the chicken pox anyway?" She shook her head. "Even being in foster care, I got all my shots."

"It's a long story," I said. Until Maisie came to Chagrin Falls to live with her grandmother, her childhood hadn't been smooth sailing.

"Morning! Morning!" My mother swept through the door with all of her usual chipperness. She had a cloth bag in one hand and held the side door open with the other.

"I present to you all of my hard work!" she said, and in came Denise Swanson, rolling a metal grocery cart.

"Hey, Soror!" she said. A big grin on her face. Soror, a colloquialism for sorority sister, was her usual greeting when she saw me. "We brought cookies."

"Twelve dozen," my mother said.

Denise Swanson, like my mother and me, was a member of Alpha Kappa Alpha, the first black sorority, usually shortened to AKA. Like my mother, she'd been an education major, too, and had pledged with my mother at Howard University in DC some thirty-something years ago. They'd been friends ever since.

An Ohio native, she served as an executive on the Cleveland Municipal School Board. Always dressed classy, she had an excitement about her when dealing with other people no matter what the conversation was about, and loved lending a helping hand.

Today, even though she'd been baking with my mother, she looked like she was on her way to a luncheon at a board of directors meeting. She had on a charm bracelet that dangled, clanked, and probably would have gotten in the way of making up cookie batter. She had on salmon pink trousers and a matching blouse (she loved our sorority's colors—salmon pink and apple green— and wore them often). Her shoes were low-heeled and sensible, but shiny. She kept her hair short, almost in the same style as mine.

I chuckled. "You helped?" I asked Denise.

"Of course she did," my mother said. "I told you, I've been working on them for two days."

"I know you did," I said. "I just didn't know Mrs. Swanson had helped."

"I mostly kept her company," Denise said.

"She did not," my mother said. "The peanut butter ones are all her."

"Now what are you going to do with so many cookies, Bronwyn?" Denise asked. Always the teacher, she didn't do nicknames even though she'd heard my family call me Win my whole life.

"Ice cream cookies," my mother said before I could answer. "Win's going to sell them on the new ice cream truck."

"I heard about that. It's not like the usual 'Turkey in the Straw'–playing ice cream truck, is it?"

"It's a *food* truck that sells ice cream," I corrected proudly. I didn't want anyone thinking we'd be driving up and down city streets with kids chasing after us. I wanted it to be trendier. "And no." I chuckled. "We don't play 'Turkey in the Straw.' It's like the food trucks that are on Walnut Street on Wednesdays."

"I love Walnut Wednesdays. I go all the time," Mrs. Swanson said. "Happy then to be taking part in this." She snapped off her bracelet and started rolling up her sleeves. "Okay, Ailbhe. Show me what to do."

"What do you want me to do?" Candy asked. She'd been standing there idle. She'd put her earbuds back in. She'd been in her own world and I'd nearly forgotten she was there.

"Mrs. Swanson," I said, forgoing giving Candy directions to introduce her. "This is Candy Cook. She's working here while she finishes high school."

"What grade are you in?" Mrs. Swanson asked.

"I'm in the twelfth grade now," she said. "Finally. I'd been trying to get here for a long time."

"Well, you made it, which is an accomplishment," Mrs. Swanson said, even though I wasn't sure if she knew Candy's story.

"We'd better get cooking," my mother said. She grabbed two aprons off the rack. "Here, Denise." She handed one to her. "Put this on. You're the only person I know who dresses up to come and cook."

She laughed. "I didn't know you were going to rope me into working this early in the morning. I thought we were going to drop off the cookies and go to breakfast."

"Mom," I said, thinking I'd give her and Mrs. Swanson light duty. "You can make the ice cream sandwiches. Use the chocolate and vanilla. Two scoops between the cookies. Roll the outside in nuts, but only on half of them. You know, because some people have nut allergies."

"Okay," she said. "Denise and I will do those first. C'mon." Mom waved her over. "We have a special area for non-nut products so they don't get mixed up."

"That's gotta be tricky," Denise said. "It's easy for nut powder or dust to contaminate the other products in the kitchen."

"It is," I said. "And I keep a sign up saying that we do make them in the same kitchen. But we're really careful." I looked over at Candy. "You'll make the peanut butter and chocolate ice cream once they're finished."

"Make ice cream?" A big smile curled up the side of her face. "You're gonna let me make ice cream?"

"You want to?" I asked.

"Yes!" she said, eyes bright and wide.

"We'll let them get finished with the no-nuts ice cream sandwiches. Meanwhile, you can help me with the blueberry and yogurt pops."

"Okay," she said. "What do I do?"

"We'll make up the mixture and pour them into the molds. Then put them in the blast freezer."

"So this was a great time to initiate your food truck, Bronwyn," Mrs. Swanson said as she stood at the sink with us, waiting her turn to wash her hands. "I heard that news trucks are going to be stopping by all weekend, especially on Sunday for the hot-air balloon show."

"The Festival will be on TV?" Candy asked.

"They're making a big deal out of it, it seems," Mrs. Swanson said. "Putting Chagrin Falls on the map."

"Why?" Candy asked. She pushed up her glasses with the back of her hand.

"We've always been on the map," my mother said and swatted a hand at her friend. "This year is special, though. It's the seventy-fifth anniversary of the Harvest Time Festival. Longest-running annual event of its kind in Northeast Ohio." My mother was proud of her home. "Good news about us for a change."

"Oh, that was awful, the story Channel 6 did on the village after the Mini Mall Fiasco," Mrs. Swanson said.

Candy let out a laugh. "The Mini Mall Fiasco," she repeated.

"That's what they called it," Mrs. Swanson said. "Even had that one reporter that was from Chagrin Falls do the story."

My mother waved a hand. "Don't even say her name. She knows she could have done a better job highlighting the village. Her family lives here."

"It was about murder," I said, not sure how a better job could be done highlighting that.

A Dallas company had tried to come in and buy up property and land in our little town, and the person they sent as a representative was killed. Murdered right behind the very shops they were trying to purchase. They wanted the real estate in order to build a mini vertical mall. It had been a fiasco. Hence the name. The news got that part of it right.

My mother put a proud smile on her face. "This news cycle the story will be special. I'm sure they won't be able to mess it up. The long-lasting Festival *and* the first year for the Crewse Family's ice cream truck!"

"Food truck!" Denise, Candy and I said in unison.

chapter

TWO

"S he's a beaut." My grandfather let out a long, low whistle.

"PopPop, you've seen her before."

"Not in action," he said. "That's one fine food truck."

Unlike my mother, I never had any trouble with PopPop calling it what it was. It was Sunday, the second day of the Festival, but the first day PopPop had come over to the park to visit.

"Baby Blue," as I called her, had been very popular on her first-ever Festival run. She had a dipping case, similar to the one in the store only smaller, a state-of-the-art mini blast freezer, a walk-in freezer (really a "step-in" freezer because you could only step inside of it) and a prep table on the back wall. The outside was, of course, baby blue, with a big vanilla ice cream cone on the side with *Crewse Creamery* painted in yellow. It went perfectly with the baby blue and yellow awning over the large serving window that matched the one over the store.

My grandfather had turned the management of our family's

business over to me and had given me full control. I was happy that he approved of the changes I made and my plan to keep our business alive and thriving.

PopPop had always been supportive of me and he was still my loudest cheerer in my cheerleader squad, in a quiet sort of way. PopPop, like my father, had a certain calmness about him. Not too many things ruffled his feathers. He was best described as grumpy. Extra grumpy, saying just what was on his mind. It seemed like the older he got, the more things, in general, irritated him. There were two things I knew of, though, that brightened his demeanor. Me. And the woman standing next to him.

"Hi, Safta," I said. "You enjoying the Festival?"

Rivkah Solomon was Maisie's grandmother and the Jewish owner of the local Chinese restaurant, the Village Dragon. Like Maisie, I called her Safta, Yiddish for "grandmother."

"Too many people," she said and turned up her nose.

She was a perfect match for my grandfather. Just as grouchy as he was. "That's good, isn't it?" I asked. "We want people to come."

"More people for you to feed at the restaurant," my grandfather said.

She smiled. "Yes. That'll be good."

Rivkah loved to feed people. She thought food could cure anything, and make better any bad situation.

"Can I get you guys some ice cream?" I asked.

"What you got?" PopPop asked.

I pointed to our chalkboard sign. Almost a replica of the one hanging in our store.

"We'll take a scoop of the vanilla," PopPop said.

"Feeling adventurous, huh?" I said and gave him a smirk.

"Besides your grandmother's rocky road cake, and a scoop of pralines and cream, I like it simple. Vanilla will do, unless you got one of the other two."

"Two scoops of vanilla coming up," I said. I nodded at Candy that I'd get them. All the while thinking that I'd have to fish out my grandmother's recipe box and find the ones for my grandfather's favorites. I didn't know what was wrong with me. I should always have some of them on hand for him.

I watched them walk away, Rivkah fussing that the scoop on his cone was bigger. I saw him trading his for hers.

"How cute," Candy said. "All the time I've been working at the ice cream parlor, I hadn't realized they were dating."

"They're not," I said. I cocked my head to the side and watched them as they made their way to the lemonade truck. "At least I don't think they are." Not that I hadn't wondered about that.

"They should," Candy said. "They seem perfect for each other."

"May I get a sundae, please?" Another customer came up to the window before I had a chance to digest what Candy had said, or even think about if I liked the idea.

What would Grandma Kay say?

I shook off that thought. "Sure," I said. "What kind?"

"Hot fudge," she said. She pushed her cheek-length, blond-streaked hair behind her ear and looked down at her crisp, white button-down shirt. I pictured her getting a big chocolate stain on it. She pointed to the menu board. "Mmmm. That chocolate peanut butter ice cream sounds good. Do I have to have vanilla with my sundae?"

"Nope," I said. I shook my head and smiled. "Pick whatever flavor you like."

"Okay." She licked her lips and rubbed her hands together. "I want two scoops of the chocolate peanut butter, hot fudge . . . do you put whipped cream on it? And a cherry?"

"Yep. You can have the works. And our whipped cream is made from scratch. You'll love it."

I started to go and make her sundae when another customer came up. One I'd known a long time.

"Hi, Win," she said. "I see you're still selling ice cream."

It was Kaitlyn Toles. Chagrin Falls High School alumna and my classmate. She was a former Harvest Time Festival Queen, current Channel 6 news reporter, and *the* creator of the Village Mini Mall Fiasco story.

She also was and had always been to anyone and everyone who had ever dealt with her—a constant pain in the butt.

"I see you're still needing to reassure yourself that you're better than everyone else," I said, giving her my best customer service smile.

She rolled her eyes at me. "It's a good thing it's good. And your food truck is cute." She took a sip from her covered coffee cup and batted her eyes at me over the brown top.

I wouldn't describe my food truck as "cute," but I guess its meeting her approval, at least in her eyes, made it good. I knew that was the closest thing to a compliment I was going to get from her.

"Thank you," I said to her, then turned to Candy. "Would

you make her sundae, please?" I pointed to the woman who'd walked up before Kaitlyn, which made her take notice of the woman.

"Sure," Candy said at the same time Kaitlyn let her brand of "joy" spread.

"Avery," Kaitlyn said smugly to the hot fudge sundae customer. "What are you doing here?"

Avery, as Kaitlyn called her, looked at Kaitlyn sideways through her heavily mascaraed eyelashes and arched a brow. "The same thing you are."

"I'm doing a feature," Kaitlyn said. "Covering my hometown." She smacked her lips. "You aren't from here. You have no business here."

"I do," Avery said. "And I'm in the same boat with you. No camera operator. No crew. Just our wits."

"Avery Kendricks, your wits couldn't get you a job as a production assistant on a late-night infomercial." Kaitlyn ran her hand down her high ponytail. "And I do have a cameraman. The Grey Wolf. My truck got a flat, so he's over at the mechanic's shop with it."

That seemed to deflate Avery some.

"Are you getting ice cream?" I asked Kaitlyn. Thought I might need to intervene before a catfight broke out.

Candy handed Avery her sundae and Kaitlyn pointed at it. "I want one of those."

"A sundae?" I asked.

"Yep. Just like that one. Chocolate ice cream. And *two* cherries on top." She took another sip of her coffee.

Always trying to be bigger and better.

"That's peanut butter chocolate," I said, remembering Kaitlyn was one of those people we'd talked about earlier. She had a nut allergy.

"I want chocolate. Plain chocolate," she said. She knew I knew without saying. When we were younger, she'd always come to our ice cream parlor even though she never had any conversation for me, and greeted me with an upturned nose. "And one scoop of something coffee-ish." She held up her cup. "Do you have that flavor?"

Even stuck-up girls liked ice cream.

"We've got mocha fudge."

"Oh!" She hunched her shoulders and let her eyes roll back in her head. "That sounds divine." She wiggled her fingers at me. "Okay, get to making it. I need my sundae fix."

"I'll make it," Candy said. Out of the corner of my eye, I saw her pick up the scooper from the tray of warm water used to rinse them. The same scooper she'd used to dip up Avery's ice cream that contained nuts.

"Not that one," I said and walked over to her. I dropped the one she had back into the tray and grabbed a clean scooper from the drawer. Candy didn't know about Kaitlyn's allergy, and that rinse water could have some nut residue in it.

By the time I'd finished her sundae and come back to her, another familiar face stood at my counter.

Cameron Toffey.

He, too, was from my high school days. And someone else whom I wasn't too fond of.

There'd been only a handful of blacks at our school, Cameron and I being the only two in our graduating class. But that hadn't forged any camaraderie between the two of us.

He'd been the salutatorian to my valedictorian. Which set him off-kilter. All through high school he'd competed with me academically from the first time I'd received an award. And it seemed to get his goat when he didn't beat me, although he always came close. I never understood why he had the need, though. He played football, was our class president and had the prettiest girl in school wearing his promise ring.

Kaitlyn Irene Toles and Cameron Aaron Toffey had been the 2000s version of Kim Kardashian and Kanye West. They were high-profile, controversial and the only interracial couple at Chagrin Falls High. She was petite and sandy blond. He was six-three and big. And I mean muscularly big. Most times, he'd carry her around piggyback style. Caramel-colored skin, he was clean-cut and a gentleman.

They were known as "KitCat," which spelled out their initials and because, as a couple, they were as cute as a kitty cat.

At least that was what other people said.

"Hi, Cameron," I said, setting the sundae in front of Kaitlyn.

"I was going to get you one of those," he said and pointed. "I just saw Avery with one. Thought you'd love it."

"Hers was chocolate *peanut* butter," Kaitlyn said as if he couldn't have been thinking she'd eat that. If I didn't know better, I would think she was using her I'm-better-than-you voice on him.

"I'm back." A man approached Kaitlyn, a camera sitting on his shoulder.

"Hi, Gary," Avery said, batting her eyelashes and smiling coyly at the flabby, sweaty cameraman.

He returned her attentions with a grunt.

Was this whom Kaitlyn had called the Grey Wolf? Maybe it was his camera skills that had gotten him the name.

"I can see you're back," Kaitlyn said, throwing a dismissive hand his way and ignoring Avery's comment to him. "I'm not blind." She looked at me. "I have to go. Work calls. Cam." She didn't even let her eyes acknowledge his presence. "Pay Win for my sundae."

I guessed her cameraman had gotten the flat tire fixed.

And her boyfriend was paying her way.

She had people waiting on her hand and foot.

Kaitlyn started to leave and then turned back. "Oh!" she said and held up her sundae. "I should do a spot with this. In front of Win's truck." She walked back over and put her Java Joe's coffee cup on the counter. "Watch that," she said, placing it precariously close to the edge before turning to go back to her cameraman. I grabbed it and pulled it back to the center of the counter.

Kaitlyn glanced over her shoulder at me and gave me a wicked smile. "I may even do one by your store. May as well get some publicity going on all your hard work remodeling it."

Leave it to Kaitlyn to think that the ice cream parlor needed her to get business. Especially during Festival time. There was no shortage of people ambling around Chagrin Falls.

But deep down I knew a nod on Channel 6 couldn't hurt.

Kaitlyn brushed down the front of her light blue top and Capri pants. She looked down as she planted her leather, multicolored sandals firmly in the sparsely grassed dirt underfoot. She took the microphone from her cameraman and ran her finger down her ponytail, and pressing her lips together to even out her lipstick, she put on that signature smile of hers. I think she had started practicing it back in high school.

My eyes left her and landed on Cameron, who I was surprised to see was watching me rather than Kaitlyn. "That'll be seven dollars," I said and stuck out my hand.

"For a sundae? Two scoops of ice cream? Really?"

"And two"—I held up as many fingers and flashed a fake smile—"cherries on top."

He pulled money out of his wallet, laid it on the counter and walked away.

Candy, Avery (who hadn't moved) and I watched as Kaitlyn did her little spiel with ice cream sundae in hand in front of her cameraman. I didn't hear all she'd said, but I heard "Crewse Creamery" come out of her mouth. I'd have to be sure to catch her story when it aired.

"What a jerk," Candy said after Avery, Kaitlyn and Gary, the cameraman, had moved on.

"Who?"

"That lady's boyfriend."

"Cameron." I chuckled. "Always has been," I said.

"He watched you the whole time you were making her sundae, but didn't watch her when she was filming. At first, I thought he was going to hit on you. Then when I found out he was *her* boyfriend, I thought, way not to be supportive."

"I don't know." I shrugged. "Usually he's overprotective of

Kaitlyn. Maybe she doesn't like him watching her work or something. It was weird, though."

"Toxic," Candy said and shook her head. "That's the word I would pick. Now those two, unlike your grandfather and Mrs. Solomon"—she looked at me—"shouldn't ever be together."

chapter

THREE

We had a pretty good line of customers going for most of the morning. I wondered how the store was doing. I smiled at the thought of the food truck doubling our business.

"Hi." A smartly dressed woman stood in front of the counter. She had on a white pantsuit with gold buttons that had the emblem of an anchor on them. She had on no stockings and at least four-inch white heels. She definitely wasn't dressed for a day at a festival.

She had long, sandy brown hair and striking hazel eyes accentuated with the smoky eye makeup look—eyeliner, a dark espresso powder surrounding her top and bottom lashes. Her nails and lips were a bright red.

She had stepped aside the line and was holding a business card in one hand, her cell phone in the other.

"Welcome to Crewse Creamery," I said. "The line starts over there."

She paid no attention to where I pointed. "I'm looking for the owner of Crewse Creamery," she said. "I had stopped over to the store on . . ." She looked down at her phone. "On North Main when I saw the truck. Very bright and attention-getting, I may add."

"Uhm . . . Thank you," I said. I was pretty sure that was a compliment, although her face didn't show it. "Crewse Creamery is a family business. I'm the manager."

"Good," she said and stepped closer to the counter. "Gwendolyn Baxter. CEO. Baldwin Media Limited." She stuck out a hand.

"Bronwyn Crewse," I said and reached out my hand to shake hers.

"We are an event planning and promotion company," she announced, "among other things, and we'd like to invite you to participate in our first Ice Cream Crawl."

"An ice cream crawl?" I said. "Is that like a bar crawl?"

"Exactly," she said and gave me a smile that barely moved her lips. It said she appreciated not having to explain what she meant. "It's set for next summer. We will be traveling by party bus and visiting about seven of Cleveland's best ice cream spots."

"And Crewse Creamery is one of the city's favorites?" I changed that so it didn't sound like a question. "We're one of the city's favorites."

"Of course," she said. "And we'd like for you to be the anchor store. We'd end the crawl here. Thank our contributors, do a little speech. Eat the ice cream."

"Oh. Okay," I said.

"This is a benefit for Children's Hospital. A fundraiser."

I was very familiar with Children's Hospital. It was part of

Lakeside Memorial Clinic, where my father practiced as an orthopedic surgeon.

"We'd be happy to take part in that," I said. "Thank you for thinking of us."

"You might not thank me when you hear what you have to do." She was no nonsense. All business. "It's a lot of work. We'd be hijacking your store for our event and we wouldn't compensate you."

"But we can sell ice cream, right?"

"Of course," she said. "But all proceeds go to the hospital."

"We're in." I nodded my confirmation.

"Good PR for you. Maybe we can work this truck into it somehow." She let her eyes wander around the interior of it. "You're the only ice cream store on our crawl that has a food truck."

"It's new," I said, trying to keep from blushing. "We just got it."

"Smart addition," she said. "There'll be meetings that you may have to take part in. Several people you need to meet." One compliment and she was back to business. She started typing something on her phone. Her nails clicking on the screen. "Will that work for you?"

"Sure," I said.

"I've emailed the doctor at the hospital who hired us," she said, still pecking away on her phone and not looking up at me. "It was his idea to have an anchor store, and with yours being out the farthest from the city, and the falls, beautiful falls, I should add, as a backdrop, we thought Crewse Creamery would be perfect."

"We think it's perfect, too."

She looked up from her phone at me and smiled. "Here." She passed me her business card. "If you have any questions, just call me. But someone should be contacting you soon. Probably Dr. Hayes." Her eyes went back to her phone. "He's in charge."

"Okay," I said.

"Okay," she said and looked up. "I guess that's it. For now. You have any questions for me?"

"No," I said and looked at the card she'd handed me. "Thank you for including us, Ms. Baxter."

"Call me Gwendolyn."

"Gwendolyn. Would you like some ice cream?"

"I'm not doing carbs today."

"I have some Popsicles made only with fruit and yogurt."

"Really?"

"Really. On the house," I said and turned to get her one out of the freezer. "Consider it a taste test." I passed it over the counter.

"Thank you," she said and smiled and tipped the Popsicle toward me. "I can remember coming to your ice cream parlor when I was a little girl." Her eyes sparkled with the memory. "I already know its reputation."

Gwendolyn left, but my smile didn't. I went back to waiting on customers with it plastered across my face.

"I thought you were minding the store," I said to my brother Bobby. He'd knocked on the door of the truck wanting entrance, and I'd opened it for him.

"Why are you smiling?"

I touched my face. "I'm not smiling."

"You were when I passed by the truck. You were just standing there smiling."

"Some lady just asked for us to be part of an ice cream crawl. A benefit endeavor for Children's Hospital."

"Are you going to do it?"

"Of course we are," I said. "It's for a good cause and it's Daddy's hospital."

"Which reminds me. Dad came to help Mom out." Bobby stepped up into the truck. "They were acting like teenagers at a 1950s corner soda shop who'd just gotten pinned. That's why I left. Came to see if you need help and you're over here smiling, too."

I giggled. "I'm not smiling because of love. And they weren't old enough to frequent a soda shop when those things were out."

"I wish somebody'd tell them that." He closed the door behind him and huffed. "Then PopPop and Mrs. Solomon came in. What's up with the two of them?"

I didn't have an answer for that inquiry.

"Love is in the air," Candy said. She was definitely a fan of the two of them being together. I was close to both of them but didn't have a clue as to whether they were a "thing." Bobby didn't seem to like the idea too much, though.

"Hi, Candy," Bobby said. She threw a hand up in return.

"I thought Mrs. Swanson was coming back to help," I said.

"Yeah." He pointed to my apron, signaling he needed it. "I don't think Mrs. Swanson could take all the sweetness coming out of that sweet shop either." He shook his head. "So I came over here. Figure I could give you a break."

"I thought you were offering a late-night clinic?"

"I am," he said. "The park closes at dark and the food trucks pull out. But people hang around sick from too much food, drinking, whatever. There are a ton of injuries even after the Festival day is technically over. Falls, cuts, bruises and belly-aches. They need somewhere to go close to get bandaged up. I'm going to fulfill that need."

"When are you going over there?" I asked.

"When you get back."

I was the youngest in the family. Three older brothers, Bobby was the one next to me. He was a nurse practitioner and ran a clinic for the underserved in our, and in neighboring, communities. He was all about helping the needy. He also was a big tattletale. One didn't go with the other, I know, but that's how everyone thought about Bobby whenever he was mentioned. He told things like he was still five years old. It was usually our father or grandfather he'd run to tell, but now he was telling on them.

"Okay," I said. Untying my apron, I pulled it off and handed it to him. "I won't be long." I grabbed my knapsack and slung it over my head and across my shoulder.

"Take as long as you want," he said. "I was checking out your food truck competition when I walked over. You should, too."

"I'm not competing," I said.

"Still, you gotta know. You know, if you want to give your customer the best experience."

Maybe Bobby was right. I probably should check out my competition, and my mind was set on that when I walked down the steps, adjusting the strap on my knapsack, out of the side of the trailer and right smack into O.

The nickname of Morrison Kaye, who, so the story goes, was always saying "Okay" when he was a kid, the "kay" part was dropped, and everyone just started calling him "O."

"What're you thinking about that you can't see where you're going?"

"Sorry!" I said.

"That's okay." Seemed like he still liked using the term.

"I was lost in thought."

"I can tell." He smiled at me. "Where're you going?"

"Uhm . . ." I shrugged. "Just around Triangle Park, I guess. Check out the food trucks."

He nodded. "See what your competition is like."

I smiled. He had the same idea Bobby had.

"Mind if I walk with you?"

"Nope." I gave him a friendly smile, didn't want him reading anything into it. "I'd enjoy the company."

O was a law professor at nearby Wyncliffe University. He'd been hanging around the ice cream parlor practically every day since we'd reopened after the remodel. I just couldn't imagine how high his glucose levels were.

My family and friends constantly teased that he liked me, but I had other things on my mind. Like a family business to run.

I couldn't remember the last time I'd had a boyfriend. Probably even before I went to live in New York. My job at Hawken Spencer, one of the boutique ad agencies in Manhattan, didn't give me the time to do it. And running a business, especially family owned, was more than a notion.

I didn't know when I'd ever have time to date.

I didn't know when I'd ever want to.

I looked at O and realized I might one day need to tell him that. It seemed like love was in the air—at least around me. Pop-

Pop and Rivkah. Kaitlyn and Cameron. My parents. But not for me . . .

"Seems like I had perfect timing," O said. "You coming out right when I was coming over to see you."

"Or else Bobby told you."

He was also on the "O likes you" bandwagon.

O chuckled. "You really are a good detective."

"Just as long as me being a detective doesn't have to do with murder, I'm fine being called that."

"Didn't you enjoy your sleuthing?" he asked.

"No."

"Finding out whodunit?"

"No." I was answering before he even finished asking.

A mock surprised look came on his face. "I thought you did," he said. "I really did. You seemed to be so interested. And invested. All except for the part where you were almost killed."

"Twice," I added. "And it wasn't something I *wanted* to do."

"Even Liam said you were good at it, although he isn't so keen on you doing it."

"You can tell your friend, Mr. Detective Liam Beverly, that he doesn't have to worry about me doing that anymore. I'm hanging up my deerstalking hat and pipe and canceling my subscription to *Ellery Queen Magazine*."

chapter

FOUR

O and I strolled around Riverside Park, the area next to the half of the falls across from our store. Behind our store was the true falls. The one that brought people to Chagrin Falls.

I told O about the invitation Crewse Creamery had gotten to participate in the ice cream crawl as we ambled around the food trucks parked in the triangle in the middle of downtown.

"That sounds like fun," he said. "I've never heard of it, though."

"I hadn't either," I said. "But I'm thinking I should do something really special. Special ice cream. Special decorations."

"I'm sure their planning committee has their own ideas about that."

"And I'm sure their planning committee will need my help with those ideas."

"Okay," he said, laughing. "I'm sure they will. Do you want something to eat?" O asked.

"No, thank you," I said. I didn't expect him to buy me anything, and after KitCat's interactions, I didn't want to appear selfish. After all, I wasn't offering him anything in return.

"You're not hungry?"

"Not right now," I said.

"Oh," he said and pointed. "I've been meaning to go to the bookshop to see if my order came in."

"What book did you order?"

"*A Dead Man's Honor* by Frankie Y. Bailey. You know that book?"

I shook my head. "I don't think so."

"I'll share it with you when I'm done." He glanced at me. "You'll walk over with me?"

"Sure," I said.

"It's about a law professor who solves crimes. Thought I'd pick up a tip or two."

"Are you planning on doing some amateur sleuthing yourself?" I asked.

"Who knows," he said, a smirk crawling up his face. "Might need to help out a friend." He gave me a sideways glance.

I just shook my head.

I heard the roar of an engine and looked up to see a black Charger. It had darkly tinted windows and a double red stripe going up the center of the hood.

"Why is that car driving around over here?" I said. "People are walking around. The food trucks are here."

We watched as it parked, practically on the sidewalk, and a guy hopped out of it and disappeared between the food trucks.

"Oh. No wonder," I said. "Cameron Toffey."

"You know him?" O asked.

"I went to high school with him. Just saw him this morning. Hasn't changed one bit. Same girlfriend. Same attitude." I pointed to the car. "Still likes to do what he wants."

"Bad boy?"

"No." I crunched up my face, trying to figure out how to describe him. "He was polite to teachers and stuff. Played sports." I shrugged. "Just arrogant, you know? The stereotypical kind of jock guy."

"Oh," O said and nodded.

We headed over to the Around the Corner Bookshop owned by Amelia Hargrove. A woman who had been high on my list of suspects in my last murder . . . well, I guess I could call it an *investigation*. Although I more or less stumbled on the killer. Or rather, the killer stumbled onto me. With a gun in hand no less.

Ha! Just shows how good a detective I was. I had Amelia pegged as the killer, or at least one of them. I was 100 percent wrong!

Maybe I should pick up a detective novel, too, while we're at the store . . .

The village's bookstore was small, quaint and stuffed with books. The shelves ran parallel to the door so you could walk along the rows and get lost in them and to the outside world. O went right up to the desk to inquire about his book, but I stayed behind and browsed the shelves. It was a mix of genres, books old and new. A vanilla scent permeated throughout, reminding me of the vanilla bean plants in Maisie's greenhouse.

I found a little table in the corner covered with old books. The sign stated they were all one dollar or fill up a canvas bag for seven. I didn't have much time for reading these days. I sometimes worked twelve-hour shifts. Up at the crack of dawn to make ice cream, turning in before midnight after totaling the day's receipts. Still, I loved the feel of them in my hands and the look of them on my shelf.

I perused the table and picked up a few to leaf through. One caught my eyes. *Recipes from Chagrin Falls*.

"How cute," I mumbled as I picked it up and opened it, flipping through the pages. The book appeared to have little handwritten notes scrawled along the margins and inserted in the text. I didn't bother to read them, flipping to the front of the book to see where it had been published. And right inside the front cover was an inscription that started: *To Kaylene Crewse*.

I ran my hand over the writing.

That was my grandmother. Had this been her book?

It was a first edition print, a worn drab brown cover, no more than 5 by 7 inches with gold lettering and no more than a half inch thick. The author was one Madeline Markham, whose name I didn't recognize, and Grayscale Publishing had printed the book in 1972. I wasn't even born yet.

I had to have that book. I scurried up to the counter, holding the book close to my chest, and found O just finishing up his purchase.

"You ready?" he asked and looked down at the book I was holding.

"I just want to get this book," I said, then placed it on the counter and looked into the eyes of the store clerk.

It was the owner, Amelia Hargrove.

It was the first time I'd seen her since I'd thought she was a murderer. *Awkward*.

"Hi, Win," she said. "Did you find what you were looking for?"

"I wasn't looking for anything in particular," I said. "I just came in with O and found this." I patted the book. "It was on the table in the corner." I pointed toward the back. "It's a dollar?"

"Sure is," she said. "Plus tax."

"Okay, I'll take it." I reached into my knapsack to get my wallet.

I didn't know that Amelia knew that I had suspected her of murder. But from the rumor mill, which is quite alive and rampant in Chagrin Falls, I'd heard how she'd been upset by all the news surrounding the Mini Mall Fiasco.

It seemed that Kaitlyn had singled her out, reporting, possibly erroneously, how Amelia was instrumental in initiating the gentrification, as Kaitlyn called it (and as had my activist brother, Bobby). And how, after she decided to stay, people perhaps shouldn't patronize her bookstore. According to Kaitlyn's story, we should band together and put her out of business since she wasn't happy with her location.

I didn't know if her business had suffered, but that murder and the trouble it brought didn't do any of us much good.

"You guys going to watch the Balloon Glow?" she asked, making small talk, I assumed.

I glanced out the window. It wouldn't be long before it was dusk.

"That would be fun," O said, a hopeful smile on his face. "You wanna walk over there with me?"

I looked at Amelia, who seemed to be waiting for my answer as well. "That'll be fun," I said. "But I'll have to stop by the truck and drop off my book first."

"Oh, your book," she said. "That'll be one dollar and seven cents."

"I got it," O said, his change still in his hand from his purchase.

"I got it," I said. "There's an inscription in there to my grandmother. I want to pay for it myself."

"An inscription to Kaylene?" Amelia said and flipped it open. "Wow." I saw her eyes scan the page, reading it over. "I didn't notice that there. How nice." She smiled at me.

"Yeah, I thought so, too." I beamed at the thought.

"How about I just give this to you," she said. "Seems like it belonged to your family in the first place."

"Really?" I said.

"Yep. Go ahead." She pushed the book toward me. "It belongs with you."

"Thank you, Amelia."

I don't know why I was thinking she hated me, or something. It hadn't been like she'd known what I was thinking.

Amelia put my book in a small paper bag, and O and I left the store. We walked back over to the truck.

"What kind of book is it?" he asked.

"A recipe book written by people in Chagrin Falls."

"And one of your grandmother's recipes is in there?"

I chuckled. "You know, I don't know." I glanced down at my package. "I flipped through it, but when I saw her name, I didn't look any further. I just decided to buy it."

When we got back to the truck, I walked to the serving window and put my book on the counter. Candy was waiting on a customer and my brother was wiping down the prep table.

"Bobby, we're going to watch them fire up the balloons. You okay to stay here?"

"Sure," he said, coming over to the counter. He pointed at my package. "What'dya get?"

"A book," I said. "I think it might be Grandma Kay's. I'll show you later. Would you put it behind the counter for me?"

"Okay," he said. "And I'll help Candy close up and drive the truck back to the store."

"I can do that," I said. "When I get back."

"It'll be completely dark by the time the Balloon Glow ends."

I looked up toward the sky. "You're right."

"Hi." I turned to see Kaitlyn's cameraman, then swung around more, expecting to see her. But she was nowhere in sight.

"Hi," I said and smiled.

"I came back for ice cream. I wasn't able to get any earlier."

"We've got plenty of it." I nodded my head toward my brother.

"We got footage of your ice cream truck and your shop." Gary patted his camera. "If you want to see it."

"Now?" I asked.

"Sure." He chuckled. "But I thought maybe I could download it and you could use it for marketing."

"Oh yeah," I said. "That would be good. Thank you."

"No problem." He reached inside his shirt pocket and pulled out a card. "Just give me a call or email me."

"Okay, I will."

"You ready?" O asked.

"Yep." I nodded. "My brother Bobby will help you out, Gary." I glanced at his card to make sure I'd gotten his name right. "It's on the house."

"Anything?"

I could see him salivating. "Yep. Whatever you want."

He slapped his hands together and rubbed them back and forth. "I know exactly what I want."

O tugged on my arm and we headed back over to the high school baseball field. Glancing back at Gary, a huge smile on his face, I was sure I was going to regret giving him free food.

It was a good thing we'd be closing soon. Otherwise we might not have anything left to serve anyone else.

THE BALLOON GLOW on Sunday evening was a light show—and every year it got better. At dusk, on the night before the parade, balloonists came from all over Ohio and inflated their hot-air balloons with fire from gas burners—off and on, creating a dance of lights. It was dazzling. Colorful. And spectacular. A night show not to be missed.

I was glad I would be there to see it.

"Have you ever been up in a balloon?" O asked as we walked over to the high school.

"Sure," I said. "I've lived in Chagrin Falls all my life."

"I've been around here, too," O said. "But never went up in one."

"You should try it," I said. "They launch on Monday. For the parade."

"Do they offer rides?"

"During the morning of the parade, just for exhibition, the balloonists, or aeronauts as they like to be called, go up alone. They don't fly in the afternoon, it's too hot, but late afternoon they offer rides."

"Maybe I'll go up," he said. "What are you doing tomorrow?"

"Working," I said. "Like I do every day."

We neared the field and could see the balloons set in a circle and hear the *whoosh* as the burners started to go off. It was dark now and the only light was from the first balloons that had been gassed up.

"Business is really picking up, huh?" O asked, his voice getting louder to make himself heard over the nearing crowd.

"We always did good business, it just wasn't ice cream business," I said, letting my voice level meet his. "My Aunt Jack had another, uh, I don't know, *vision*, I guess, for the store."

"You turned that around. And you're being modest." He smiled at me. "Your grandfather told me the store hasn't had this much business in a really long time."

"He said that?" I could feel a blush coming on.

"He did." He nodded. "And said he loved the food truck."

"I know! It turned out so nice. And I get to be a part of all the fun out here."

"What other plans you got for it? You taking it around Cleveland?"

"Look," I said and pointed to the balloons, the burners lighting up one after the other. I quickened my step and O followed suit. I wanted to get closer to see. "Isn't it beautiful!"

"What did you say?" O got closer to me and extended his head so his ear was close to me.

"I said—" But my words got lost in a loud-pitched shriek.

"Oh my God!" someone shouted. "I think she's dead!"

chapter

FIVE

People started running toward the woman who'd screamed. It seemed to come from right near the balloons, but it didn't stop the light show.

I stood on my tippy-toes to try to see what was going on, then jumped up and down, bouncing to make myself higher than the crowd. But it didn't help.

"Someone call 911!" I heard another person shout.

"What happened?" a woman asked me. Someone who'd been standing next to me the entire time I'd been there.

"I don't know," I said, wondering why she'd think I would.

"Is anyone here a doctor?" An echoed train of the question passed along the onlookers.

"What's going on?"

I huffed and turned to look at another person asking me that question.

It was Bobby.

"Oh!" I said. "They need a doctor."

"Where?" he said.

"Over there." I pointed to the crowd.

"Alright," he said and sprinted off. He turned around, running backward, and put finger to mouth and thumb to ear. "Call Dad. He's on his way here."

"Who's minding the store?" I yelled after him, but he was gone. "And the truck," I muttered.

"You wanna walk over to the store?" O asked.

"Okay," I said. "I'm sure Bobby would have put the truck to bed before coming over here. He knows no food trucks are allowed in the park after dark."

We started to head out when I remembered I needed to call my father. My father was an orthopedic surgeon at the Lakeside Memorial Clinic, one of the two major hospital systems in the area. He also helped Bobby at the clinic on occasion, doing general medicine, helping bandage and heal whoever walked in the door.

"Hold on," I said, stopping abruptly. As I pulled out my phone, I was pushed from the back and right into O. He reached out a hand to steady me.

"Oh! Excuse me," she said when I turned to have a look at what was going on. It was Avery who had pushed me. The other Channel 6 reporter Kaitlyn had talked to at the truck.

"It's okay," I said. "No problem." I pulled away from O, who was still holding on to me.

"Trying to find Gary," Avery said, her eyes darting around the dark field.

"Gary?" Then I remembered. "Oh. Kaitlyn's cameraman?"

"He's mine now," she said. "And I want to get this story." She jerked a finger over her shoulder.

Knowing Kaitlyn, Gary was with her and they already had the story, especially if someone was really dead.

"What story?" O asked Avery.

"The one going on over there?" I pointed across the yard where all the commotion was taking place.

"The story where I tell how she got what she deserved." A slick little smile crept up her face.

"Who?" O and I both asked.

"What who deserved?" I added.

"Kaitlyn Toles," she said, starting to walk away. She turned her head back toward us to finish. "She's dead and finally out of my way."

"Oh my," I said, watching Avery's back as she pushed through people milling about. "Did she say Kaitlyn is dead?" I held my head with my hand and slowly turned around to look where the crowd had gathered. I started blowing air out of my mouth. I couldn't believe what I'd heard. I'd just seen her.

"You know this Kaitlyn person?" O asked.

"Yeah . . ." It felt as if I didn't have enough breath to talk. I looked down at my other hand and realized I was still holding the phone. "My dad." I punched in his number. "I was supposed to be calling my dad."

My head was pounding, and just the ringing of the phone caused me to squint from the throbs. It was like someone was beating inside it with one of those percussion mallets used on a kettle drum.

"Hello!" My father was shouting through the phone. "Win, are you there?"

"Dad?"

"What's wrong with you? You call and don't say anything."

"Sorry. I guess I zoned out." I realized my voice had gotten shaky. "It's Kaitlyn, Dad."

"Who?"

"You know, Kaitlyn Toles, from high school. From Channel 6."

"What about her?"

"I don't know, Dad." I swallowed and lowered my head. It seemed if I didn't, I might fall over. "Someone said she's dead."

"Dead?"

"Are you coming to the field?"

"I'm here. Where are you?"

"I don't know. Can you . . . Maybe you can just follow the crowd? I guess that's where she is."

"Okay. I'll call you back."

As soon as he hung up, I heard sirens. They were still a ways away, but they seemed to be coming fast.

I looked at O. "She's the same age as me." I closed my eyes to stop my head from swirling. "I wonder what happened to her."

Tears welled up in my eyes. I had a knot forming in my throat.

"C'mon," O said. "Your dad's coming, right? And your brother is here. The ambulance is here." He pointed to the flashing lights on the parked truck. "Nothing you can do." He laid a hand on my shoulder. "Let's go and see what's going on with Crewse Creamery."

"I want to go over there," I said. "I just saw her. Gave her ice cream. We went to school together."

I felt like I was rambling, but my thoughts just wouldn't coalesce. Something turning over in my stomach that sent a buzz all through me told me I needed to know. To find out for sure what happened to Kaitlyn or I might not be able to do anything else.

"You sure?" O asked.

I nodded slowly as I walked over with dread spreading all through me. It all seemed surreal.

As we got closer to the balloons and the crowd, I could hear the sirens blaring in my ears. They were right up on us. Two EMT techs jumped out of the truck and pulled a gurney out of the back. Pushing past us, they jogged over and the crowd opened up like the Red Sea to let them pass.

I watched them as they made it to the center of the crowd. The burner lights made it bright as day. I could see my dad. He was standing next to Cameron, who appeared to be sobbing. And right next to him was Shannon Holske, another Chagrin Falls High School alumna. She, too, seemed to be comforting him.

And Kaitlyn—I recognized her bright baby blue pants and top—was on the ground. She had only one shoe on. The other lay a few feet away. Nearby was that coffee cup she was always holding. It was like an extra appendage.

Cameron looked up, presumably at the incoming EMTs, but when his eyes caught mine, he raised a hand, pointed at me and said, "It's her fault, she did it." Everyone turned my way as he blurted out, "Win killed Kaitlyn."

I GASPED.

I clutched my chest with my hand and locked eyes with Cameron and we glared at each other.

Why would he say that about me?

I watched as my father pushed Cameron's hand down, and Bobby, who had been assisting clearing the crowd, came over to join them. They circled around him, ending our stare-down.

"C'mon," O said. "Let's go."

"I didn't do anything to Kaitlyn. Why would he say that?"

"He's just upset, I'm sure," O said, turning back to look. He still held on to my arm, keeping me moving forward. "Who is he?"

"Kaitlyn's boyfriend."

O shook his head. "He's just racked with grief. I'm sure."

We didn't say anything else as we walked from the high school field back to Crewse Creamery. I pulled open the door and the jangle of the bell sent a shiver down my spine. I was so jumpy.

My mother took one look at me. "What's wrong?" She watched the door to see if anyone else was coming in. "Where's your father? And Bobby? I heard an ambulance." She came from around the counter, taking off her apron as she walked.

"No, Mom. They're okay. I'm okay."

"Then what is it?"

"It's Kaitlyn Toles, Mom. She's dead."

"I just saw her," my mother said. She pointed to a spot on the floor as if Kaitlyn were still standing there. "She came by to do a story . . . put us in her story about the Festival. I was nice to her even though I wasn't too happy about her doing that Mini Mall Fiasco story." My mother swiped a hand across her forehead. "I watched her coffee cup for her while she did her little report. She shoved it into my hand. I remember thinking it was a good thing it had one of those cardboard sleeves on it. It was really hot."

I shook my head. "She was over by the balloons. That coffee cup was right at her feet." I hunched my shoulders and felt tears welling up in my eyes again. "Lying on the ground. Dad and Bobby were there, but I don't think they could do anything for her."

"Oh my Lord," my mother said. "You saw her?"

"Win was wondering where the truck is and if everything was okay here," O said. I guess he was trying to steer us away from the sad conversation.

"Of course everything is okay here," my mother said. "Bobby brought the truck back before he went over for the Balloon Glow. I thought it was a little early, but . . ." Her voice trailed off.

"Candy go home?" I asked.

"Yes. I sent her home. It was slow here. Everyone's watching the Balloon Glow. Your father went over to meet Bobby. They were planning to hang out there before going over to the clinic." My mother's eyes went toward the door, and she called out before the bell even had time to ring. "Bobby!" she said. "What in the world is going on?"

"Kaitlyn Toles died," he said. He looked at me. "Cameron said you gave her some ice cream with nuts in it."

"What!" my mother said.

"I did not," I said. "I know she has a nut allergy."

"What happened?" Bobby said.

"She came to the truck for ice cream," I said. "Cameron was there. He saw what she had. I gave her one scoop of chocolate and one scoop of mocha fudge." I coughed back a knot in my throat. "And two cherries."

"So why would Cameron say that?" my mother asked. "He has always been a little troublemaker." She balled up a fist and stomped a foot. "Heck, we've been feeding Kaitlyn ice cream all her life. We all know better."

"It's just what Cameron *said*," Bobby said. "Doesn't make it true."

"Wouldn't she have had an EpiPen?" O asked. "On her?"

"She always had one," my mother said, nodding.

"I didn't see one," Bobby said. "I don't know. She may have tried to use it."

"What did your father say?"

"He told Cameron to calm down. That Win hadn't done anything wrong."

"Where is he?" my mother asked.

"He stayed around until they took the body," Bobby said. "I don't know." He shook his head and looked at me. "Before she died, she was vomiting and complaining of nausea. People said she was clutching her chest and acting like she couldn't breathe."

"What does that mean?" I asked, feeling defensive.

"It means that those *are* symptoms of a nut allergy."

"I didn't give her any nuts," I said, my voice cracking and tears streaming down my face.

"Those are also symptoms of a heart attack," O said. "It could have been anything."

"I'm not blaming Win," Bobby said and held up his hands. "I'm just stating what happened."

"You're stating it like it's my fault," I said.

"No, I'm not," he said and tried to put an arm around me. I shrugged him off. "C'mon, Win. That's not what I meant."

"We'll just have to wait and see what happened," my mother

said. She went back behind the counter as a customer walked in the door. "Win, you should go home."

"I'm fine," I said. "I have to see about the store."

"We got this," she said. "Bobby'll stay here with me."

I looked at Bobby. "I thought you were opening up the clinic tonight."

He shrugged. "Changed my mind. I'll stay with Mom. You go home." He looked at me, remorse in his eyes, but he didn't touch me. "I didn't mean you did anything, Win. You know I wouldn't say anything like that."

chapter

༄ ༄

SIX

O asked to walk me home, I told him no, but my mother insisted he did. They may not have actually believed I gave Kaitlyn nuts, but they sure were treating me like I might break. Handling me with kid gloves. Acting like I was in a fragile state.

Okay, so I did feel kind of broken. Sad.

And maybe a little bit guilty . . .

I let the scene play over in my mind. Hadn't I given her ice cream from a clean scoop? Hadn't it been plain chocolate I'd given her?

And why was I doubting myself?

"You know, people don't typically die hours later from anaphylactic shock after ingesting something they're allergic to," O said. Had he sensed what I was feeling? "It almost always happens right away."

They were the first words we'd spoken to each other since we'd left the ice cream parlor, and we were practically at my house.

"I know," I said. I'd been walking with my head hung low. I picked it up, adjusted my knapsack across my torso and gave O a weak smile. "It's just sad and I know Cameron is heartbroken."

"I'm sure he is, and I'm sure he didn't mean what he said."

"Cameron and I have always had this . . . I don't know, kind of *animosity* toward each other. He was always trying to beat me at something and I was always making sure he didn't." I looked up and we were at the old Victorian where I rented out the second floor. "This is where I live," I said and pointed.

O looked up at the house and smiled. "That's a big place."

"I live upstairs. A small carved-out apartment."

"Oh, okay," he said and chuckled.

Feeling awkward, I said, "I'm going in."

"Okaaay." He drew the word out, letting it linger for a moment. "You want company?" he asked.

"No. I'm good," I said. "But thank you."

"You're welcome."

"I mean for everything. For looking out for me over at the field, for taking up for me, and getting me home. It was nice of you and you didn't have to do it."

"I don't mind doing it. I want to do it," he said.

Feeling more awkward by the second, I said goodbye and headed into the house. But the walls of my "carved-out" apartment started closing in on me as soon as I climbed the steps and closed the door behind me.

I was feeling on edge. And antsy. And like I needed to do something. But what could I do?

Nothing.

Kaitlyn was gone. It wasn't my fault, but I felt bad. Other than my grandmother, no one I knew and was close to had died. I can't say that Kaitlyn and I were *close*, or even friends, but I'd known her all my life. She was so young and it just didn't seem right.

I took my knapsack off and laid it on the table in the hallway, then walked around the house and flipped lights on. I just didn't seem to know what to do with myself. I ambled into the kitchen, opened a couple cabinets and closed them back. I opened up the refrigerator and took out a dozen eggs and a loaf of bread. I couldn't remember the last time I'd eaten. I set them on the counter and stared at them for a long moment.

"I'm not hungry," I muttered and put them back in the refrigerator. I went to the sink, filled a glass with tap water and drank it. Then I went to the bathroom and ended up just standing in the middle of the floor. There wasn't anything to do in there either. Looking at my watch, I saw that it was close to ten thirty.

"I could just go to bed," I announced to the tub. It didn't seem to care one way or the other what I did.

I turned off the lights in each room as I padded back down the hallway, figuring I'd just turn in for the night.

But that didn't work out either.

I got to my bedroom and did a U-turn.

I threw my hands up. "I've got to get out of here."

I hurried back down the hallway, picked up my knapsack and went back down the stairs. I cracked open the door and peeked outside to make sure O wasn't still lurking around. I didn't want him to see me. He probably was going to give a full report on how he'd gotten me safely inside for the night.

Chagrin Falls was like living in Manhattan—you walked a lot. I had a car, a not-so-new little blue Toyota Corolla, which stayed parked at the back of the house more than it took to the street, but tonight I was driving. I wanted to go back over to the field where the Balloon Glow was being held, and I didn't want anyone to see me.

I pulled my blue car into the parking lot and walked over to the field. I didn't know what I was expecting to see. Caution tape? Kaitlyn's one multicolored sandal? Evidence that she'd tried to use her EpiPen? Maybe Cameron still there somewhere? I looked around the field for him. Even trying to make out a figure in the wooded areas beyond the outfield. Then, if I saw him, I'd be able to tell him that I hadn't done anything wrong.

There was nothing and no one there. Nothing that would let me know what had happened to her. The only things there were the markings on the ground where the balloon baskets had rested and the tire tracks from the ambulance.

The balloons probably were the reason that Kaitlyn had been there, trying to get her story. I walked around the large circle where the balloons had been when Kaitlyn was there and then back over to my car. I turned on the ignition, adjusted the seatbelt and took off.

I ended up on Hickory Hill Road. The street where Kaitlyn's parents lived. I hadn't been over to her house since fifth grade. Riya, Maisie and I had gone for Kaitlyn's birthday party. Jack Walters had managed to get the last seat in a game of musical chairs. That didn't sit too well with Riya. She thought she should've had it.

Riya Amacarelli, my other best friend, had a temper that was set on high, and a low tolerance for the long list of things that irritated her.

After she showed Jack Walters she could flip him and the chair he'd stolen from her and ruined Kaitlyn's pony-riding, bouncy house birthday party, she wasn't invited back to any more. And of course, if she couldn't go, Maisie and I weren't going either.

The lights were on in their house. And there were several cars parked in the driveway and down the street. I guessed people had been streaming through to offer their condolences ever since the news broke.

The news. That's where Kaitlyn had made her life. And it probably was going to be where she would be appearing, one last time, tomorrow.

I felt tears welling up in my eyes, and I realized I was sitting, staring at that house, and clicking my nails like a stalker. I drove farther up the street and found a parking space. I needed to go in.

I got out of the car and started walking toward the house, but my knees had a different idea, and they seemed to win over my stomach. I didn't know how far this invasion would go. I slowed down, my knees weak, feeling like they'd falter any minute. Butterflies set off in my belly that seemed to turn into bats. Gnawing on my insides, bumping around. My mouth was dry. I was afraid.

Afraid they might believe Cameron. Blame me for Kaitlyn being dead. Afraid that I might not find the right words to say when I started to speak. Afraid that I would only make them more upset by being there.

I stopped. Clicking my nails, I looked at the house, then back at my car. It seemed like a better place to be.

I piled back in the car and went to the ice cream shop, and as soon as I went through the door, I knew what would make me feel better.

Yes. Usually it was just being there, making ice cream and reliving memories of my Grandma Kay, but not tonight.

I grabbed a bucket, sanitizer, industrial-strength cleaner and cloths and threw them all into a 30-gallon plastic garbage bag. I dropped in a few extras of those, too, and went out the door.

Bobby had closed down the food truck. He would have had to come to the shop to get the keys for it, and I knew my mother would have told him where to park it.

River Street.

I headed that way, and as I turned the corner off North Main, I saw her there in all her glory. That did put a small smile on my face.

I pulled open the door, switched on the light and took in a breath. The first thing I spotted was the book I'd gotten from Amelia's Around the Corner Bookshop. Grandma Kay's book. She'd been there waiting for me, knowing exactly what I needed to do. I tucked the book down into my knapsack and blew out that breath.

First thing I did: I dumped all the ice cream down the drain.

Just in case, somehow, it had been contaminated.

I filled the bucket up with hot, sudsy water and I cleaned from the top of that truck to the bottom. Countertop. Dipping case. Prep table. I packed up all the scoopers and the trays and put them into one of the garbage bags. I washed the walls, the floor, and cleaned out the mini cooler and blast freezer. I rehung the red-and-white *Food Allergy Warning: Our Food May Contain Peanut or Tree Nut Products* sign several times in several different places to try to make it more conspicuous and ended up putting it back where it'd been in the first place.

I stood in the middle of the floor and looked around. Everything was clean. Nut free. That made me feel a little better.

Then I remembered my mother said Kaitlyn had come to the ice cream parlor and even had had her watch her coffee cup.

Did watching include touching?

I packed up all my supplies, used trays and scoopers, put my knapsack across my shoulder, locked up the food truck and headed over to the shop.

I stared down at all the glistening ice cream.

I had dragged my bag through the door, dropped it and my knapsack on the floor and flipped on all the lights.

How, I had thought, *am I going to scrub all of this down by myself?*

I headed to the front of the store and flipped on the lights in the dipping case. And that was where I stood. If I threw away all that ice cream, I'd have to spend the rest of the night, and morning, making more.

I spun around and let my eyes scan over the countertop and the white-topped tables. I grabbed the tray of red velvet ice cream and headed to the back to the sink and hot water.

It had to be done.

"What are you doing here?" A voice came out of nowhere unexpectedly.

I dropped the tray and clutched my chest. I let out a scream, mostly from being frightened but partly because the ice cream that splattered all over me was cold. Really cold.

"Riya!" I screeched at her. "What are *you* doing here? You scared me half to death."

"I saw your car, the lights on, and when I came to the side door, it was unlocked. What is wrong with *you?*"

"I'm cleaning up."

She looked down at the floor and let her eyes travel slowly from the mess up to my face. "Is that what you're doing? Because it doesn't look like that to me."

"Kaitlyn Toles died today." I just blurted it out. No need to sidestep around it.

"Oh my," she said. Her eyes straying off, she stood perfectly still and didn't say anything else. I didn't either.

After a full minute or two, I felt the ice cream melting. It felt sticky and cold.

"I need to get all of this off of me and off the floor." I circled my finger around. "And clean up."

"I've got an extra pair of pants and a shirt in the car," Riya said. "I keep them for when I stay over at the hospital." She shook her head. "I'll get them and then you can tell me about Kaitlyn."

I was in the bathroom when Riya got back with her duffel bag. "I've got sweatpants. They should fit you," Riya said through the door. "And a T-shirt."

"I wear the same size as you, Riya," I said.

"Only in your imaginary world." She opened the door and handed me the duffel bag, then pulled it shut again.

Riya was all about exercise and fitness. Me, well, I lived and breathed ice cream. Still, at nearly thirty I was a size six, just more of a lumpier six than Riya.

"So what does Kaitlyn dying have to do with you in the store at midnight covering yourself in ice cream?" she asked through the door.

"I'm only covered in ice cream because you scared the living daylights out of me," I answered from the other side. I tore off a mess of paper towels and turned on the water.

"I was worried about you." I could tell she raised her voice to be heard over the running water. "I thought something might have happened to you."

"You happened," I yelled. "Nearly giving me a heart attack."

"Is that what happened to Kaitlyn?"

I carefully pulled off shoes and pants and wiped down one leg before I answered. "I don't know what happened to her," I said.

"What? I can't hear you."

"I said, I don't know what happened to her." I turned my face toward the door and talked. "Cameron said I gave her nuts."

"She's allergic to nuts."

"I know that." My voice went up about three octaves.

Riya opened the door and looked at me. "Did you give her nuts?"

"No, Riya, I didn't." I blew out a breath. "The person before her got ice cream with peanut butter in it, but I made sure to get a clean scooper before I got hers."

"So why did he say that?"

"I don't know." I flapped my arms and smacked them against my bare thighs. "*That* is the question of the day." I rolled my eyes toward the ceiling and held out a hand in explanation. "He was hysterical. He was standing over her body. Crying. I don't know." I shook my head and closed my eyes. "But I feel so bad." Tears came again. I don't know why, but they just did.

"Don't cry," Riya said, pulling the door shut again. "You know I don't do tears."

chapter SEVEN

I came out of the bathroom and Riya was wringing out the mop. She'd cleaned up the spill and put the tray in the sink.

"Thank you," I said.

"No." She dipped her head. "I'm sorry about making you spill it. I should have knocked or something." She glanced over at the side door, where she'd entered, tucking a lock of her dark brown hair behind her ear. "Although you were in here with it unlocked and *that* scared me."

Riya, Maisie and I had been best friends forever. They were like the sisters I'd never had. Riya had just finished her residency in the emergency department (she hated it when I called it the emergency "room") at the hospital where my father worked. And even though I was the only one of my siblings who hadn't gone into the medical field, sometimes, through Riya, I felt as if I'd at least gone through all the ups and downs of medical school and graduated right alongside her. I'd heard her rant about her professors, quizzed her for pharmacology and neuroscience exams, and was her guinea pig, letting her examine, prod and poke me.

But Riya was one tough cookie. She'd saved my life. Literally. But when it came to emotions, she wasn't sympathetic nor did she get teary-eyed. She would usually explode. Her fight-or-flight response was never the latter.

Maisie, on the other hand, was a vitamin-pill-popping, community-garden-eating, I-never-get-sick proclaimer (although she *was* sick now), the complete opposite. She thought she could fix everything with food. She would have appreciated my tears and probably would have cried with me.

"It's okay," I said and waved a hand. "I was all set to throw all the ice cream away anyway."

"None of it killed her, you know."

"I know." I tugged at the drawstrings on the sweatpants she'd given me. "I went to see her parents," I said sheepishly.

"Kaitlyn's?"

I nodded.

"That was nice. What did they say?"

"I couldn't go in."

"They wouldn't let you in?" Her eyes got big.

"No. I got too nervous to go in."

She frowned. "Why?"

"Because I felt bad."

"Because of what Cameron said?"

"Yep."

"He was a jerk in high school, Win. I'm sure he's still a jerk now."

"I saw Shannon Holske at the field with him. You know, after it happened."

"With who? Cameron?"

I nodded.

"Is he dating her again?" she asked. "Because why did he say you did something to Kaitlyn if he is? Why does he care?"

"No!" I shook my head. "He's not dating Shannon. He and Kaitlyn were together." My brow crinkled. "But I'm sure if he were dating Shannon, he'd still care what happened to Kaitlyn, Riya. I mean, I care." I shrugged. "And Shannon was probably just there for the Balloon Glow and saw what happened."

"Oh," she said.

"I felt so bad seeing him standing there."

"Why?"

"I don't know. I feel like I had something to do with it."

Riya tilted her head and looked at me. "You didn't. Isn't that what you just told me?"

I huffed and swiped a palm over my eye. I could feel the sting of tears welling up again.

"C'mon," she said.

"C'mon where?"

"We're going to find out just how Kaitlyn died. Help you past all of this, because if I see one more tear fall . . ." She shook her head and yanked my arm hard enough that my feet rose off the floor.

"What! How?" I blinked my eyes and tried to put up some resistance, but we ended up in a human tug-of-war. "Where are you trying to take me?"

"The hospital. I know the pathologist on shift tonight."

I managed to grab my knapsack as she pulled me out the door.

THERE WERE ONLY two major hospital systems in Cleveland. They had satellite offices and suburban hospitals dotted all around the greater Cleveland area, and each of them had a main campus. That was where, according to Riya, a dead body would go for an autopsy if the coroner wasn't involved. Riya figured since my dad had been there, and her death wasn't a crime, he'd know to wait until they'd gotten to the hospital to call her death. We had a 50-50 chance that the EMTs had taken Kaitlyn to Lakeside Memorial Clinic, the hospital where Riya worked.

We zoomed through the city in Riya's little red Chevy Camaro like we were trying out for a part in *The Fast and the Furious.* Tinted windows and shiny exterior made us stand out even in the dark night.

People glanced our way as we rolled and wound through downtown. I didn't get around Cleveland proper much. Chagrin Falls was a self-contained suburb. About the only thing we didn't have was a movie theater. But Chagrin Falls had restaurants, clothing boutiques, a pharmacy, a gas station and a grocery store—everything a person would need to lead their daily life. And of course, my family store, so I didn't even have to leave the village to go to work.

Staring out the window as Riya drove down Euclid Avenue, everything looked so different from the last time I'd ventured out. Old buildings torn down, new ones erected. Streets blocked.

Some divided by newly cemented median strips. There were coffee shops, contemporary eating establishments and colorful, swanky apartment buildings. All, it seemed, not there the last time I'd ventured this way.

Illuminated only by streetlights and flashy signs, I gazed out onto the dark streets and wondered what wonders I'd see coming in the daylight. Then I thought about Kaitlyn, how she'd never see daylight again.

"WHAT DO YOU mean, I can't see the report?"

"I mean you can't see it. And you are going to have to go. I don't want to be overheard talking to you about it."

Dr. Riya Amacarelli's hospital "in" was getting ready to get us thrown out.

Riya's skin color had gone from olive to beet. Her fists were balling up at her side, and I knew any minute she was going to explode.

We'd lucked out. Kaitlyn Toles' body had been brought to Lakeside Memorial and we'd been in the morgue for a good ten minutes, Riya chatting up her friend Michael, the pathologist. His nametag included the last name, Kenneth, with an MD behind it and an ID photo that showed a much younger version of him. He was at least six-two, and a hundred eighty pounds. He looked about forty, had pasty-looking skin and wore a long ponytail on his head and a pair of light gray Crocs on his feet.

Riya said she was warming him up, so we could pump him for information.

But all her chewing the fat with Dr. Pathologist hadn't helped one bit when she'd gotten to the question we came to have answered.

"It's okay," I said to Riya, using a calm voice. I didn't know if her "friend and colleague," as she'd introduced him to me, knew about Riya's temper, and I wanted to keep it that way. "I don't need to know how she died."

Maisie and I had been taking meditation classes with her and I stood in front of her, trying to get her to focus on me.

"I can't understand why he won't tell me," she said to me, then turned to him, stepping closer to him. "What's the big deal?"

"Because there is more to it than she just died," he said. He seemed frustrated with her, but not mad. "You should understand that."

But she didn't seem to understand. And if he knew what I knew about Riya, he would try to make her understand, and not in a way that it would escalate to mad.

"How can there be more?" Riya said, her voice rising toward a shriek, her hands up in the air.

"Just breathe, Riya." I tried to hold on to her, but she tugged away.

"She died!" she said, her voice escalating. "And there is noth . . . Oh . . ." Riya dropped her arms, her mouth still opened from the last remark. But it seemed like all the tenseness had left her body. Then she turned and looked at me. "Oh," came out again, but this time it was like she had to push it out. She closed her eyes momentarily and turned back to Dr. Kenneth. "There is more to it, huh?"

He raised an eyebrow as if to say, "Finally, you get it."

Riya came over, stood next to me and took my hand. She turned her head to the side, settled her eyes on mine and said in almost a whisper, "There's more to it because Kaitlyn Toles was murdered."

chapter EIGHT

While mum was the word on any information about how Kaitlyn had died, Dr. Kenneth freely gave us the information on how we could find out. An investigation had been opened, according to a detective on the case. The teller of that truth? One Chagrin Falls police officer by the name of Liam Beverly.

We'd slowly walked the long, expansive halls of the hospital to find an exit on Wade Park, then crossed East Boulevard to get to the covered concrete garage where we'd parked Riya's sporty two-seater.

I buckled myself into the leather bucket seat, slumped down and started clicking my nails. Quietly under my knapsack so as not to annoy Riya any more. I turned back to gazing out the window as I'd done on the way there.

Riya took her eyes off the road for a moment to glance at me. "I'm sure you didn't have anything to do with that," she said.

I sighed. Guess she'd heard my nail clicking. I pulled my

hand from under my knapsack and propped my elbow up on the door to balance my head on a fisted hand. "I know I didn't have anything to do with it," I said, indignation swimming in my voice. "It's just that I don't even know how to digest all of this. Maybe you can't understand." I looked over at her. "You know, like why, all of this? Why did it happen to her? Why did it happen with me around? I hadn't seen her, other than on television, in forever."

"There is nothing you can do about it, so don't worry about it. You need to just let it go."

"You're right." I sat up straight in my seat and turned to give her a weak smile. "All I need to do is make ice cream, seeing that I threw away all that was in the food truck. And I'm probably a few trays down for the parlor, too." I glanced over at Riya.

"Sounds like a plan to me," she said and gave a curt nod.

"Did I tell you we were invited to participate in an ice cream crawl?" I asked, trying to turn my thoughts around.

"Like a bar crawl?"

"Yep," I said and sniffed. "I'm real excited about it."

"Yeah, I can tell," she said sarcastically.

I rolled my eyes at her. Then I thought, maybe it was a good idea to start thinking about it. "You wanna take me to the grocery store?" I asked. I gave her a puppy-dog-sad-face look. "I think that I'm going to need some different ingredients for flavors I have in mind for the store, but maybe, I'm thinking I could come up with some ideas for the crawl."

"A grocery store?" She glanced at the clock on the dashboard and pointed. "Do you see what time it is?"

"Yes. I know," I said, pulling my wallet out of my knapsack to make sure I had funds to shop. "But the Giant Eagle on Mayfield in South Euclid stays open twenty-four hours. Do you mind?"

"Nope, not at all." She flashed me a smile.

Silence fell over the car as we drove, and I tried to keep my mind off the events of the day—well, of yesterday. Yep. It was a new day. I had to push forward. I was truly sorry about Kaitlyn, but Riya was right, there was nothing I could do about it.

Then why did I still feel so bad?

"So are you gonna be in a funk like the whole rest of the night or what?" Riya said as she pulled into a parking space.

"I'm not in a funk," I said as we climbed out of the car, both of us slamming the car doors shut at the same time.

"What do you call it?" she asked, waiting for me to come around the car. "You're throwing away ice cream, looking all sullen and clicking your nails. Let me see." She grabbed my hand. "Do you have any nails left?"

"I know. I know." I tugged my hand away from hers. "But you have to admit, it is just so weird how it all happened. And now to find out she was murdered!" I shook my head. "Another murder in Chagrin Falls. That's just crazy."

"Yeah, I know," Riya said. "Looks like we'll be known from now on for more than being Tree City USA.

"So what are you buying from here?" Riya asked as we headed toward the automatic doors. The store was filled with light and activity.

"Oh, I don't know," I said. I chewed on my bottom lip and tilted my head. "I was thinking maybe I could make some blood orange sherbet." I tilted my head the other way. "Or maybe some black licorice sorbet."

"Oh my God." Riya stopped walking and threw up her hands. "It sounds like you're making ice cream for a funeral. Blood orange. Black licorice. Have you lost your mind?"

"No," I said, as if I really needed to answer that question. "I don't see any—"

She cut me off before I could finish my sentence. "We are not doing this." She came up behind me, placed her hands on my shoulders and turned me around. "Not tonight. We are going back to Chagrin Falls. I'm sure there is something at the shop that you can make ice cream out of. Something a little more happy. Your fridge and pantry are always full."

She clicked the unlock button on her fob, pointed to the passenger side and ordered me to, "Get in."

"I'm fine," I said, sliding into my seat and reaching for the seatbelt. She gave me a sideways glance. "I am. Really. I just wish I knew what she died from."

"Are you ever going to turn this loose?" Her words were pleading. "Why do you need to know?"

"Because we knew her. She was a friend." Riya squinted and grimaced. "Okay, sort of friend," I said, letting a little more of the truth seep into my statement. "I've known her practically as long as I've known you."

"She didn't like you," she said.

"She didn't like *you*," I said. "She treated other people, me included, the way she did because she was a snob."

"If you really want to know, if you really think knowing will make you feel better," Riya said, "we could ask that detective guy."

"What detective guy? Wait." I frowned. "Are you talking about Detective Beverly?"

"Yes." Riya licked her lips and I could see a gleam in her eye when she glanced at me. It shone brightly even through the darkness of the interior of the car. "I wouldn't mind seeing him again."

"Why would you want to see him again?"

"Because, you know . . . He's cute," she said and started smiling and blushing. "And you never know"—she hunched her shoulders—"when you might need a homicide detective."

My whole face scrunched up. "No one should ever *need* a homicide detective, Riya."

"Well, it just so happens that *we* do." Her eyes were batting a mile a minute. "We need one right now."

"Oh my, Riya. You want a homicide detective just so you can *see* him?" Just the thought of that made me chuckle.

"I can't help it if he's cute."

"Well, we can't see him now." I mimicked her earlier action and pointed at the clock. "It's two o'clock in the morning."

"I have a phone number for him."

"He's not at work, remember? We just talked about that."

"I mean his cell number." She raised an eyebrow. "You know, like his personal, private number."

That made me chuckle even more. "And how, pray tell, did you get that?"

"I don't kiss and tell," she said. A sly little grin crawled up her face. "But let's just say he's been to Lake Memorial a time or two and had to give personal information."

"Riya! I don't even think that's legal! Or lawful, whichever one it is when you break HIPAA laws." I shook my head. "You are going to lose your license to practice medicine. I thought the only thing I had to worry about was your temper."

"I'll have you know that meditation has made me temper-*less*." The last word tumbled out with hesitation, as if she wasn't sure it was a word.

"Is that what I witnessed tonight? Temper-*less*-ness." I said my new made-up word with the same hesitation.

"He was just being a pain," she said, then muttered under her breath, "The little jerk." She sucked her tongue. "Ugh! We talk about stuff all the time. Patients. In general, you know? Granted, I know I asked about a specific person this time, but she was dead! What can be wrong about that?" She looked at me, and her face softened into a smile. "And there's no need to worry. I didn't really take that detective's number out of the file. I'm not that bad." She punched my arm. "He brought his nephew in the other day to the ED. I was the attending."

"That's still not right if you copied it down."

"I didn't," she said and glanced my way. "I can't help it if I remember things I see."

"We're not calling him."

"Okay," she said and held her hands up in surrender. "Even though this is the perfect opportunity for me to speak to him. The perfect reason to give him a call. Like the one I'd been waiting for." She put her hands together like she was praying. "I mean, I couldn't have made up a better excuse."

"Hey! Hands on wheel," I said. "And no. Good reason or not."

"I'm just saying . . . But if you ever need to, you know, talk to him . . . meet with him, or anything, just let me know. I'm your contact girl." She glanced over at me. "The only thing I ask is that you include me."

I laughed. "I hope I never need to talk to him. And it doesn't matter now anyway. About talking to him. It's enough knowing what we did find out." I let out a long sigh. "I don't want to know anything else."

"So you're good?" she asked. "Because you were really worrying me."

"I'm good." I nodded. "I'd be even better if when you take me back to the ice cream shop, you'd help me make ice cream."

"Now? Tonight?"

"I thought you wanted to help me feel better? Making ice cream does that."

"We'll be up all night."

I nodded to that dashboard clock we'd been referencing all night. "We already have been."

chapter

NINE

Riya and I stayed up the rest of the time it was dark out. We'd driven back past the high school and now could see the yellow crime scene tape flapping in the wind. Dr. Kenneth was right—the investigation into Kaitlyn's murder had begun.

Inside my kitchen with the shiny aluminum appliances, exposed brick walls and the warmness from the smells of the fruits and spices, I felt at home. We set to work and in no time had made ice cream bases for five different flavors. There wasn't a lot of chatter between the two of us. Which was fine with me. There were only two things on my mind. One of them, I knew either one of us didn't want to talk about. The other thing was ice cream, and I was making that. So there was no need to discuss it.

Plus, it would make me worry. I had no idea how I was going to make up all the ice cream I'd thrown away the night before and get it frozen in time for the store opening.

Riya tuckered out about seven fifteen, but my mother showed

up fifteen minutes later. She was bubbly and cheery and had so much energy I'd thought maybe she'd taken an entire bottle of B_{12}.

"Mom, can you slow down, you're making me more tired than I am," I said with droopy eyes. I was running on fumes.

"I still can't understand why you dumped all the ice cream. You'd have to know that Kaitlyn probably died from a heart attack. What else could it have been?" She shook her head. "The girl was so thin and she ran on coffee."

I didn't say anything. Didn't want to tell my mother what I'd found out the night before. She would question me to death and I didn't have any answers for her.

"How do you know that?" I asked.

"She had a cup with her when she came in here. She smelled like coffee. Old coffee. And she sent her cameraman across the street to the Juniper Tree to get her more." She shook her head. "Caffeine is not good for you. Makes your heart race."

I decided I'd better change the subject.

"Crewse Creamery was invited to be an anchor store in an ice cream crawl next summer."

"What is an ice cream crawl?" she asked. "And what does it mean, an anchor store?"

Everyone else knew what a crawl meant, except my mother, so I had to explain everything to her.

"Oh wow!" she said, her eyes wide. "Are we doing it?" she asked, excitement already dancing in them.

"Yes," I said. "Of course. I mean, if we all agree to it. With everything that's been going on, I haven't had a chance to discuss it with PopPop yet."

"I'm sure he'll agree. You're taking Crewse Creamery on such adventures. Ice cream socials, food truck rendezvous and now a crawl!" She clapped her hands. "Whatever that is."

"I just explained it to you," I said, frowning.

"And knowing you," she spoke over me, "you're going to go all out. Come up with some new ice cream flavors." She planted her palms on the sides of her face. "It's going to be so much fun!"

I laughed at her excitement. "It will be, and you're right, I am going to try and come up with new flavors," I said, a smile beaming across my face. Nothing like making ice cream to change my mood.

"Maybe you could do something with your Grandma Kay's recipes?" She nodded over at where I kept the box. "You said you were going to make a Kaylene line of ice cream, remember? Maybe you could start that?"

"I still have to talk with one of the organizers, though," I said, not wanting her to get overenthused about something that might not be a part of the hospital's plans. "Ms. Baxter, the woman who came and talked to me, said someone will call me."

"You'd better put on your thinking cap."

"Thinking cap?" I laughed. "I haven't heard that in a long time."

"It can't be anything plain," my mother said. "I want you to start thinking about it. It's got to be something not ordinary."

"When do I do ordinary?" I said, protesting. "Just today Riya and I made salted caramel, key lime pie, and bourbon vanilla and chocolate truffle ice cream. And then we made watermelon and black sesame sorbet, and strawberry and cream pops." I planted my hands on my hips. "That undertaking was extraordinary."

"Well, that's not good," my mother said, a furrow carving through her forehead.

"What?" I said.

"Making all that hard stuff when you're tired and it's late." There was no pleasing her. She went over to the cooler and pulled out a gallon of milk. "What's wrong with just vanilla?" She put it on the aluminum table and went into the pantry.

I didn't do "just" vanilla. That was what was wrong with it. But I was too tired to argue.

She came out of the pantry with vanilla bean pods and bananas. "Or how about vegan banana ice cream? You just freeze them and blend into ice cream. No fuss. No muss."

I knew how to make vegan banana ice cream, and it was smart to make something easy.

"And how about if we make a double batch of vanilla. Take the second one, swirl in some chocolate, throw in some Spanish peanuts and you've got tin roof." She disappeared back into the pantry.

"I was trying not to make anything with nuts in it," I said to her after she'd emerged.

Her mouth was fashioned in an O, but nothing came out. She looked down at the can of peanuts she'd found in the back, up at me, and did an about-face.

"How about some regular chocolate?" She came back with a chocolate bar.

I chuckled. "Good idea, Mom," I said. "What do you want me to make?"

"Nothing. You go home. You need to get a few hours of sleep."

"I'm good."

"No. You go. I got this. You've made enough of the fancy stuff. I'm just going to freeze bananas and mix up vanilla beans, sugar and milk. Nothing could be easier."

"What about the food truck?"

"I'll call Bobby," she said. "It's not going out until eleven, same time as the store opens, right?"

"Yeah. But I like to go early."

"We'll figure it out," she said. "You just go. Bobby should be here soon. Your dad has the day off and so do your brothers. I'll have plenty of help."

"I'm sure they'll want to go to the parade."

"They'll help if I ask. It's still a family business, Win."

"I know," I said and looked around the kitchen. "I still worry."

"Don't."

"You sure?"

"I am."

"I'm thinking about hiring someone to run the food truck full time," I said. "At least when it's good weather. But I'm still formulating that idea."

"That's nice, sweetie," she said, busying herself with stuff other than me. "Think all about it on your way home."

I looked around the kitchen. It was a wreck from Riya and me making ice cream in a hurry and with little energy, but we'd gotten it done. My mother was peeling bananas and laying them on a tray.

I guess I could go home and take a nap . . .

"Oh," I said and snapped my fingers. "I've already taken the batches we made out of the blast freezer and put them in the freezer. They should be ready before it's time to open."

"Bye, Bronwyn." She kept her eyes on her task.

I knew she meant business when she called me by my full name. It was time to go.

But before I could get out the side door, we heard someone beating on the front window.

"What in the world," my mother said. She wiped her hands on her apron and tried to peer out front through the plexiglass partition. "Don't they know we're not open yet?" She didn't move from where she stood.

"Only one way to find out," I said. I walked to the front of the store and saw Cameron Toffey standing in front of our window, hands cupped. He was trying to see inside. His face lit up when he saw me.

What does he want?

"Who is it?" my mother called from the back. "Someone we know?"

"Yes, Mommy. Someone we know."

"Who?" she said. I could hear her voice getting closer. She must've decided it was safe to venture out from the back.

"Cameron Toffey," I said.

"Oh my!" I could hear the agitation in her voice. "What does he want?"

She didn't like being bothered with anyone who was having a rift with one of her children. Although we were all adults, she still felt the need to protect us.

"I don't know," I said. "I was just wondering the same thing."

When he saw me come to the front, he moved over to the door and stood there waiting for me to open it. I couldn't imag-ine what he wanted. To accuse me again? To accuse me of something even more egregious? Although I couldn't imagine what that could be. I knew I didn't have the strength to deal with his accusations this morning. But I also knew the man was grieving and I couldn't turn him away.

I unlocked the front door and let him in.

"Cameron," I said, trying to keep my voice steady, "we're not open yet."

"I know. I know." He sounded out of breath like he'd been running. But he'd only been standing at the window. I hoped he wasn't having some kind of heart attack. "I needed to talk to you."

"About what?" I asked.

"Cameron, do not come in here starting anything. Do you understand?" My mother used her best, strictest teacher voice. "You saying anything about Win is not going to happen."

"I'm sorry," he said to my mother, then turned to me. "I'm sorry, Win." He swallowed and shook his head. "I don't know what I was thinking. You know. It just happened and I was, like, why? She's so young. And then I thought about her allergy." He was talking fast. His hands were cupped in front of him like a beggar, but it seemed it was forgiveness he wanted. "You have to understand." His eyes searched mine. "Can you? Will you?" He shut his eyes. "Please, Win, forgive me."

"Cameron—"

"No. No. Look. Before you say anything." He dug down in his pants pocket and pulled out a velvet box. "I was going to ask her to marry me on the balloon today. Well, make it official. We'd already made the commitment to each other and we were just going to seal it. With the ring." He held it out to me, but I didn't want to take it.

"I thought giving her the ring on a balloon ride at the village's Festival would be the perfect event to mark the beginning of our life together. So I rented one. It was at the Glow last night. But I was going to wait until today . . . until we were up in the air." He lowered his head, his voice cracking with his last words. His next ones were barely audible. "We were going to tie the knot next month. Nothing fancy, and then spend two lazy weeks on a sandy beach, just the two of us. Together."

"It's okay, Cameron," my mother said, her attitude doing a one-eighty. Forgetting all about how upset she'd been with him earlier. "C'mon. Sit down."

"No." He shook his head vigorously. "I can't sit. I've been up all night. I can't be still. I can't sleep. I just wanted to come and tell Win I was sorry for saying what I did last night and to ask a favor."

"Sure," my mother said, not letting me do any of the talking. "What is it?"

"I just need Win to help me find out what happened."

He could have knocked me over with a feather. He couldn't be asking me to do what I thought he was asking.

"What do you mean?" my mother said.

I forgot she didn't know.

"I've heard about her solving murders," he said, looking at me sheepishly. "I thought she could help with this one. She could help me."

"Wait." My mother steadied herself by grasping the back of one of the parlor chairs she was standing near. "Are you saying that Kaitlyn was murdered?"

"Oh," I said and flinched. "I knew but I didn't want to tell you, Mom."

"Oh my Lord," she said and pulled out the chair she was holding on to and sat down.

"Yeah. So I was thinking Win would help." Cameron kept going, not concerned how the news had affected my mother. I went and stood next to her. "It could be like old times," he said. "Us working together. We were the two smartest ones in school." He looked at me expectantly. "The doctors wouldn't tell us what killed her. Only that it wasn't natural and it had nothing to do with her peanut allergy. That's probably where we should start. Don't you think?"

We'd never worked on anything together. He was always working *against* me. And I definitely didn't want to work on another murder. With him or anyone else.

The last two I had anything to do with had almost gotten me killed.

chapter

❦

TEN

I t took all my strength to convince Cameron he couldn't persuade me to help him investigate Kaitlyn's murder and to get him out of the ice cream parlor. My mother was no help. She seemed like she was in shock.

But I told him in no uncertain terms that I was not going to help him do any sleuthing and that he should leave everything to the police.

He didn't like that answer, saying that they'd drag their feet on everything and never solve Kaitlyn's murder. And even if they tried, the Village of Chagrin Falls wouldn't be able to help because he'd already heard that I was the one who had solved the only murder cases we'd had in our quaint little village.

He didn't know Detective Beverly. He was smart and far from being incapable.

But either way, there was *no* way that I was going to get involved. The first murderer I'd encountered tried to stab me with a knife. The second one tried to shoot me. Nothing had made me more afraid than I had been when I stood face-to-face with a killer. I swore to myself that would not ever happen again. And I looked Cameron in the eye and told him just that.

Sometimes the fear I suffered in those moments, facing death due to nosiness, I'm sure, would have sent me to therapy if it hadn't been for my family and Maisie and Riya, who had all helped me through. They'd saved me. PopPop and Riya had saved me. Literally.

After that I was more cautious than usual and could get jittery over the smallest things, so Riya took my mom, Maisie and me to her meditation class. Then Maisie and I enrolled in a tae kwon do class. Riya was a black belt. The ones we got on signing up were white. Her parents had tried to curb her anger problem with martial arts, but that didn't work. Although Maisie and I fumbled our way through the only three classes we'd taken so far, Riya showed the patience I never knew she possessed in helping me learn how to defend myself. "You won't be so scared," she had said, "when confronted with danger, if you understand all the strength you have inside." She'd patted my chest over my heart. "Right in there."

I didn't know if that was true, but I found just going through the motions in martial arts left me feeling empowered.

Cameron finally left, and I got my mother settled back down, didn't want her having any parking lot moments. She'd had that faraway look in her eyes. Whenever she was depressed or anxious, she'd drive to parking lots and sit in her car. For hours.

After I left the store, I stopped by where the truck was parked. I wanted to check on it one more time before I went home. I didn't know why. It hadn't even been six hours since I'd been there and scrubbed it down. Still. I wanted to make sure it was ready for the day. And for Bobby. I didn't want him to have to do anything but flip open the serving window and sell ice cream.

I heard the motor of the tow truck, a low rumble and squeaky brakes as it came to a halt.

"Hi, Win," he said, hopping off his truck. "I saw your food truck parked here a couple of times."

It was Mike Spirelli. He owned Spirelli's, a mechanic's shop up the hill from our store. It'd been there for years, just like our shop. And his father and grandfather had run it before him. Graying around his hairline, crow's-feet around his brown eyes. I'd rarely seen him out of the pinstriped work shirt, gray chino cargo pants and tan-colored safety boots.

"We just got her," I said, patting the side of the food truck. "So proud of her." I was grinning from ear to ear. I loved talking about the truck.

"She's a looker. Where you having your maintenance done?" he asked.

I chuckled. "She's brand-new," I said. "I hope we don't have to have her serviced anytime soon."

"Never too soon to start," he said. He walked toward the truck and nodded at the front of it. "May I?"

"Sure," I said. I opened the door to the truck. "I'll pop the hood."

He lifted the hood and stuck his head under it. I could see him screwing off tops, giving a shake on hoses and cables and checking levels, then he got down on the ground on his back and, with his feet, pushed himself underneath.

Mike had worked on all of my grandfather's cars for as long

as I could remember. I'd even taken my car to him during summer breaks at home.

He came out from under the truck, pulled a rag from his back pocket to wipe his hands before closing the hood.

"Looks good," he said. "You need to put some antifreeze in for the winter. Not sure where you're going to store it in the winter months, but there's only water in the radiator now."

"Water?" I asked.

"Yep." He nodded. "That's normal for the summer. But that antifreeze will keep it from freezing over during the cold months. I've got some antifreeze at the shop. Just drive it by and I'll change it out for you. No charge."

"Okay," I said.

He smiled, more wrinkles creasing into his face. "You've done a lot for your grandparents' business. Good job."

"Thank you," I said. "I'm trying."

"Wish my business was doing as well," he said.

I didn't say anything to that.

He looked down and shook his head. "Everybody around here going higher end. Taking their car back to dealers or foreign car specialists. And who's to say that I can't do the same thing. We've been fixing cars in our family for a hundred years, since the first one rolled off the assembly line and found a home in Chagrin Falls. Service. Respect. Ability. That's what should matter."

I nodded. It seemed like he just needed to vent.

"Now don't get me wrong. Business is still coming, but it's not the way it used to be. Hey, I just got to work on the Channel 6 news truck. Fixed them right up. No wait. If they come to us, then why shouldn't anyone else?"

Oh, I thought, *that was who fixed Kaitlyn's truck.* She had mentioned it to the girl who worked with her. Avery.

"Well, I'll bring the truck over," I said. "Get some antifreeze in it."

"Thank you," he said.

"And if anyone asks me about a good mechanic," I said, "I'll send them your way."

"Much appreciated," he said. "Tell your grandfather I said hey."

"I will."

After Mr. Spirelli had left, I gave the side of the truck one more pat and hoped she'd be okay with Bobby.

By the time I made it home, it was close to eight a.m. I was mentally and physically exhausted. The last thing I remembered was falling across my bed.

chapter

ELEVEN

I slowly opened my eyes to a buzzing sound in my ear. My head was on my knapsack and something inside it was making a noise.

"What in the world," I said sleepily. I could barely open my eyes, they were so heavy. I dug inside and found my cell phone. With one eye opened, I looked to see why it was making noise.

"Maisie," I grunted out loud. I swiped the Accept icon. "Hello?"

"Win!"

"Hey, Maisie, you okay?"

"Okay? Are you kidding me? Did you know that Kaitlyn Toles was murdered?"

I stretched my eyes and tried to right myself in the bed. I had to stretch my neck. It had a kink in it from sleeping in such an awkward position.

"Uhm. Yes. I knew."

"Why didn't you tell me?"

"Because I just found out about it like at one o'clock in the morning."

"Well, that was more than twelve hours ago . . ."

She was still talking, but the only thing that registered with me was that she'd said that one o'clock *a.m.* was twelve hours ago. That meant it was past one o'clock in the afternoon. I bolted straight up and looked at the alarm clock on my night table. It said two fifteen. I pulled my phone down from my ear to check that my clock was right. It was.

"Oh man!" I said, putting the phone back up to my ear. I cut Maisie off. "Maisie, I have to go!"

"Go where?" she said.

"Work! I fell asleep."

"No one is in the store?" she asked.

"Yes. Yes. Someone is there. I think. I hope." I scrambled to get out of my clothes. I needed to at least change clothes and brush my teeth. "Maisie, I have to call you back."

"No!" she yelled through the phone so loud I had to hold it away from my ear. "Tell me what happened."

"I can't tell you now," I said. "But I'll come over later and tell you everything I know."

"What time?"

"I don't know," I screeched. "I don't even know what's going on at the store. Or at the food truck." I grabbed a towel out of the linen closet on my way down the hall. "I promise I'll come see you, but for now, I have to go."

I pressed End, threw the phone down, put on a plastic cap and hopped in the shower. It took me all of three minutes to lather, scrub and rinse. I was out putting on clothes before I was completely dry. I brushed my teeth as I stuck a foot in each tennis shoe and brushed a hand over my hair, which was a hard thing to do. Both hands wanted to go in the same direction.

My first instinct was to go to the food truck. I had left my mother at the ice cream parlor, so I could trust more that everything there was fine. There'd been days when my Grandma Kay first took sick and my mother was on summer break from her job teaching third graders that she'd run that shop all by herself while PopPop tended to my grandmother. But she didn't know the first thing about my "ice cream truck," as she called it, and I was sure with people coming for the parade and hot-air balloon rides, we'd have plenty of business.

Panic rose in my stomach and I had a dry mouth the whole way down the hill from my house. I was so upset with myself for sleeping that long. But when I got to the truck, I blew out a sigh of relief and felt a big smile come across my face. PopPop, my dad and Bobby seemed to have everything under control. It was the original Crewse Crew.

"Hey, Pumpkin," my father said as I walked up to the front window. He handed a couple of scoops of what looked like vanilla ice cream to a customer.

"Hi, Daddy," I said. "Any room for me inside that truck?"

"Sure is," he said. "We were just waiting for you to wake up."

"Sorry about that," I said. "I guess I was more tired than I thought."

I had pulled many an all-nighter in my career, especially when I worked in New York as an ad exec. Deadlines and creativity didn't always sync. My team and I would be up all night making sure we got our presentation right on the night before the client meeting.

"You're fine," my PopPop said. "This is a family business, little girl. We're all in this together."

I loved my family.

"Dad and PopPop are going to watch the parade," Bobby said. "I can stay with you."

"You don't have to," I said. "Candy is coming to help me out here"—I glanced at my watch—"and Wilhelmina will be at the store in an hour or so." Then a thought hit me. "If you guys are here, who's helping Mom now?"

"Her soror," my dad said and grinned. "Denise came to watch the parade, Ailbhe put her behind the counter and put her to work."

"Oh," I said. I hated to impose on her like that. "Maybe I should call Wilhelmina to come in early?"

"What you're going to have to do," PopPop said, "now that you've got this food truck, is get more help."

"I know," I said. "I agree. I was just thinking about that today."

"Don't think too long. Or too hard," he said. "This food truck can't go out in the winter, but while you've got good weather, hiring someone else is a good idea." He folded his arms. "Plus, it'll give you help so you don't have to stay in the shop all day, every day."

"I don't mind, PopPop."

"I know you don't. But it'll wear you out. Practically everyone has gone their own way now. Not like when your grandmother and I were running it. There was always family available."

"C'mon, Dad," my father said. "We need to get going. I wanted to sit down and have a bite to eat before the parade starts at three."

"I'm ready," he said.

I walked around to the side of the truck. The two of them came down the steps one at a time and planted a kiss on my cheek. The last one out held the door open for me.

"See you guys," I said.

I stepped up in the truck, hung my knapsack on the hook on the door and put my apron over my head. When I got it past my eyes, the first person I saw standing at the counter was Shannon Holske.

Blond hair. Blue eyes. A Kaitlyn look-alike. She hadn't changed much since high school.

Just the sight of her gave me a flashback to the night before. Her standing next to Cameron and the two of them standing over Kaitlyn's body.

I wondered if that sight would ever go away.

chapter

chapter

TWELVE

I'd seen the body of the first murder victim in our village. Ste-phen Bayard. He was at the bottom of the falls when I'd gone down to get snow to make ice cream. But it had been dark, and he was more or less just a lump on the ground that I tripped over.

Kaitlyn, I'd seen in full, living Technicolor.

"Hi, Shannon," I said, not wanting to let my thoughts show through in my demeanor. "Welcome to Crewse Creamery. What can I get for you?"

"Not for me," she said. "It's for the little one." She pointed down.

I had to lean forward standing on my toes to see the little chubby toddler standing under the counter. "Well, hello there," I said and grinned at him. "You come for ice cream?"

"Ice team," he said and clapped his hands.

"How cute," I said. "Is he yours?"

"Yes. That's my little Ronnie. Everyone asks me that because he looks just like his father. Don't you think he does? He didn't get one thing from me."

I didn't quite know what to say to that. Did she expect me to know his father? I racked my brains trying to think whom she dated that I knew.

I could only come up with Cameron.

Oh no, I thought. I took another peek over the counter. That would mean Shannon *had* gotten back together with Cameron after graduation.

And where was Kaitlyn when that happened?

"All I see is cuteness," I said, trying to dodge the matter entirely. "What can I get him?"

"Just a scoop of vanilla. If you have it. It's about the only thing that won't make such a visible mess."

"Cup or cone?"

"Cup."

"And you sure you don't want anything?" I asked and turned to get started on her order.

"No," she said and gently brushed a strand of hair back in place. "I'm on my way to the float. I'm riding as one of the past queens."

That stumped me for a minute, but I tried not to show it. I glanced at her and for the first time noticed that she was all done up. Her hair was curled and stuck in place. I suspected she'd used tons of hair spray. Her face was full of makeup—smoky eyes, dark rose-tinted cheeks, and full-on glossiness covered every inch of her lips. Even outside the lines. Perhaps she'd had help from the toddler coloring them in.

Shannon Holske had never been a Harvest Time Festival

Queen. The year we'd graduated, that honor had been bestowed on Kaitlyn Toles.

Ohhh . . .

She was taking Kaitlyn's place.

I glanced over at her, lifting my head up from the dipping case. She had always tried to have what Kaitlyn had. Cameron. A Harvest Time Festival crown. And even being captain of the lacrosse team. I can't say they were rivals because Kaitlyn never gave her a second thought. Kaitlyn Toles didn't compete, she just *was. Was* the best. *Was* always first.

I grabbed a plastic spoon and napkin and walked back to the counter thinking Shannon would make a good murder suspect.

Wait . . . Why did I just think that? *I am not getting into solving a murder!* Plus, getting to ride atop a float as Queen of Harvest Time, ten years after the crown had been given, did not a motive for murder make. And if the little one that I was handing ice cream to was Cameron's, it seemed like she'd finally gotten something that Kaitlyn didn't have. She didn't need Kaitlyn out of her way.

"That'll be two dollars," I said.

Shannon paid me and the two of them left. I tried to push anything murder-ish out of my mind.

For the next few hours, Bobby and I worked side by side like we did when we were kids and waited on a steady stream of customers. When we got a lull, I found more ice cream in the freezer and put it out. I don't know why I was surprised everything had gone so smoothly without me. PopPop had run the ice cream shop for nearly fifty years. I rinsed out scoopers, dumped the contents from the tray we used to rinse scoopers and filled it back up with hot water. And got the trash together.

"I'm going to take this over to the dumpster," I said and held up the trash bag. "Be right back."

"Hello." He was standing there when I opened the door to the food truck, and as my grandmother used to say, he scared the stew out of me. I'd never known what that meant, but I knew how it felt. I jumped, stumbled down the step outside the door and dropped the trash bag I was carrying.

At least it wasn't ice cream.

"What the hey!" I screamed.

Liam Beverly thought the little fright he gave me was funny.

"Sorry," he said, still laughing.

"Why are you standing outside my door?" I asked. "We serve ice cream from the serving window." I jabbed a finger that way. "Around the front."

"I was just getting ready to knock when you came out."

"What are you doing here?"

"I just wanted to say congratulations." He shook his head. "Leave it to you to somehow be involved every time there's a murder in Chagrin Falls."

"Oh!" I grunted. That took my emotions from fear to terror. "Murder?" I just wanted to scream, "I didn't do it!" at him.

"Don't tell me you didn't know." He stooped and picked up my garbage bag and handed it to me. Then swung around looking about the area. "Where's Maisie? Picking up your magnifying glass from being cleaned?"

I sucked my tongue. "She has chicken pox, so she's at home. In bed. And I know nothing about murder. And Maisie and I have never used a magnifying glass to solve one."

"You mean to stumble upon who committed one."

I opened my mouth to say something, but realized that was a fair statement.

"Whatever," was the best comeback I had.

"That's not what the pathologist, Dr. Kenneth, down at Lakeside Memorial said." Detective Beverly looked at me questioningly.

I rolled my eyes upward. Riya was right. That guy was a jerk.

"I didn't do anything," I said.

"You didn't?" he asked. That familiar smirk on his face like he had the upper hand, or knew something bad about me. Something I didn't even know.

"No. Of course I didn't." I crunched up my nose. "Why? Do you think I did? Is that why you're here?"

"Looks pretty clean in there." He leaned around me and looked into the food truck. "Pristine. Like it just had a scrub-down."

I looked back at the door. I had neglected to close it after coming out because he'd startled me. I walked back up the two steps and pulled it shut. "It's a food truck. I have to keep it clean."

He smiled and slowly nodded.

"Anything else?"

"I hadn't thought you did anything. You know," he said, "concerning the murder. At least not until you told me you *hadn't* done anything."

"I didn't."

"My advice." He raised an eyebrow. "Until someone actually asks you a question, never offer that you don't know anything, because that only makes you seem more suspicious."

I swallowed hard and, taking his advice, didn't offer any response.

"I think I'll go around to the . . . what is it called?" He looked at me out of the side of his eye. "Serving window? And get some ice cream from your very fine, very clean establishment."

"Ugh," I muttered as I watched him round the truck chuckling.

"THIS IS MY nephew, Nevel Ray." Detective Beverly patted the tall, lanky boy standing next to him at the window on the shoulder. "Told him you had the best ice cream in Cleveland."

Okay, I couldn't help but smile, even though it was Detective Beverly who'd said it.

"That's right, we do. All homemade from fresh produce and fair trade products," I said, not at all too ashamed to brag.

"I'd prefer to be called Quincy," was what he said in response.

"It's his last name," Detective Beverly said. "He's my sister's son."

"Okay, Quincy," I said. "What kind of ice cream would you like?"

"I like your food truck. I've never seen one that sells ice cream."

Before I could answer, Detective Beverly interrupted.

"Bronwyn," Detective Beverly said, a note of seriousness in his voice. "Do you mind if your brother serves Nevel Ray?"

"Quincy," Nevel Ray corrected.

"Quincy," Detective Beverly corrected and kept talking. "I do need to ask you some questions."

"Sure," I said. I only agreed for fear of the man arresting me for obstructing justice. I didn't want to talk to him and had thought I'd dodged an interrogation when he came around front for ice cream. "Bobby?" I looked at my brother. His face said he knew exactly how I felt.

"No problem," Bobby said and stepped up to the counter.

"You want to talk?" I said, stepping to the side and looking at the detective.

"Let's go back around to the side of the trailer." He pointed. "A little more privacy there."

"Okay," I said and internally rolled my eyes. I went back to the side door, and opening it, I came down the steps.

Why hadn't he just asked me what he wanted when we were standing here before?

And as if he'd read my mind, he said, "I didn't ask you any questions before when we were here because I had frightened you. I didn't want you answering my questions under stress. Tend to get better and more complete answers when people are calm."

"How do people stay calm when they are talking to a police officer about a murder?"

"Good point." He chuckled. "But at least your heart isn't racing now. You ready to answer some questions for me?"

"Yep. Ask away."

But that's not what I was feeling inside. Inside I was screaming and wanting to wrangle myself away from the whole situation.

One thousand questions bombarded my brain of what he might ask and none of them boded well for me.

"You served Kaitlyn Toles ice cream the day she died?"

See. There was one of those questions . . .

I gulped. I needed to open up my throat, which was beginning to close. I coughed into my hand before I answered. "I did." I blew out a breath. "But it didn't have any nuts in it."

"Nuts?" he said and looked at me sideways.

"She had a nut allergy."

"Oh," he said. "I didn't know that." He pulled out a small notebook.

I guess this was one of those times he'd just warned me about. What was it he said? Don't volunteer information.

"What kill . . . I mean, what happened? What did she die from?"

"I can't share that information now," he said, glancing up at me from what he was writing. "And if you don't mind, I'll ask the questions."

I nodded even though I did mind.

"Was there anyone else here yesterday with her?"

"You mean when she got ice cream?"

"Yes," he said and tilted his head, waiting for my answer.

"Uhm. Her cameraman. I think his name is Gary something or other." I pointed over my shoulder with a thumb. "I have his card if you need it."

"Nope. Don't need it." He didn't even look up at me. "Anyone else?"

"Someone named Avery, who I guess worked with her?" I let my voice go up at the end, to make it into a question.

Now. Should I tell him about the animosity between them? How Avery said she was glad Kaitlyn was finally dead?

Oh wait . . . No volunteering of information. Right.

I didn't say anything else about her.

"And then there was Cameron Toffey. Her boyfriend. And that's it."

"Boyfriend," he said with a jerk, like he'd just gotten a jolt. He thought about that for a minute, tapping on his notebook with his pen.

"Anything unusual happen while she was here?"

I considered who he was talking about. "Nope," I said. Remembering that Kaitlyn had just been her usual annoying, selfish self and people were reacting to her just as they always did.

"And why did you scrub your truck so clean? I'm assuming you did it last night. After she was killed?"

"You act as if I keep my places of business in disarray. I always clean."

"That place is *sparkling* clean. Like I can see the little gleaming stars on it."

"Okay, I get your point."

"I came by yesterday," he said, "before all of this happened. It didn't look like this then. And you've got all new flavors of ice cream."

He really was a detective.

"I felt bad about Kaitlyn," I said. "I'd given her ice cream and a few hours later she was dead. I just couldn't stop thinking about her nut allergy."

"I see," he said.

But I wondered if he really did. No one could know how it felt to think that you may have harmed someone. Harmed them enough that they died.

"I can tell you that she didn't die from eating your ice cream."

I felt a rush of relief come over me. Even though deep down I had known it had nothing to do with me. Even after being told by Cameron in his quest to have me help discover the truth of what happened, it still felt good for it to be confirmed officially.

"I know," I said, my voice not fully showing the confidence I'd wish it did.

"Yeah," he said with a smirk. "I could tell you hadn't been the least bit worried about that."

"But how did you know she was here and ate ice cream?"

"Because that and coffee were the only things the pathologist could find she'd ingested."

chapter

❦

THIRTEEN

When I went back in the food truck, Bobby was still talking to Nevel Ray or Quincy. Whatever his name was.

"What was that all about?" Bobby asked.

"He wanted to question me about yesterday when Kaitlyn came by to get ice cream."

"What did you tell him?"

I shrugged. "Just that she was here and so were Cameron, Avery and Gary, her cameraman."

"Who is Avery?" he asked. "You never said anything about her."

"I didn't have a reason to talk about her," I said. "Heck, when they were here, I never thought I'd have a reason to ever tell anyone anything about it."

"So now you do. Who is she?"

"She worked with Kaitlyn over at Channel 6. She's the one who had the chocolate peanut butter ice cream."

"Oh." He nodded, understanding. "The one you served right before Kaitlyn."

"Yeah," I said.

"Did he mention that? Ask what kind of ice cream Kaitlyn had?"

"No," I said. "Just commented on how clean the truck was."

"What is that supposed to mean?" Bobby asked. That comment seemed to irritate him.

"Nothing," I said. "Just being the detective that he is." I ran some water in one of the paper cups we kept and drank it. Not getting enough sleep and having to deal with Detective Beverly was enough to make anyone's mouth feel parched.

"So did he tell you how she died?" he asked.

"He wouldn't tell me anything. Just said to let him ask the questions."

"I know how she died."

Bobby and I looked out the serving window. Nevel Ray was standing with his hands in his jeans pockets and a cheesy grin on his face.

"Are you going to tell us?" Bobby asked.

"Sure, if you'll give me a job on this food truck."

Bobby and I looked at each other, then back at Nevel Ray.

"A job?" I asked.

"Yeah. Bobby tells me he's a nurse practitioner and runs a clinic. I know he doesn't do this full-time. And when me and my uncle stopped by earlier, two old men were in here fumbling around."

"Hey!" Bobby said.

"That was our father and grandfather," I said, talking over

Bobby. "They know what they're doing. My grandfather started this business."

"I didn't say they didn't know what they were doing, just that you might need help." He took his hands out of his pockets and held them up in the air. "I'm available."

"Won't you get in trouble with your uncle for telling me how Kaitlyn died?"

"Death certificates are public record," he said. "Anyone can pick one up and see the cause of death if you know the name and date of death."

"Have you ever worked in an ice cream store before?" Bobby asked, steering the conversation back to Nevel Ray wanting a job.

"How hard could it be?" Nevel Ray said.

"Do you have a driver's license?" I asked.

"Sure do."

I looked at Bobby, who looked back at me expectantly. "Okay," I said and went over to shake his hand. "You're hired, Nevel Ray."

"That was the easiest job interview I ever had," he said and grinned. "And please, call me Quincy."

"Oh yeah. Sorry," I said. "Nevel Ray is such a unique name that it stuck in my brain."

"Why do you want to be called Quincy?" Bobby asked.

"Quincy is my last name. One day I'm going to be famous and will go by a monym. My legal first name wouldn't work. It's two names."

"Oh," Bobby and I said at the same time, our mouths open, heads nodding.

"Okaayyy," I said once I'd finished processing what he'd said. "When can you start work?"

"I'm ready to start now. I've got nothing else to do."

"Great," I said. "C'mon around, I'll let you in."

"Our deal isn't completed yet," he said.

"No?" I asked.

"I owe you information."

"Yes." I nodded and smiled. After that whole I'll-Be-Famous-One-Day-and-Use-Only-One-Name discussion, I'd forgotten he'd promised to tell. "You do. So how did Kaitlyn Toles die?"

"She died from ethylene glycol poisoning. The stuff that's in antifreeze. Somebody spiked her coffee with it."

SO POISON KILLED Kaitlyn Toles.

I mean, I knew it must have been. I hadn't seen any gunshot wounds and I wouldn't suspect that someone could've strangled her and gotten away with it right in front of everyone at the Balloon Glow.

It was in that coffee she had everybody watch.

I did a quick Google search to find out about the stuff. Quincy had told me it was antifreeze. Of course, anyone would know that something that went into a car would probably kill a human. I wanted to see how someone was able to get poison into her coffee cup.

Then the question is who?

And then I realized what I was doing.

I was thinking of how to solve the murder, even without Maisie pushing me to do it.

I shook my head to clear it. I had other things that needed my attention.

Once the parade started, the line in front of our food truck dwindled down to a dribble.

Quincy, the future mononymist, was a quick study. He was friendly to the customers and bragged about the ice cream flavors and menu items like he'd made them himself. He hadn't even tasted all of them.

He and Bobby had become fast friends, too. Good thing Quincy didn't have experience and a degree in the health field, or Bobby might have stolen him from my employ. They chatted it up, letting me interject a question or two, and we learned a lot about him, where he was from and how he planned on being the rich guy who went by one name.

The only thing I dreaded was that I probably was going to have to talk to his uncle, Detective Beverly. I always dreaded conversations with him. He always had an inappropriate smirk on his face and probing questions I didn't want to answer.

"Hello, I'd like to get a sundae, please."

I looked at the window, and it was Avery standing there with Gary the cameraman behind her.

"Hiiii, Averyyyy." I drew the words out, singsongy, so that Bobby would pay attention. We met eyes and he touched his nose conspiratorially.

"You remember me?" She smiled prettily.

"Of course," I said and threw one more glance at Bobby before I moseyed up to the counter. "Chocolate peanut butter ice cream and hot fudge sundae with whipped cream and a cherry on top."

She blushed. "You do remember."

"If you're back for more," I said, "I'm all out of chocolate peanut butter ice cream."

She waved a hand, but never lost the smile. "It doesn't matter. I just need it for the promo spot."

"Promo spot?"

"Yeah, our coverage is going to be on the parade and the balloon launch. Mostly the balloon launch," she said, emphasizing the last words like she was testing them out.

"Okaayy," I said, squinting my eyes.

"Is it possible to give me the ice cream for free?" she asked, turning to look at me from the side of her eyes while she batted those mascaraed eyelashes of hers and made her mouth pouty. "Seeing that we're using it for the promo."

"No," I said, matching her plastered smile with one of my own. "Sundaes are seven dollars."

"But our spot will generate business for you," she protested.

"We get lots of business."

She looked around as if looking for the customers and then looked back at me. "Fine," she said. "I'm sure I can include it in my expense report."

I glanced at Gary. He stood at the ready, holding his camera on his shoulder. No expression whatsoever.

"Sundae, please," Avery said. I guessed I wasn't moving fast enough for her.

"I'll get it," Quincy said. "Gotta earn my pay."

Avery got her sundae, sans the chocolate peanut butter ice cream, and stepped in front of the camera much the same way that Kaitlyn had done only the day before. In fact, it seemed that she used the same words and hand gestures as had the newly departed Channel 6 reporter.

"Producers didn't want to show Kaitlyn smiling and happy

when everyone knew in a few hours she'd be dead," Gary told us. He took the camera off his shoulder and put a hand on the counter.

He and Avery had finished their "promo." She'd dumped the sundae "prop" into the trash and told him she was going to the rest-room before meeting him over at the parade, "*posthaste*," she had barked. "Don't dawdle."

"I guess that would be bad to do," I said. "I wondered why Avery did everything over the same way, though."

"Avery L'Rue Kendricks has always wanted to be Kaitlyn Toles. Probably would have killed to do it." He noticed the star-tled look I gave him. "It probably wasn't her," he added, raising his eyebrow like he was questioning the validity of that state-ment. "At least I don't think it was."

chapter

❧❧

FOURTEEN

The inside of the food truck was packed to capacity after Candy came to work, and Bobby was the first to volunteer to vacate. After the parade, the hot-air balloons were going to launch from the high school's baseball field, and I'd thought about moving the truck there, but the Harvest Time Festival select committee gave me the official "No way," shut-down signal—a thumbs-down.

I was all set to send Quincy home, thinking I'd stay with Candy and we'd close out the evening, when my phone rang. It was a number I knew well.

"Hi, Maisie," I said. "How are you doing? I know I said I'd come to see you, but we've been . . . really busy."

"I wasn't calling for that. I know you're busy."

She was being nice after yelling at me earlier to come tell her about Kaitlyn.

"I only wish I hadn't gotten sick now. You needed all the help you could get running both the food truck and the store."

I pulled the phone down from my ear and looked at it. It was her face smiling back at me and her name. But she wasn't acting crazy like she always did when it came to wanting to solve a murder.

"Are you okay?" I asked.

"Yes," she said. "Feeling better. So good that I wanted some ice cream."

"Ice cream I have."

"I know," she said and giggled. "I'm having Safta stop by after the parade and get me some. I called to see what kind you have."

"Tell you what," I said, realizing I missed my sick friend. I looked at Candy and Quincy. She was showing him stuff I'd already shown him and he was going right along with her. They'd be okay, I figured. At least until I got back from visiting Maisie. "I'll bring you some. I know just what you want."

"I don't want to wait until you close. Safta said the parade would be ending soon."

"No. I can bring it." I glanced over at the dipping case. "I'll come now," I said, flinging my knapsack over my head and pushing an arm through it. "I'll dip up the ice cream and leave right away."

MAISIE LIVED IN probably the smallest house in Chagrin Falls. It was an A-frame house that was yellow and white. She bought it with the insurance money she'd gotten when her mother died. Her grandmother had saved the money for her.

She'd planted flowers with a kaleidoscope of colors that matched her personality and sense of style perfectly. I went into the house, yelled up the stairs that it was me, before heading into the kitchen to put the ice cream in the freezer.

Her cat, Felice, came strolling into the kitchen.

"Well, hello there," I said, stooping down. I ran my hand over her back. "You're looking heavier."

Her whiskers went up and she swiped a paw at me. "Eeee-oww!"

"Okay. Sorry," I said. "I take it back." She swished her tail, saying apology accepted. "You've been keeping Maisie company?"

"Eeow." She pressed her face against mine.

"Good." I stood back up. "We've missed you at the store, but I know that Maisie needed you more."

She walked over to the cabinet and gave it a bump.

"What?" I looked down at her. "You want something in there." I opened up the cabinet. It was chock full of cat treats—chicken-flavored, catnip, tuna-flavored sticks and turkey and gravy.

"What is going on here?" I said. "This is the reason you've—"

"Meoww."

"Okay. Okay," I said. "I won't say it again. But I am going to have a talk with Maisie about all of this.

"You look itchy," I said. I was standing in the doorway of her bedroom. Felice, who'd followed me up, was at my feet.

Maisie was sitting up in bed, the cover thrown to the side. She had on bright yellow socks, a blue gown and a red bandanna tied around her head. Her different-colored red hair sticking out of it was wiry and uncombed.

Her pale skin was covered in red spots that had brownish tips, on top of which she'd slathered, it seemed, an entire bottle of calamine lotion. Streaks of it having caked and hardened.

"Don't even say the word," she said. "I will go into another scratching frenzy." She looked at me. "Where's my ice cream?"

"In the freezer," I said. I walked to her bed, climbed in and crawled over her to the other side. I pulled my knapsack off, laid it in my lap and looked at her.

"How do you wait until you're twenty-eight years old to get the chicken pox?" I asked.

"How did you get to leave your ice cream truck? I was sure you guys would be swamped."

"We were," I said and eyed her. "You didn't seem too worried about that earlier when you were ordering me to come over."

"Yeah," she said and leaned her head on my shoulder. "Sorry about that. I think the fever I had made me delirious."

"'Delusional' would be a better word for how you were acting." I patted her leg. "It's okay, though. I'd go crazy cooped up, too." Felice jumped up on the bed and into my lap with a thud. "Ow! What have you been feeding this cat?"

"Just some tuna. A little salmon."

"Yeah. Right," I said. "She's gained ten pounds in the week she's been here with you."

"She has not."

"I wouldn't be surprised," I said. Maisie lifted up her paw like she could determine how much she weighed.

"Back to how you were able to come over," she said, letting go of Felice's paw. "Who did you get to work?"

"I hired someone," I said with a proud smile. "Another employee for Crewse Creamery."

"Who?" she asked. She reached over and rubbed Felice behind the ears.

"Detective Beverly's nephew. Of all people."

"Really? Are you firing me?"

"No. He's going to work in the food truck. At least while the weather holds."

"And then what?"

I shrugged. "Hadn't thought that far ahead," I said. Although I was sure I'd need him in the store. Just didn't want to upset Maisie with that news even though he wouldn't be replacing her. "But it's a good thing I did, because that's how I got to come and see you."

"Was Candy there, too?"

"Yes. She said hi. Said she misses you and Felice. But she was kind of concerned that I was going to catch the chicken pox, bring it back and contaminate everybody else."

"Didn't you tell her I'm not in the contagious stage anymore?"

"I did," I said. "And she's had her shots. I don't know why she was worried." I hunched my shoulders. "Probably just kidding me about it."

"So what does Detective Beverly think about you hiring his nephew?"

"I don't know. I haven't talked to him yet." I scratched my arm. "I'm sure he'll be okay with it. Quincy, as he likes to be called, who is from Steubenville, is taking a gap year before he goes to college."

"And he came to Chagrin Falls to do that? Isn't he supposed to travel around Europe or something?"

I shrugged. "I guess he'd rather work on a food truck, which was good fortune for me."

"He know anything about ice cream?"

"No. But who does? It's not like it's a fast-food restaurant and

ice cream parlors are on every block. Where would he have gotten experience?"

"Breeeow," Felice interjected like she had the answer.

"Either way, he acted like he knew stuff. Caught on so
quickly, he was even suggesting ice cream recipes. Oh!" I pushed
the fat cat off my lap and reached down in my bag. "I got this at
the Around the Corner Bookshop." I pulled out the Chagrin
Falls recipe book and opened to the inscription inside. "Look."

She took the book from me. "Wow. This was your Grandma
Kay's book?"

"I'm guessing so," I said. "Wasn't that a good find?"

"It was," she said. "Is Grandma Kay's recipe inside?" Her last
words were drowned out by the ringing of her cell phone. She
looked at it and mouthed "Safta" to me.

"Hi," she said into the phone. She closed the book, laid it in
her lap and patted it as she talked.

I sat and stroked Felice while Maisie was on the phone. She
nuzzled close and purred in satisfaction.

"Okay, I will," she said, trying to end the conversation. "Really, I don't know anything about it and hadn't given it a second
thought." She paused, then, "Okay. Yes. Okay." She gave the one-
word answers after listening to whatever orders her grandmother
was giving. "Yes, Safta. I'm sure Win will feed me." And with
that, she hung up.

"Your grandmother worried about you eating?"

"That and that I might try to solve Kaitlyn's murder from my
sickbed."

"You should let her know that her cat is definitely eating.
That would make her happy."

"I haven't been feeding her a lot," Maisie protested.

"You talking about solving Kaitlyn's murder when you said you haven't given it a second thought?"

"Yep."

"Maisie," I said. "That's not true."

"Yes it is," she said, her face serious. "After you said you'd fill me in, I didn't give it a second thought. I knew you'd stay true to your word."

So tell me," Maisie started. "How do you kill a person with antifreeze?" She turned up her mouth. "Doesn't it taste horrible?"

That was the first question about the murder in her 300-mile-long string of questions.

"I looked it up," I said, settling in. I knew from the onset we'd be talking about the murder for a while. Even Felice knew better than to hang around. Soon after Maisie's third or fourth question, she hopped off the bed and strutted out of the room.

"Yeah?"

"It seems that ethylene glycol, the poisonous compound in antifreeze, is sweet tasting and odorless. I read that now manufacturers of it are being asked to include additives to make it taste bad. Bitter."

"Really?"

"Uh-huh." I nodded.

She frowned up at me. "How do you know all of that?"

"I looked it up after I found out it was used as the murder weapon."

Maisie nodded, satisfied with my answer.

"It was put in her coffee," I said. "Evidently whoever killed her got their hands on the one without the bitter taste."

"Obviously."

"And it doesn't kill right away." I was trying to anticipate her questions. Get them out of the way. "It can take up to twelve hours."

"Oh wow." I had her rapt attention. It was like she was engrossed in one of those Acorn TV shows. "So why didn't she go get help?"

"Good question," I said. "Maybe she didn't know she'd been poisoned."

"What are the symptoms?"

She got me on that one. "Didn't look that up."

I pulled out my phone and she leaned in. A quick inquiry to Google gave us the answer. "Says it affects the nervous system. Slurred speech. Dizziness. Nausea."

"Was she acting drunk?" Maisie asked.

"Drunk?" I tilted my head to the side. "Ohhhh. Yeah." She looked at me, eyes wide. "I mean no." I shook my head. "I don't know. I was just saying that *is* how someone acts when they're drunk. She didn't act like that when I saw her." I gave Maisie a sidelong glance. "She did have coffee, though."

"Oh my." She slapped a palm to her cheek. "That might have been the cup with the poison."

"Could be," I said. "But maybe she'd already drunk the poison by the time she came to the Festival."

We talked for an hour—well, mostly I answered questions for an hour—about Kaitlyn Toles' murder. Although I'd spilled everything I knew when I struck up the conversation, it wasn't enough to fill up ten minutes, but Maisie found a way to draw it out.

"Are you going to solve the murder?" I had hoped she would run out of questions before she got to that. "It is kind of what we do now," Maisie said. Her words were exact as if she was speaking a known fact.

"Maisie," I said with finality, trying to get her to stop with all her murder questions. "I'd be more interested in finding out about the story behind this recipe book"—I patted the brown book still sitting in her lap—"than I would be about solving Kaitlyn's murder." I looked at her—pink lotion streaked across her face, the red bumps pushing through. I started scratching *my* face. "And it's not 'what we do.' We make delicious, mouthwatering frozen treats."

"You know what I mean."

"I do," I said and reached out to pat her leg buried under the cover. "But without you, it wouldn't be any fun. Plus, I didn't have any motivation to do it."

"What do you mean?"

"I know you're always gung-ho and ready to solve a mystery because you think you belong on Acorn TV, but not me. The only reason I wanted to help with those murders is because they involved someone I cared about."

"Your father and Rory," she said.

"Right. On that first murder, Detective Beverly was ready to throw my father in jail and toss away the key."

"Yeah, but on that second one, he wasn't going to arrest Rory."

"No, but you would have thought he was, the way she was so upset. And then he threatened her, saying he was going to charge her with stuff. Stuff that O said he couldn't do."

"In this one, you know Cameron."

"Cameron isn't accused of anything, and he is not somebody I care about."

"You and him were friends in high school."

I frowned. "We were not. Do you have a fever?" I picked up her limp wrist. "Because you're hallucinating."

She tried to chuckle but it came out in a cough. "You two were always competing."

"Competition does not a friendship make," I said.

"You liked Kaitlyn," Maisie said.

"I was probably the only one."

"Except for Cameron, he adored her."

"Did I tell you, he was all set to ask her to marry him? Take her up in his balloon and propose."

"So sad." Maisie shook her head. Her eyes were droopy, but I didn't think it was due to her having any sympathy for Kaitlyn and Cameron. I thought it was because she was sick.

"Do you want to get some sleep?" I asked. "I can come back tomorrow."

"No." She grabbed my wrist and held it tight. "Don't go."

"Okay," I said. I glanced at her and felt so bad. "What can I do to make you feel better? You hungry?"

She nodded. Pitifully.

"How about"—I got on my hands and knees and crawled over her—"I get you some real food. I don't know what I was thinking bringing ice cream."

"Safta brought chicken noodle soup over earlier."

"Is that good for chicken pox?" I'd never heard of that. I knew it was good for colds and the flu.

"Chicken noodle soup will cure just about everything," she said, her voice now weaker than it had been.

"Okay then." I gave a firm nod. If she thought it would work, I wasn't going to argue. "I'll heat some up."

"Can I look at your recipe book?" she said and pointed to the nightstand on the other side of the bed where I'd laid it.

"Sure," I said. I walked around the bed and grabbed it, handing it to her, and then headed out of her bedroom toward the kitchen of her small house.

"Bring me ice cream, too," she said. "Maybe that'll help with the fever."

That was something else I hadn't heard of.

I came back with a tray. A bowl of piping hot chicken noodle soup and a cup of chamomile tea I'd found in her cabinet. I knew it was used to soothe and cool irritated skin, thought it might do the same on skin irritated by a virus like what she had.

Then I dipped up a bowl of the chocolate ice cream I'd brought her, making one for each of us. I knew it was a bad combination. Hot soup and cold dessert. Either the soup would get cold while she ate the ice cream or the ice cream would melt waiting for her to finish the soup.

It was easy to see, I wasn't the best caretaker.

"Win," Maisie said when I walked back into the room. She was sitting straight up, her knees bent, the open recipe book I'd bought resting atop them.

"Didn't you tell me that you made Kaitlyn a sundae?"

"Yeah, I did," I said and placed the tray on the bedside table next to her. "Why?"

"Because I think I may have just found your motivation."

"What?" I asked.

"There are handwritten notations in each of the recipes."

"I know," I said. "I saw that."

"Did you see that they were on how to make them lethal?"

"Le ... What?" My brows creased together. "Lethal?"

"And there's more," she said, looking up at me, seemingly sorry she had to be the bearer of this news. "There's one for a hot fudge sundae that calls for the addition of ethylene glycol. The stuff that killed Kaitlyn."

chapter

SIXTEEN

No way," I said, my eyes nearly bulging out of my head and the words getting caught in the back of my throat.

"Way," she said and pushed the book into me.

"How could this be?" I said and plopped down on the side of her bed. I flipped through the pages and saw what she meant. It felt as if someone had just taken a large stone and thrown it into my stomach. The handwritten notes knocked the wind out of me. "My grandmother would never do anything like this."

"I know," Maisie said. "Is that how you make your Grandma Kay's hot fudge?"

I read over the recipe. There was one for vanilla ice cream, one for hot fudge and one for whipped cream. Sure enough, all of them were ones I recognized. The ones I used. In fact, I had just served the hot fudge and an extra dollop of the whipped cream to Kaitlyn the day she died.

"Yes. These are her recipes," I said and then pointed to the top line on the page. "Which isn't amazing seeing that, I'm just noticing, the recipe is called Kaylene's Hot Fudge Sundae."

"Your grandmother's name."

"My grandmother's name."

"But how did those additions of poison get in there?" Maisie asked.

"I don't know." My voice went high-pitched and shaky. "I bought it from the bookshop."

"Is that your grandmother's handwriting?"

"I don't know. I can't tell."

"She made marks like that on her recipe cards."

I popped off the bed. "Lots of people do, I'm sure," I said. "Why would anyone do this to her book?"

Maisie hunched her shoulders and slowly shook her head.

"I swear. Can my world get any more unreal?" I covered my face with my hands. "I keep getting tangled up in murders and now my grandmother's book has murderous scribblings in it."

"Who gave her that book?"

"I don't know," I said. "I guess the person that wrote it." I turned the book to look at the spine. "Madeline Markham."

"Did she know her?"

"I don't know. I guess she must have in passing. Grandma Kay is sharing one of her coveted recipes in this book."

"Maybe that Madeline Markham stole the recipes from Grandma Kay."

I tilted my head to the side and put hand on hip. "And then what? Grandma Kay killed her?"

"I guess that wasn't a good guess at what happened."

"I would agree with that."

"Maybe," Maisie said and pointed at me like she'd just figured it out, "this Madeline chick inserted the poisons *before* she gave it to your grandmother."

"That wouldn't make sense either," I said. "Why would Grandma Kay want, or take, a book with recipes added on how to kill people?"

"Yeah, I guess you're right."

"I just wish I knew what this is about."

"Especially since it has a sundae with the poison that killed Kaitlyn."

"I know, right?"

"I've got an idea," Maisie said. "Let's find Old Author Madeline and see if she knows what it's about." She picked up her phone off the night table. "We could go and talk to her."

"Now there's a suggestion I'd agree with."

"Siri," Maisie said. "Who is Madeline Markham?"

"I'll search the web for information on Madeline Markham," Siri answered in the Australian accent Maisie had chosen.

"What does it say?" I walked around the bed and climbed back in with her. Maisie didn't answer. I could see her eyes scurrying over the words as her finger scrolled down the article Siri'd found. "Maisie! Does it say anything about the book?"

"Mmmhmmm."

She wasn't listening to me.

"Is she here in Chagrin Falls?" She kept reading. "Can we go and talk to her?"

Maisie lifted her eyes from her screen and looked at me. She scrunched up her eyes, like answering me was going to be painful. "She is still here," Maisie said, nodding. "In Chagrin Falls. But we can't talk to her."

"Why?" I said, annoyed.

"Because she's dead. Buried at the same cemetery your grandmother's in. She died after eating a blueberry pie made from a recipe in her *Recipes from Chagrin Falls* book. The pie was given to her by a friend."

"It does not say that," I said and snatched the phone from her blistering hands. "Let me see." I read from the article she had, and sure enough, it was what it said.

"What friend?" I asked.

"You read it," she said, her eyes big. "It doesn't say what friend."

I didn't say anything. I couldn't. I sat there with my head down.

"Was Madeline a friend of your grandmother's?" Maisie asked.

"I don't know." I held my hands up. "I don't remember that she was."

"Do you think she took her the blueberry pie?"

"I'd never known my grandmother to make anything but sweet potato pie. I bet she didn't even know how."

"Unless . . ." Maisie's eyes wandered down to the book.

"Oh my gosh." I handed her phone back and closed my eyes. "Do you think there's a recipe in there for poisoned blueberry pie?"

"I don't know," she said. "Look and see."

"You look," I said. "I can't."

Maisie took the book and checked the table of contents. Running her finger down the list of included recipes, she stopped at one, glanced at me before she leafed through the pages to the one she'd found. "Here," she said. "Randall's Blueberry Pie." She cleared her throat. "It says you add blueberries, sugar and, penciled in, someone's written, a spoonful of strychnine."

I rolled my neck back, my head landing on the back of the bed. I let out a loud moan, and then an "Oh my God . . ."

"LET'S CALL THE publisher," I suggested.

I'd recovered from my shock and was ready to take action and pursue the reason my grandmother's name was in this book.

"What kind of information are we supposed to get from the publisher?" Maisie asked. She opened up the book and turned to the title page. She ran a hand over their name.

"I don't know. Maybe they can tell us where her books were sent."

"All of them?" Maisie asked, disbelief showing on her face. "They can't keep up with the distribution of her books. Look at this one." She held it up and shook it. "I'm sure they don't know anything about this one."

"Maybe someone bought that book. Used it to kill the author, then put the inscription to my grandmother in it."

"How does that make sense?" Maisie asked.

"I don't know," I said and leaned back on the headboard. "I'm just going to call the publisher anyway." I picked up my phone and googled the Grayscale Publishing Company. "I found the number." I smiled.

"They might be closed," Maisie said. "It's after five."

"It's ringing," I said. I was getting excited about talking to them until voicemail came on. "I think we called too late, although they say their hours are to six." I ended the call and stared at the screen. "I don't guess I should leave a message."

"Probably not a good idea," Maisie said, handing me the book. "And they might be closed because it's Labor Day."

"Oh. Labor Day. I forgot."

"It was a bad idea," Maisie said.

"I guess it was," I said. I closed my eyes. I'd had a long day and night, and now I was just making it hard, too. I needed to be still, as my mother said. Maybe I needed a parking lot moment.

"My soup is cold and my ice cream is melted."

I opened my eyes and looked at the tray I'd brought up for Maisie. She was balancing it on her lap and spooning up the soupy ice cream, letting it drip from the spoon.

"Ugh!" I chuckled. "I'll get you more," I said, climbing out of bed and taking the tray from her. "Then I have to go. I left two newbies on the truck, neither of whom can drive it."

"And can you make me a turkey sandwich? All these recipes have made me hungry."

How she wanted to eat after reading about food with strychnine and antifreeze in it was another mystery I probably wouldn't be able to solve.

I walked home from Maisie's house after making sure she and the cat were properly fed. The streets were practically deserted. They'd been filled with people all weekend, and now that the Festival was over, all that was left were remnants of the merriments and carousing. Paper strewn about, the smell of greasy food and diesel fuel lingering in the air.

I rounded the triangle, and the first thing I noticed were the lights in the bookshop.

Maybe Amelia was still there.

I peeked through the window and saw her behind the counter. I thought I'd at least give it a try.

"Hi, Amelia," I said, coming in the door. "Glad I caught you."

"Oh," she said, looking up at me from whatever she was doing, a warm smile on her face.

"Yes. You know the book I bought earlier?"

"Yes. I remember. Off the discount table."

"Right. It was inscribed to my grandmother, but I'm not so sure where it came from."

"No? You don't think it was hers?"

"I'm just not sure. Thought I'd check with you and see if you knew where it came from."

"Can't say offhand, not for sure, but most of the books on that table are donated. I'm like the Goodwill of books around here."

"Any way to know for sure?" I asked.

"Well . . . let's see. I keep an inventory of all of my books. I have invoices for the ones I buy, a handwritten ledger for the ones that come in. But I rarely put down who gave them to me because most times they're left at the door."

She pulled a ledger from under the counter and flipped through it. "It would have had to have been in the last month or so . . ." Her words slowed as her eyes skimmed the pages. "Nope. Sorry, Win. Nothing here."

"Okay," I said. "Thanks."

"Why . . ." She drew in a breath and tried again. "What's wrong?"

"Nothing. I just wanted to know who gave my grandmother that book."

"I'm sure it was the author."

"Did you know her?"

"Madeline Markham?"

"Yep. That's her. She lived in Chagrin Falls."

"She did. Had her book signing right here. I remember she'd only gotten about seven of her recipes from people that lived here. All the others were from people that lived elsewhere. She never told anyone that, though."

"Do you know who the other people were?" I asked.

"Mostly people that owned food places. Your grandmother. The Kellers. George Draper, who used to own a diner here in the early sixties. Uhm . . ." She looked up like she was trying to remember. "I'd have to think about the others. I don't think they owned food establishments. But none of them are around anymore anyway."

"Oh," I said.

"I hope that helps you," she said and smiled.

It didn't. But I didn't have to let her know that.

chapter

SEVENTEEN

I had fooled around long enough. Chasing the answers to a book where everyone involved was dead.

I rushed back to the food truck. I had spent too much time with Maisie. It was getting dark and it was time to shut it down for the day. Other than a meetup for the float participants and celebration of the year's Queen of Harvest Time at the Over the Moon Bar and Grill, this year's Festival was over.

But what I really wanted was to get the truck tucked in and get over to the store. I had something there I wanted to check on.

I hastily got rid of Quincy and Candy after I'd gotten back. Customers were dropping by, not enough that I couldn't handle by myself, but by park rules we wouldn't be able to serve them much longer anyway. After dark, I drove over to park the food truck on River Street.

I'd rented a garage to keep it in, but PopPop didn't like the price I'd negotiated. It was probably the first thing I'd done since he handed over the management of the store to me that he disagreed with. But he assured me that it didn't have to do with my decision-making. It was only that he felt the owner of the garage overcharged me because I was a woman. He wanted to talk to him. I didn't know if that made it any better or not—a man, Pop-Pop, having to handle it for me. But he grumbled so much about it that I just let him handle it.

I jerked the truck into gear. I was on a mission.

I had learned how to master it like a pro. We'd gone down to the Ohio DMV like we were in an episode of the *Brady Bunch*—PopPop, my parents, my brothers and I to get our commercial driver's licenses. I could barely get my brothers in the store to help out, but they were all ready to help with the food truck.

Grandma Kay's recipe cards were in a cabinet in the kitchen of our ice cream parlor. I rushed back, hoping that the store wouldn't be too crowded. Just enough to keep whoever was working the front in the front and me able to spend time in the back.

I wanted to compare handwritings. I needed to know if Grandma Kay's scribblings matched the ones in the book.

I knew my grandmother was turning over in her grave.

How could I even think such a thing? I groaned and hung my head low as I walked up the alley between the florist shop and our building. I didn't want to think anything of the sort. But I just needed to know.

I unlocked the side door of the shop and glanced over at the cabinet. My fingers were itching to get to those cards, but I had to keep my actions undercover, so the first thing I needed to do was check on the store.

I walked in front and found two of my brothers, James Jr. and

Lew, serving customers. I looked around to find PopPop or my mother. No way, I thought, would they leave those two in the store alone.

James Jr. was the other medical doctor in the family. He worked in sports medicine. Lew was a dentist. I didn't think they'd worked in the store since their last year in high school.

Okay, maybe I was overexaggerating, but I knew it had been a while.

"What are you two doing?"

"Taking up where you slacked off," James Jr. said. He looked at Lew. I don't know why we added *Junior* to his name when we spoke of him or to him. Sure, he was a junior, named after my father, James Graham Crewse. But everyone in the family called my father Graham. It's not like we would have ever mixed up the two.

"I don't slack off," I said. "I thought Mommy was here."

"She can't work twelve hours like you do," Lew said. "We gave her a break."

"I thought Wilhelmina was here."

"She said she went to bed at eight," James Jr. said. "She had to go."

"She did not," I said, unsure if that was the truth or not. She did tell me she was an early riser and she was in her midseventies, but I'd never heard her say that before. Then again, I'd never really asked her to work late. Still, she hadn't complained.

"Well, I'm here now if you guys want to take off."

"We're good," James Jr. said, smiling. "Feels good hanging out in the store like we used to. PopPop used to always leave us here to run it."

"I doubt that," I said.

Those two were goof-offs when they were younger. They liked to get into mischief. Since then, James Jr. had gotten serious. About everything. But tonight he seemed like he was all smiles.

The store was open until eleven p.m. I didn't know if they'd last that long. But they'd give me enough time to check out the cards against the writing in the book.

"I'm in the back if you need me," I said over my shoulder.

"We were running this store when you were still in diapers," Lew said. "We're fine."

I heard a customer chuckle.

My brothers were overprotective of me, I was their baby sister, but they didn't mind giving me the blues at the most inopportune times.

The recipe box was over my makeshift desk. I'd sit there and reconcile receipts at the end of the day, place orders for ingredients and fill out the work schedule for the following week. I took in a breath and looked around before I reached for her tin.

My memory of the pale green tin box with citrus fruit and leaves painted across the top and spilling over the rim of the container went back a long way. I can remember, my knees in a chair and my arms folded on the table, watching my Grandma Kay write down her recipes. "For safekeeping," she'd say and pat the box.

Now they were evidence.

Oh, how I hoped the writing didn't match.

And what if it does, I thought. It wasn't that she could have killed Kaitlyn. Grandma Kay had been dead for more than ten years.

But what about that blueberry pie...

I blew out a few quick breaths. All of this murder stuff going around was making me crazy.

I opened up the tin and fingered my way through them. I wanted one that had a lot of additions to it. Grandma Kay had been meticulous in typing up her recipe cards when she first started keeping them, but after she'd gotten older and found ways to perfect her recipes, she'd just pencil in her changes.

I needed one that had a lot of changes.

I found one for her cake batter ice cream.

Cake batter hadn't started out tasting like cake batter. She'd perfected it over the years. So there were a lot of additions.

I opened up the brown book and turned first to Kaylene's Hot Fudge Sundae recipe. There were only the three words added, a caret inserted to show where in the recipe the anti-freeze was to be put in.

Grandma Kay didn't use any carets on her index cards. She crossed out stuff. Wrote above it. No insertions.

At least not on this card.

I decided to look at a few more cards.

"Why are you back here? Making your brothers work."

It was Bobby. I was concentrating so hard, I nearly fell out of the chair. The book went tumbling on the floor and the tin box almost followed behind it. That would have been a disaster. I caught it in time, juggling it between two hands, trying to keep it from spilling over.

"What is that?" Bobby asked. He reached down for the book and I kicked it with my foot.

"Nothing," I said.

"Is that the book that you started telling me about? The one that was Grandma Kay's?"

"Yes. I was just checking her recipe on her cards to the one in the book," I lied.

"Why? You know all of her recipes by heart."

"No I don't," I said and smirked. "I still check the cards for stuff."

"Like what?"

"Why, Bobby?" He was frustrating me. Bobby was not the brother to be caught doing anything sneaky in front of.

"That's my question to you. Why?"

"Why what!"

"Why are you hiding the book?"

I huffed. "I told you. I forgot the recipe. Well, I really didn't, but the one in the book wasn't the same as the way I remembered Grandma Kay making it." I looked up at him while I closed the recipe tin and placed my hand on top. I protected the book with my foot. "And I felt bad." I was making this story up as I went along. "I thought I hadn't been making it right all this time."

"Really?"

"Yes. And I found out that Grandma Kay had changed it to the way she taught me. It's just that the one in the book is how she *used* to make it."

"Then why are you so jumpy?"

"Because I felt bad and I didn't want anyone to know I was second-guessing myself."

He stared at me for a moment. Then cocked his head and looked at me sideways. He was weighing my story.

"You shouldn't feel bad, Win. You're doing good. Nobody makes Grandma Kay's ice cream as close to hers as you do."

"Thank you, Bobby. I want to do right by her."

"You are. She'd be proud. Now go get some chamomile or lemon balm tea, to help you not be so jumpy."

"Okay," I said sheepishly.

I slumped in my seat after he'd left.

Grandma Kay would definitely not be proud of me if she knew what I was doing. She'd ball up her little fist, shake it at me and say, "Bronwyn Renee Crewse, I think you done lost your cotton-picking mind!"

chapter

EIGHTEEN

After Bobby had left, I put the book and recipe cards away. I was letting my imagination get away with me, and it was making me nervous and was a waste of energy.

I glanced up at the clock. I had a few hours before the ice cream parlor closed, and I figured I may as well put that time to good use. I went into my walk-in pantry and took inventory of what I had.

I was going to make ice cream.

That always calmed my senses and me.

I came out with an armful of stuff. Chocolate. Brown sugar. Coffee beans. Then I went to the fridge. I opened the door and stared into it. It was getting low, but there were enough fruits and dairy products to make an assorted array of ice cream flavors.

I didn't need to restock the food truck. I would dump what little was there. I laid everything I'd collected on the table and looked at it. Tilting my head from one side to the other, I thought about what ingredients I could put together and what flavors I could make.

I tapped my fingers on the tabletop and realized I'd forgotten something. I went back into the pantry and grabbed several bags and put them on the table.

Nuts.

I was going to make something with nuts in it.

I was done being worried.

We had signs everywhere about our products and I had always been cautious. Plus, Kaitlyn hadn't died from a nut allergy.

I hummed as I worked. James Jr. and Lew stayed in front. Bobby had hung out with them for a bit, but I knew he was tired. He'd been a big help and I felt bad he'd caught me in the act of checking up on my grandmother.

In time I had made up batches of pralines and cream, tin roof, strawberry shortcake, and lemon-lime sorbet. I stuck them in the blast freezer and headed out to clean out the truck.

I told my brothers just to shut off the lights and lock the door. I could come back if need be and run the report on the cash register.

CLEANING UP THE food truck was a breeze. Before I knew it, I was ready to head back out and up to the ice cream parlor.

I opened the door to the side of the food truck and screamed.

I was going to have to put a window in that door. Every time I opened it, someone was standing there.

"Oh my God, Maisie! What do you have on your face?"

I'd finished cleaning and dumping all the ice cream. I'd put what I could still use in a black trash bag and had been going to haul it back over to the store when I'd run into her.

Maisie was standing there, under the streetlight, her face glowing like a jack-o'-lantern with a candle inside and darkness all around her. After I'd composed myself, I leaned in close and swiped a finger down her face. I turned my finger over and looked at it. "What is that?"

"I put on makeup," she said. "So the blisters wouldn't show."

I didn't want to laugh. I was sure she had good intentions.

"What kind is it?"

"I only had Bronze Glow. You know, the kind that gives you a tanned look."

Maisie didn't wear makeup. I wasn't even sure why she had any at her house. She hadn't put it on any better than she'd put on the calamine lotion. It was darker in some spots and uneven. But true to its name, it did glow.

"Just so you know," I said, "you can still see the chicken pox pustules."

"Oh," she said and lifted a finger to touch her face.

"I can't let you in my truck," I said.

"I'm not contagious."

"I know, but you *are* scary." I shut the door behind me and locked it. "And it just wouldn't look good to have you around food. C'mon."

I gave her sweater sleeve a tug and we started walking down River Street, heading toward my store. I didn't know what I was going to do with her there, since I wasn't letting her in there either. I glanced at her and realized how she was dressed. I had been so distracted by her face.

She had on brown and yellow plaid flannel pajama pants, and had changed out of the yellow socks, which would have matched, to purple ones and Nike rubber slide-ins. She had on a red T-shirt with the word *Smile* written in glitter across the front and a brown sweater that went to her knees. At least her red bandanna, the same one she'd had on earlier, matched her shirt. Otherwise, with her golden glow, she looked like a rainbow coming out after the rain, and her face was the sun peeking through.

"Why are you here?" I looked at my watch. It was nearly midnight.

"I can't stop thinking about who murdered Kaitlyn."

"I just bet you can't," I said, although I had to admit it had been oozing through the crevices of my mind, too, filling up the spaces. "Nothing to do while you're recuperating and getting your fill on your murder mystery shows, huh?" I wasn't going to let Maisie know I was thinking about it.

"Yeah, I'm watching television and a real live murder pops up." She raised her eyebrows. "Can you believe it?"

"That's almost as scary as you look."

Her eyes were big. "I know!"

"Maisie, we're not doing the murder, remember? We need to find out about this book." I patted my knapsack.

"Did you compare it to your grandmother's handwriting?"

"I tried. But I got distracted."

"So you don't know?"

"No. Not for sure. I mean"—I looked at her—"I do know for sure that my grandmother didn't poison anyone. I just don't know for sure who wrote those notations in her book or why."

"That's the thing to find out."

"I agree," I said. "I went to see Amelia after I left your house."

"At the bookstore?"

"Yep."

"Why?" Then she nodded. "To see who'd given her the book?"

"Yeah. But she didn't know."

"Maybe it was her." Maisie looked at me expectantly.

I didn't know what she was expecting, because I didn't get what she was saying.

"What was her?"

"Maybe it was her who murdered Kaitlyn."

"Oh no," I said, my tone fussy. "Why would she do that?"

"Because of the Mini Mall Fiasco. Kaitlyn really made her look bad. All over the news."

"That is true," I said. Realization hitting, I changed my attitude.

"And the coffee came from the Dixby sisters' coffee shop," Maisie added, smiling like we'd hit on something. "Easy access for her."

"You don't know that the coffee came from the Juniper Tree."

The only coffee and tea shop in Chagrin Falls, the Juniper Tree was owned by a set of elderly twins. Two women who didn't have the best disposition and people Maisie and I even suspected in the last murder. The one about the vertical mall. The one that Kaitlyn had written about, making things look worse for some than it really was.

Maisie knew just what I was thinking.

"Maybe they are all in it together. The Dixby sisters and Amelia." Nodding in agreement with her own conspiracy theory, she smiled at me. "Revenge is best served up cold. Dead cold."

"Oh my," I said. "You are scary."

"It's possible," she said.

"And where would they have gotten the poison?"

"We'd have to figure that out."

"We've got other things to figure out," I said and patted my knapsack.

"I was thinking the book could wait," Maisie said and ducked her head. "I mean, it has nothing to do with the murder, and we should work on that first."

"No we shouldn't." I looked at her. "I don't know, but I'm thinking you probably shouldn't even be outside, let alone going around talking to people."

"I'm fine." She waved a dismissive hand at me. "You wanna know who I think the murderer is?"

"No," I said, knowing she'd tell me anyway.

"I think it was Shannon Holske."

"Shannon? I thought you just said it was Amelia and the Dixby sisters."

"I'd formulated the theory about it being Shannon before you went and talked to Amelia."

I nodded, admitting that that made sense. Maisie was going to push her ideas on me whether I wanted her to or not. May as well make it easy on myself. "So why Shannon?"

"All the clues lead to her."

"What clues?" I thought her fever had affected more than her ability to pick out clothing. "We haven't found any clues."

"We have." She lowered her voice. "All the things you told me."

I didn't remember telling her anything, but I was sure she'd fill me in on that, too.

"She was conveniently at the Balloon Glow right when it happened."

"Scores of people were at the Balloon Glow," I tried to interrupt. She kept going.

"She has hated Kaitlyn since high school. Ever since she found out she was Cameron's standby."

"Standby?"

"Yeah, during that time KitCat was at a standstill."

"Huh?"

"When Kaitlyn and Cameron broke up. Cameron really was just biding his time with Shannon until he could get back with Kaitlyn."

"Oh," I said, nodding. Basically that was what had happened. And surely, love and jealousy were common reasons for murder.

"She has Cameron's love child." Maisie was still listing off her reasons. "But even with that, he was still going to marry Kaitlyn. And now Shannon, finally, has gotten to be Harvest Time Festival Queen, something she has coveted since she was a young child, and ride on the float. Even if it was only to honor past queens for the seventy-fifth celebration."

"How do you know she's coveted that since she was a child?"

She shrugged. "I made that part up. But she did want it in high school."

Maisie was right about that, Shannon did want it in high school, and she'd made valid points, even ones I'd thought of, although I'd dismissed the one about doing it to ride on the float.

"So you don't think it was Ari Terrain who killed Kaitlyn?" I asked teasingly.

"Why would I think Ari did it?" she asked.

"Because every murder that we've had in Chagrin Falls so far, you've concluded, right off the bat, that Ari did it."

"Do you think he did it?" she asked and stopped walking. Even with her "evidence" against Shannon, she still seemed to be considering the possibility.

"No I don't," I said and pulled her into motion. I poked her with my elbow. "I was kidding!"

I probably shouldn't have teased Maisie about Ari. He was her old boss when she worked at his restaurant, Molta's, and for some reason she didn't like him. To me, he was nice enough, but Maisie liked to keep him at arm's length.

"You know that there's the meetup tonight."

"I know," I said.

"Since Shannon rode on the float, she'll be there."

"I know," I said.

She pointed down the street. It was her "new" beat-up pickup truck. "We could just hop in there, start her up and, oh, I don't know, go and see what's going on over there."

Maisie had owned the cutest little green VW Bug. But when she decided to expand her community garden, she'd exchanged it for a truck. She said she'd need it to cart dirt and seed. The truck was old, but as Maisie said, "New to me." She was happy with it, but not the circumstances around why she hadn't put it to good use yet.

The Mini Mall Fiasco had thwarted her plans. At least for now. She'd been unable to buy the building she'd wanted because the company wanting to build a mall had. She was in the process of trying to get it back.

"So you came all the way over here in your scary makeup so we could go to the meetup and find Shannon?"

"I was thinking that we'd just follow her. See where she goes. I'm not really dressed to go in anywhere."

I chuckled. "She'll probably go home to bed, where I'm going. I told you I was up all night."

"I don't want to miss out on solving this murder," Maisie said.

I pointed to her face. "I'm thinking you might have to sit this one out."

She rolled her head back. Clearly agitated.

"How about if we play sleuth this time?" I said. "Not trying to solve a murder, but trying to find out why my grandmother has a book with recipes *for* murder in it." I nodded, trying to convince her it was a good idea. "We probably could do that without you taking time away from recuperating. What'dya think?"

"I think that idea sucks."

eard you hired somebody to work the food truck."

I smiled. "Yep. I did."

We were sitting in PopPop's kitchen. I'd come a little later than usual, seeing I'd already made ice cream for the day. He was drinking his morning coffee, his folded newspaper on the table next to him.

I'd slept well the night before. After staying up all night worrying about Kaitlyn the night before that, and staying busy all weekend with customers, making up for the thrown-away batches of ice cream and running the food truck for the first time, I was out cold when my head hit the pillow. Slept so hard I didn't even have nightmares about Maisie and her ghoulishly made-up face. This time, though, I remembered to change into my pajamas and not take my knapsack to bed with me.

"And all in time for Walnut Wednesday."

"You're going to try and park there tomorrow?" His voice went up a couple extra octaves at the end, showing his surprise. "You think your help is ready for that?"

"I hope so." I chuckled. "You remember Detective Liam Beverly?" I asked.

"Yeah, I do." He looked at me over the rim of his cup. "I hope you didn't hire him."

"No." I laughed. "I hired his nephew."

"Where'd you find him?"

"He came up to the truck and asked for a job."

"While that detective was questioning you?"

I frowned. Curiosity and anxiety grumbled in my stomach. How did he know that? And was he upset about it?

"Only because Kaitlyn had come by and gotten ice cream right before she died."

"I heard you were upset about the nuts."

"She was allergic," I said.

"I heard," he said. "Does he know how to drive a food truck?"

I had to stop and think for a moment. PopPop had changed conversation topics on me and I had to remember who we were talking about. Certainly not Detective Beverly.

"I don't know if he knows how to drive one, PopPop," I said. "But he catches on quickly. He can handle selling ice cream out of it."

"You'll work on getting him a CDL?"

"Sure will," I said.

"I can drive him anywhere you need him to go. Help him sell ice cream, too."

That made my face beam. "Thank you."

He took a sip of his coffee. "The way business is going, you might have to hire a couple of more people."

"I know, if my brothers hadn't chipped in and helped during the Festival, it would have been rough sailing."

"Adding that food truck added more work and the potential for more customers."

"It did," I said.

"Just don't hire any more women that want to date me," he said and winked.

He was referring to Wilhelmina. She'd started working there and was all grins whenever PopPop was around. Batting her eyes, making little comments with a soft voice and purring at him more than Felice did when it was time for a treat.

"I can't help it if the women find you charming," I said.

He grunted.

I stood up and bent to kiss him on his cheek. "I have to get going."

"I got one more thing to talk to you about," he said. "Sit down." He pointed to the chair I'd just vacated.

I sat.

"What do you think your grandmother did?"

"What?" I asked. My eyebrows shot up.

"Something with her recipes and a book or something?"

Bobby.

That little tattletale.

"It's nothing, PopPop." I closed my eyes and shook my head. I was going to choke that boy when I saw him.

"What kind of book is it?" he asked.

There was no getting around it. He wasn't going to let me out the door until I told him.

"And why were you being sneaky about it?" he asked.

I reached down into my knapsack and pulled out the thin, old brown book. Such a little thing causing so much disruption.

"It's a recipe book written by a woman named Madeline Markham," I said.

"*Recipes from Chagrin Falls*," my grandfather said, taking the book from me. "I remember this. Your grandmother was so excited about one of her recipes being in a published book."

"There's actually three of her recipes in there," I said. "And one of them has a slight addition to it."

"Oh," he said and opened up the book. "She probably wouldn't like that." He chuckled.

"I'm sure she wouldn't," I said.

"Uh." He wasn't paying attention to me. He was looking up her recipe. "Practically all these pages are written on. Not nice to mark up a book like this."

"Somebody added poison to the recipes."

"What?" He looked up from the book at me. His brows creased.

I took the book from him and turned to Grandma Kay's page. "Somebody added ethylene glycol to the recipe."

"Oh," he said. "Well, that wasn't nice."

"Ethylene glycol poisoning is what Kaitlyn Toles died of."

"Is that the girl you knew from high school?"

Bobby didn't leave anything out.

I flipped back through the pages until I got to the blueberry pie recipe. "And that's what Madeline Markham died of."

"Blueberry pie? Your grandmother took her a blueberry pie . . ." he said, his words trailing off as he balanced the book at a different angle so he could see it without putting on his reading glasses.

He read through the recipe, his finger pointing to every word, until it stopped on "strychnine." Then he looked up at me.

"You think your grandmother did this?" A look of disgust on his face I'd never seen when speaking to me nearly broke my heart into pieces. "Is that why you were comparing her recipe cards to the book?"

"No. I don't think that," I said, feeling the pain of it by hearing the words spoken, more than I'd ever felt when I just thought about them. And if that wasn't the reason I was comparing the writings, then what was?

Shameful, as my grandmother used to say.

"This isn't your grandmother's book," my grandfather said.

"It has her name in the front of it." I didn't want to flip the book to the inside cover. I didn't even want to touch it again.

"I don't care what it has," he said and got up from the table. He disappeared into the front of his suite without another word to me.

I sat there. Turning several times to see if he was coming back. I didn't know how I was going to make this up to my grandfather.

I started clicking my nails.

Was he not speaking to me?

I turned again and looked toward the front of his suite. There weren't but a few rooms in the house. Where had he gone?

"Here," he said, finally coming back. He seemed winded, but satisfied with himself. He'd come with another copy of the cookbook and had laid it on the table. "That's your grandmother's book."

I picked it up and flipped through it. There was a bookmark on page seventeen. The page where her recipe was printed.

"How?"

I didn't say anything else. I didn't want to say anything to show that I doubted that this book, the one my grandfather had, was my grandmother's. I believed it. But where did the book come from that had her name in it?

My grandfather must've read my mind.

"Madeline's granddaughter mailed out the books she'd inscribed. Two of them got mixed up. Your grandmother got one that was supposed to go to someone else."

"Who?" I asked.

"Don't know. I don't know if anyone else ever reported back to Madeline that they'd gotten the wrong book." He took the book from me and folded it shut. "So Madeline promised her another signed copy. But before Kaylene got over there to get it, Madeline fell ill." PopPop stood up and took his coffee cup over to the sink. "We went to see her, your grandmother and me, to return the one and get another one. Kaylene took her a blueberry pie. From the *bakery*." He emphasized the word, looking at me. "But by the time we went over, she was too sick to sign it. So that's why there's no signature inside."

"Oh," I said.

It wasn't my grandmother's book.

"And for your information," he said, tossing the scrambled eggs he'd just made down the drain, "it wasn't blueberry pie that killed her."

TWENTY

Bobby!" I yelled into my phone. It was his voicemail getting the brunt of my agitation, only because he wouldn't pick up. "I know you're up." Holding the phone in front of me so I could talk directly into the speaker, I glanced at the time.

Six fifteen a.m.

Okay. So maybe he wasn't.

"Stop telling PopPop everything!" I said, continuing my rant to the air on the other end of the line before punching the icon to end the call. His contact info lingered on my phone and I yelled again at the screen that showed his name. "Act your age!"

The screen went black and I could see my reflection in it. It made me chuckle. I was acting just as childish as he was. Thinking the worst about my grandmother. Making my PopPop upset with me with what was going to be an otherwise perfect day.

I was going to put the matters of the book, Kaitlyn and murder behind me. But no sooner had I unlocked the side door and switched on the lights in the kitchen than the last came to haunt me.

Tap. Tap. Tap.

There came a knocking on the front window of the store. Just like it'd happened the day before. And just like the day before, it was Cameron.

Still ignoring the store hours clearly posted on the door . . .

I didn't bother to turn on the lights up front as I passed through. I unlocked the door, swung it open wide and gestured him in with an exaggerated sweeping of my hand.

"Cameron. What are you doing here?" I was sure he could sense the annoyance in my voice. Irritated, but, I noted, today's visit didn't bother me as much as it had done the day before.

"I was wondering if you'd found out anything yet," he said.

"About what?"

"Kaitlyn. About who killed her."

"Cameron." I closed my eyes and pulled in a breath. "I am not going to do that. I told you that yesterday."

"You worked on the other two murders. Why won't you do this one?"

"I didn't really work on the other ones voluntarily," I said, thinking about Maisie thinking she was the newest amateur sleuth on Acorn TV and I was her sidekick. And the first murder had my father as a suspect. "I just kind of keep getting sucked into them."

"And you don't want to get 'sucked' into this one?" he asked, doing air quotes. "Don't you care?"

I wanted to tell him the truth, that it wasn't that I didn't care. Of course I did. What could be worse than people senselessly losing their lives? But I didn't care to get tangled up in it and al-most lose my life in the process.

And with Maisie (mostly) stuck in bed with a face-altering virus, I was safe.

"Her funeral's today, you know," he said. It seemed as if he was trying to fight back tears. "I can't go."

"I didn't know they'd have it so quickly," I said. "It's only been two days . . ." My voice trailed off as I thought about the funeral. The finality of it all. "Why can't you go? Where is it?"

"It's right down the street at the church on South Franklin."

The redbrick church, I thought. I'd want mine to be a small white chapel like in the movies . . .

"Win!" He raised his voice. "Are you listening to me?"

"Sorry," I said.

I couldn't believe I was thinking about my own funeral. It was what happened, I was sure, when one was always surrounded by murder.

"Did you hear what I said?" Cameron asked.

"Could you say it again?" I said. "I'm sorry, but when you said 'funeral,' my mind just went sideways."

"So you can imagine how I feel then. Can't you?"

"I can," I said.

"I wouldn't be able to sit through that funeral," he said. He sniffed. "Not without my heart breaking all over again." He closed his eyes and stood in place. His stance and the lack of light seemed to put him off-balance. He spread his legs and blew out a troubled breath.

"What do you want me to do, Cameron?" I asked. I didn't feel as if there was anything I could do, but I felt compelled to ask. "I think we should just let the police take care of it."

"Maybe that's true," he said. He covered his head with his arms, his hands on top of his head. He started pacing. "I just feel like I should be doing something. I keep thinking that maybe I could have stopped it. You know?"

I nodded. I knew exactly how he felt. That was the way I'd felt when she first died.

"Did you see anything?" I asked. I didn't know why.

"No." He shook his head vigorously. "Nothing." He stopped pacing and tilted his head as if he was thinking. "She was there. Coming over to my balloon and then she . . . fell," he said. "I thought she'd tripped. I ran over to her but it was too late." He looked at me. "Just like that." He held his hands out as if he was searching for the answer. "Just that quick. She was gone."

"I really am so sorry for you," I said, not knowing what else to say.

"I just thought you'd help me find out who did this." He was walking between the tables, turning around and walking back, then doing it again. "Who took my life from me? She was my world, you know."

"I don't mean to sound . . . crass," I said. "Or hurtful. But what good would it do you?"

He stopped and dropped his hands and stared at me. Nothing was said between the two of us for what seemed like forever. I started to say something to break the silence, but he beat me to it.

"I don't know." He seemed to be admitting he didn't know

why he wanted me to find out. "I just heard you solved murders and I thought you'd solve this one, too."

"I don't really solve them." Now it was my turn to make an admission. "I really just kind of *stumble* on the answers. The killer thinking I knew something when really I didn't."

"You didn't find out the clues?"

"I mean, after I knew who it was, I did realize certain things," I said. "Clues, I guess . . . in hindsight. But to be honest, no"—I shook my head—"I didn't pick up on any breadcrumbs before the fact that would have led me to the gingerbread house."

I saw a small grin on his face. "I should have known," he said. "If the answers weren't in the back of the book, you couldn't solve the problem."

I frowned. "I never looked for answers in the back of the book," I said, knowing he was referring to our high school days. Then I decided I wasn't going there with him. "Cameron, I have to get back to work." I took a couple of steps toward the door, hoping he'd do the same. "Was there anything else you wanted . . . Needed?"

"No." He drew in a sharp breath. "I'm good." He turned the knob and pulled open the door. "I don't know what I'm going to do now." His voice cracked. "But I'm good."

When he'd left, I felt as if I couldn't move. I felt so bad for him. For Kaitlyn. But contrary to whatever it was he was thinking, I knew there wasn't anything I could do.

I finally stopped staring out into empty space and shook my concern for Cameron off. I went into the back and sat down at my desk.

I needed to scan in some invoices and put in a couple orders to our suppliers. I figured I had enough ice cream for just the store, and the food truck wasn't going anywhere today. I had different plans for it tomorrow, though.

But after sitting down, not even getting a good headwind into my paperwork, the side door opened. My mother and Riya came in, disrupting my flow.

"Morning," my mother said in her usual "greeting the classroom" voice. "Look who I found lurking around outside."

"Morning, you two," I said. "What are you doing here, Riya? What you got?" I nodded at the zippered garment bag Riya was carrying over her shoulder.

"My dress for the funeral. Figured I'd dress at your house."

"What funeral?" my mother said.

"I'm not going to the funeral," I said at the same time.

"Who is having a funer... Oh." My mother looked from Riya to me. "Is that today?" she asked, lines creased in her forehead. "Seems so soon."

"Same thing I said to Cameron."

"Cameron?" they said in unison.

"Yeah," I said. "He stopped by this morning."

"Again?" my mother said. "What did he want this time?"

"I'm not sure," I said. "I do know that he realized, by the time he left, I wasn't the one to help with anything he might need."

"He was the one who told you about the funeral?" Riya asked. "You didn't already know?"

"No. I didn't know. And yep. He told me. Said he wasn't going, though. It was too much for him."

"Oh," my mother said and grabbed her heart. "That is so sad. Their life together cut short. I couldn't imagine."

"Well, we're going," Riya said.

"We who?" I asked.

"Me and you," she said.

"I'm not going," I said.

"Why not?" my mother asked.

"Yeah. Why not?" Riya said.

"How could you not go?" my mother said, asking another question before I got the chance to answer the first.

"Didn't you say you went to see her parents?" Riya asked.

Now they were just double-teaming me.

"You didn't tell me you saw the Toleses!" my mother said. "How were they? Upset, I know. And now expecting even more for you to show up, don't you think?"

I held up my hands. Wanting to jump in to stop their bombardment of questions. "Mommy. I didn't see them. I went and chickened out. *And*," I emphasized, "like I said: I didn't know the funeral was today." I shrugged. "But even with me knowing or not knowing, I really don't see any reason for me to go."

"No reason!" Now they were talking in unison.

I guess that'd been the wrong thing to say.

"Oh good Lord, Win." My mother lit into me first. "Didn't I teach you better than that? You've known that girl practically your entire life. From the time you started school."

"I thought you said she was your friend," Riya added.

"I—I . . ."

I was flabbergasted. I hadn't thought about going, and now

thinking about it made me as sad as it had when I thought I may have had a hand in her death. And to add to that, the two of them were pushing me to do it.

"I haven't been to a funeral since Grandma Kay's," I said, hoping that would help them understand without me mentioning the whole "I've seen enough dead bodies lately" thing. I was breathing hard and searched my mother's eyes for some understanding.

"It's a funeral, Win," my mother said. "Not a torture chamber. For God's sake." She threw her hands up. "Nothing's going to happen to you." She flung a hand at me. "You need to go. Show your respect and represent your family."

"I have to run the store."

"Because what am I here for?" my mother said, tilting her head and putting a hand on her hip. "I'm quite capable of running the store. You go."

"But—"

"Why wouldn't you want to go?" Riya asked before I had a chance to get my objection out.

"Why would you *want* to go?" I asked her. I lowered my voice as if my mother couldn't hear my words. Riya didn't even like Kaitlyn, or so she'd said. I wished I could talk it out just between Riya and me. Convince her that it wasn't a good idea. She'd come in starting trouble early in the morning.

Why wasn't she at work?

"I want to go because we should," Riya said, answering my question in a voice louder than the one I'd used. "It's the right thing to do." I glanced over at my mother as Riya reiterated her sentiments. "Kaitlyn *is* the first person we went to school with who has died."

"Please, Win, don't embarrass me," my mother said. At times she could take things so seriously and be so dramatic about them—just like the third graders she used to teach. "Don't embarrass our entire family."

chapter TWENTY-ONE

I was still trying to figure out how the weight of my entire family's reputation had fallen on my shoulders as I walked up the steps to the First Baptist Church that afternoon.

Of course I'd done as my mother asked. I left the store right after we opened at eleven. Riya and I headed up to my house to get dressed. We took her car to my house and to the church. If I was being forced to wear heels, I wasn't going to walk the hills of Chagrin Falls in them.

And Riya was right, Kaitlyn was the first to go in our graduating class. Something I just hadn't even considered. And yes, I did have the manners that my parents had instilled when raising me. I had felt obligated to go and see her parents. To give my condolences. It should have been with casserole dish in hand, and I shouldn't have chickened out. But that was as much as I'd thought about doing.

All I could do was hope the casket would be closed by the time I got in there. Seeing her dead once was enough for me.

My mother had talked on and on the rest of the morning about how she'd been Kaitlyn's brother Joshua's third grade teacher. And how my father had set her sister Melissa's arm when she broke it in middle school. And how we all had ties to the Toles family.

That was fine, I thought after her constant chiding, *she was right, someone should go.* I just hadn't wanted it to be me.

Kaitlyn's funeral was at twelve thirty. The sun was high in the sky, and even though the weather reported scattered showers, there wasn't a cloud to be found.

I shielded my eyes to look for Riya. She'd sent me in to secure a seat while she parked the car. I had to move out of the way of the steady stream of people coming into the church.

There were so many people there. People coming past me nodding, saying hello, low murmurs of the conversations they were having among themselves. I had to move out of the way several times to let clusters of people by. I thought I probably should go and find us a seat. It looked as if it was going to be standing room only.

Had these all been friends of Kaitlyn? It didn't seem the day I'd spoken to her—the day she'd died—that she'd learned to endear herself to anyone.

I scanned the crowd. I didn't know how large her extended family was, but I knew her immediate family only included two parents, a brother and a sister. The driving forces by which my mother persuaded me to come.

I spotted a woman in striped socks, brown shoes with bell-shaped heels and a buckle. She had on long, black satin opera gloves and a black hat with a veil that covered her face. I knew without any facial recognition. I knew who she was.

I went up to the woman and whispered in her ear.

"Maisie," I said. "What are you doing here?"

She jumped, obviously startled. She turned to look at me. "How did you know it was me?" she asked in a strained whisper. She pulled up her gloves and tugged down on the veil.

"I could smell your perfume."

"I'm not wearing any perfume," she said.

"No?" I sniffed. "Smells like your new scent. *Eau de Calamine.*"

She scratched her arm through her glove. "It isn't working. I itch like the devil."

"That's what you get for not staying in bed," I said.

"Who could stay in bed when there is a murderer afoot?"

"Have you been reading Sherlock Holmes?" I asked.

"No." It seemed I could make out a frown that came with her response under her netting.

"Why are you here?" I asked.

"To find out who killed Kaitlyn," she said matter-of-factly. Then she got in close, so close her fishnet veil brushed my face. "It's a known fact, the murderer comes to the funeral."

"Will you be able to pick him or her out just from their presence here?" I asked.

"Why are *you* here?" she said, not answering my question. I didn't need to see her face that time. I could hear the irritation in her voice.

"My mother made me, and Riya dragged me." I pointed over my shoulder. "She's parking the car."

"Who? Your mother?"

"Riya. My mother's at the ice cream parlor."

"Why would Riya want to come?" Maisie asked.

"Because we should pay our respects," Riya said, coming up behind me. She stared at Maisie. "Who are you supposed to be?" She turned and looked around at the people entering the chapel. Turning back, she raised an eyebrow. "Were we supposed to come in costume?"

I had to cover my mouth to keep from laughing.

"I'm covered with spots," Maisie said. "If you'd come by to see about me, you'd know."

"I work in a hospital," Riya said. "I can't come in contact with your germs, I'd infect all of Northeast Ohio. Maybe the world."

"I'm not contagious now," Maisie said.

"And I'm here for you," Riya said, putting on a smile and patting her on the back. "Now what are you doing here?"

"Snooping," I answered for her.

"Murderers always show up at the funeral," Maisie repeated.

"We should go in," I said, getting the conversation back to the matter at hand. "If we want to get a seat."

"We should be where we can watch people," Maisie said. "Their reactions. Possibly overhear their conversations."

"We're not FBI profilers," I said. "We can't do any of those things."

"We could try," Maisie said. "That's why we're here."

I gave Riya a quick glance. We both knew that wasn't true.

We got in step with the other mourners and filed into the chapel. The pews were filling up and there wasn't a spot for the three of us to fit in together.

"There." I pointed. "One of us can sit on the end, and the other two of us can get those seats in front of it, if we hurry." I started walking and the two of them followed me.

Riya passed me up and snagged the solitary seat on the end, Maisie and I took the spaces in front of her.

"You want to leave our purses here to save our seats," Riya said, "and go and view the body?"

"Yes," Maisie said and popped up.

"No," was my answer.

"You don't want to go up?" Maisie asked.

She'd missed the whole prolonged conversation about it earlier that morning. So I gave her the short version: "No."

She eyed me like she was waiting for me to elaborate.

I shook my head. "You two go. I'll watch your seats."

"Don't you want to speak to Kaitlyn's parents?" Riya leaned forward and whispered in my ear.

"I'll talk to them later," I whispered back.

Maisie scooted past me, and she and Riya went to the front, getting at the end of the procession waiting to file by the casket at the front of the church.

I watched them as they took their place in line, then I turned to watch the stream of people that filed into the church.

Some of the faces I recognized from high school, and then I saw the Channel 6 weatherman. He was dressed in the same plaid jacket and bow tie he wore on television. The rosiness in his cheeks had spread to his entire face. He was standing with a group of people all using low voices. A few of them had red eyes and there were tissues in the hands of most.

Then I saw Avery, standing near the group, but she wasn't standing with them. Nor did she have red eyes. They were smoky, but it was only due to her choice of makeup.

Avery Kendricks had gotten her dream job because of Kaitlyn's demise. A coworker that others seemingly would miss. But she seemed not to pay any attention to the matter at hand. She had her phone out, scrolling through it. Every minute or so, she'd look up into the crowd as if she was searching for someone.

It made me wonder if she was only at the funeral because, as Maisie thought, she was the killer.

"Hi, Win." The greeting startled me. I turned to see Melissa Toles standing next to me. "I'm glad you came," she said.

"Of course," I said, trying to breathe evenly. I stood up and hugged her. "I wouldn't have missed it."

I hated lying to her. But what was I going to say? That I hadn't wanted to come? It was hard on me seeing Kaitlyn like this, but I knew it wasn't as hard as what she was going through.

"How are you holding up?" I asked.

"I'm good," she said. "As good as I can be, I guess."

I nodded. Unsure what to say, "I'm going to speak to your parents," is what came out. "Give them my condolences."

"Good. They're looking forward to that. Your dad stopped by yesterday. It was so nice to see him." She held out her arm and twisted it back and forth. "I owe him a lot. It was such a bad break and he fixed it like new."

I smiled. The whole time, though, thinking what a little sneak my mother was. There was no way my father would have visited the Toleses and not told my mother. She knew our family had already been represented and she'd still insisted that I come.

"Kaitlyn had stopped by our ice cream truck that afternoon," I said hesitantly. I didn't want to bring up the whole nut allergy thing since it had no bearing on what happened, but still, I wondered how she and her family felt about it.

"I know," she said. "Your father told us. Also told us he was there with her, you know ..." She bit down on her trembling lip. I rubbed her arm. "When she passed."

"I know," I said and nodded.

"And she was getting ready to leave, you know? Move out of town and we wouldn't have seen her for a while." She turned her head, staring off toward the front of the church. "And I didn't ... I ... didn't care. My parents had a big dinner for her and I didn't even go." She squinted her eyes in disgust. "Now I'll never get to see her again. Aren't I terrible?"

"No. No," I said. "You're not terrible. You didn't know."

"I didn't. When they had the dinner, I just thought, oh, she'll be in New York. No big deal. You know?" She nodded. "Like you did. You went to New York, but you still saw your family, right? Then you came back home."

"Right."

"Plus, she was always bragging," Melissa said with a choked chuckle, dabbing a tissue to her eye. "You know how she bragged."

I nodded and smiled. "Why was she moving to New York?" I asked.

"She didn't tell you?"

"No." I wondered, didn't Melissa know that Kaitlyn and I weren't close? "She didn't tell me."

"Oh my God, I thought she'd told everyone!" A smile let loose on her face. "She got a job with a big cable news station." She cupped her hand to her mouth. "C-N-N."

"Really?" I said and lifted an eyebrow. That was news, no pun intended, to me. How could I have not heard about that? "That was cool, huh?"

"Yes. I knew there'd be no living with her once her face was splashed all over national television." She did a hiccup, then a short pause. That intermittent period must have been used to manufacture tears, because they came pouring out before she could speak again. "Now there'll be no living with her at all."

Oh my...

"I saw Cameron this morning," I said, wanting to say something. Anything. I looked around the church. "I guess he'll be around later." I turned back to her and nodded my understanding. "Said he was too heartbroken to come."

"Cameron." Melissa swiped her tears with a quick flick of her wrist. She leaned in to me and I could feel the heat rising up in her. She spat out her words. "Wouldn't know a broken heart if someone ripped his out of his chest and tore it into shreds right in front of his face."

Whoa...

"But we'll see you later, right?" she said, standing back up straight. It was like she'd been momentarily possessed—a demon passing through the church, passed through her. She gave me a pat on my hand. "Riya told me that you guys were going to come together today. I'm glad you did. My parents would love seeing you."

Riya.

That little fabricator. With all her nagging me to go, she hadn't said one word about her speaking with Melissa Toles beforehand and telling her we'd attend.

And no sooner had I plopped back down in my seat from that conversation, happy to get off my feet in those heels, than Riya and Maisie showed back up.

"She looked nice," Maisie said, pressing her skirt down with gloved hands. "Just like herself."

"Who?" I asked.

"Kaitlyn."

"What does that mean?" I frowned. "She looked nice? Like herself?"

She shrugged. "I don't know. It's what Safta says every time she gets back from a funeral."

"We stopped and greeted Kaitlyn's parents," Riya said. Taking her seat behind me, she leaned forward. "They asked about you."

"No they didn't." Now I worried that I should have gone up because I didn't know what Riya had said.

"No, they didn't," Riya confirmed. "I just wanted you to feel bad."

I rolled my eyes.

"I got to see everyone from up there." Maisie glanced at Riya to get her attention and leaned in. She nodded knowingly. "Great vantage point."

"And did it help?" Riya asked. "Did you spot Kaitlyn's murderer yet?" Her voice low, her eyes scanning the room.

"I have," Maisie said. She raised her hand close to her face and pointed inconspicuously. "She's the one standing by Kaitlyn now. The one who is sobbing uncontrollably."

chapter

TWENTY-TWO

Shannon Holske was the person Maisie was referring to. No surprise to me. Maisie had already told me that she was her number one suspect.

It looked as if Shannon wanted to get into the casket with Kaitlyn. She was bent over close, her body shaking from the sobs. Someone was standing next to her, a girl who looked familiar, maybe someone else from high school. The other woman had her one arm around Shannon's shoulders. She was speaking low to her—I could see her lips moving close to Shannon's ear. The line was backed up because of her machinations.

"Shannon?" Riya asked. "That's who you think did it?" Clearly, that assessment surprised her.

"Motive: jealousy," Maisie said as if she was talking in code.

Riya nodded. I guessed she understood the jargon. "She's crying awfully hard, though."

"Makes her even more suspect," Maisie said. "She's putting

on a show. Trying to lead everyone away from her hand in the deed."

Her hand in the deed . . .

I stretched my eyes. It sounded far-fetched to me, especially with Maisie using all of these Sherlock Holmes–esque terms. I'd agreed with Maisie's reasons for suspecting Shannon, but sobbing as a ruse didn't make sense to me.

Because, I thought, *no one, except for Maisie, thinks of her as a suspect, do they?*

I said "no one" as if there were gaggles of amateur sleuths running around trying to solve the murder. Only the police. I turned around and spied every corner of the chapel, but I didn't see one cop anywhere.

Not even a glimpse of Detective Beverly.

I narrowed my eyes at Maisie and wondered where she'd gotten the idea that murderers showed up at funerals. Certainly, the Chagrin Falls Police Department didn't concur with that theory.

"I CAN'T GO to the repast," I said for the tenth time, but no one was listening to me. We were standing down the street from the Toles house. Practically in the same spot I'd been the night Kaitlyn died.

"We're here now," Riya said. "Unless you want to walk back home in those heels." She pointed to my feet. "I suggest you c'mon."

"Ugh!"

"We won't stay long," Riya said.

"Just long enough to see what Shannon is doing."

"And for you to speak to Kaitlyn's parents."

I clomped along, walking behind the two of them. They were on a mission. I was wondering how long it'd be before I got to take off my heels. My feet were killing me.

When we got inside, it seemed as if everyone from the church had tried to cram into the house. People were milling around, talking in hushed voices. The family was sitting in the living room. Mrs. Toles sat in the middle of a large ivory-colored couch with fringe along the bottom. Flanked on her sides were her two remaining children—Melissa and Joshua. Mr. Toles was sitting in a nearby cushioned chair that matched the couch. He was red-faced but seemed to force a smile whenever anyone stopped by to greet him.

When we came through the door, I saw Melissa touch her mother's arm and they both looked my way.

The moment I had dreaded. Speaking to her parents. I blew out a breath and walked over to them. Mrs. Toles spoke to Joshua, who looked at me, then stood up from his seat. She patted the seat he'd vacated, telling me to sit there. I nodded to Mr. Toles before I did.

"I'm glad you came," Mrs. Toles said. She held my hand and I could tell she was trying to hold back tears. "It would have made Kaitlyn very happy."

I didn't know that Kaitlyn would have ever cared, still, I was glad I was there. Even if it hadn't been of my own accord. "I should have come earlier," I said. "I apologize for that."

"Don't," she said and took my hand. "I know you're busy. Kaitlyn told us about the addition of the food truck. We'd planned on stopping by, Keith and I, until . . . you know."

"She told you about the food truck?" I asked. That surprised me.

"Oh yes. She kept us informed on you. She was the consummate journalist. Keeping abreast on all the news happenings, as she liked to say."

I nodded.

"She followed you, you know."

"Followed me," I repeated. I couldn't remember seeing her "friending" or following me on any of my social media platforms.

"Yes. She was impressed how you went to New York and worked at that ad firm. What was the name of it?"

"Hawken Spencer," Melissa answered.

I looked over at her and she smiled.

"Then you came home and revamped your family's store," Mrs. Toles said. "Kaitlyn always said you motivated her."

"She said it was too bad you didn't still live in New York since she was going there," Melissa said. "She said you two could have hung out."

"She truly admired you," Mrs. Toles said.

I couldn't believe what I was hearing. I wouldn't have ever thought that Kaitlyn gave me a second thought. Heck, any thought at all.

It really made me feel bad about not coming over sooner.

"Kaitlyn also told us how you changed the scooper out when she came by your truck for ice cream." Joshua spoke this time. Standing over me at the end of the couch, he smiled down at me. "That was cool, Win. For you to remember."

"Of course," I said. "Of course I would remember."

"And all that mess, Win, that you were responsible. You know that stuff that . . ." Mrs. Toles hesitated and slid her tongue over the roof of her mouth as if getting rid of a bad taste she had. "Cameron said at the Balloon Glow—"

"We knew it wasn't true," Melissa interjected. "She'd already come home and told us about the ice cream."

"Yes, we knew," Mrs. Toles said. "And she was careful. She always carried an EpiPen with her."

"Never went anywhere without it," Melissa said.

"We didn't want you to think," Mrs. Toles said, "we'd ever think something like that. That you would do something to harm her. Our Kaitlyn was so fond of you, we wouldn't want something like that to stick with you. Tarnish the memory of your and her relationship."

"Oh no. No." I shook my head. "It wouldn't. I—I just . . ."

"It's okay," Mrs. Toles said and patted my hand. "I'm just glad you're here. She was such a good daughter." She glanced up at Melissa and grabbed her hand. "I had two great daughters. Respectful. Helpful. A mother couldn't ask . . ." Her voice cracked with her last words. I didn't know what to say to her. I didn't know what Kaitlyn had said to her—to all of them—about me. They seemed so proud of her. And I was totally confused. Their Kaitlyn, what she'd said, what she'd done, was so different than the Kaitlyn I remembered.

Luckily, someone else came over to offer their condolences and I took my leave.

Getting up from the couch, my heart was heavy and my eyes filled with tears. Kaitlyn had admired the things I'd done. She'd followed them and discussed them with her family. How had I not known? Why didn't she ever reach out to me?

I found Riya and Maisie standing near the dining room table.

It was full of food, and their little saucer–sized plates were brimming over with a good sampling of it all.

"You okay?" Maisie said.

"You're not crying, are you?" Riya said. "The funeral is over."

"Mrs. Toles told me that Kaitlyn kept up with me and admired the things I was doing."

"She did?" Maisie said.

"Melissa told me," Riya said. "That's why I wanted to come."

"Well, I never knew that. And it's so flattering and so heartbreaking. Maybe we would have been friends if I'd known."

"She didn't want you to know, evidently," Riya said. "But that is a compliment coming from her. Kaitlyn wasn't one to admit anyone did something better than her."

"It wasn't that I did something better than her," I said. I shook my head. "I don't know. And I guess I'll never know."

"Not to break up this brag fest, but has anyone been watching Shannon?"

"No," I said.

"Watch her for what?" Riya said.

"She's been flitting around like a bee, dry-eyed, not a tear to be found. Talking to everyone like she's the hostess with the mostess."

Riya and I giggled.

"She's probably all cried out," Riya said.

"And nervous about being here, so she's keeping the conversation going."

"Speaking of which, where's that baby of hers?" Maisie asked.

"What baby?" Riya said.

"She claims to have a baby by Kaitlyn's almost fiancé," Maisie said.

"Shhh!" I said. "People might hear you." I lowered my voice and stepped closer to Riya. "She just alluded to who the baby's father was. She never came right out and said that."

"Why would she be here with Cameron's almost fiancée's family if they've been messing around?" Riya wanted to know.

"Because she's a killer with no heart," Maisie said. "I'm going to talk to her."

"No!" I said. "Don't do it here." She didn't turn around. "Maisie!"

"Too late," Riya said as we watched Maisie wiggle her way through the crowd of people. "I think this time, it's Maisie who's going in for the kill."

TWENTY-THREE

I wanted to take off my shoes and walk to the car barefoot. My feet were hurting so badly. I was not used to wearing heels, not even when I worked in New York. I didn't even know what had possessed me to put them on in the first place.

When Maisie had gotten back from stalking Shannon, she'd rushed us out of the house, saying we had to leave, "Now!"

I was happy to oblige.

"I need to get home and change," I said. "I probably should get back to the ice cream parlor."

"We have to follow Shannon," Maisie said, leading the way to Riya's car. She turned back and looked behind us at the Toles house. "She said she was getting ready to go."

"She told you that?" Riya asked.

"Of course not," Maisie said. "She was talking to someone else. She said she was going home."

"Why do we care that she's getting ready to go?" I asked.

"Because we have to follow her." I could tell she didn't like repeating herself.

"No we don't." I looked down at my clothes and my four-inch heels. Certainly not stalking-wear.

"Yes. We. Do." Maisie was standing at the car door, beating us there. She was clutching the handle, waiting for Riya to click the lock. "She might lead us to the murder weapon."

I frowned.

"Murder weapon?" Riya repeated Maisie's statement as a question. She clicked the lock and got in the car. Maisie pulled the door open and piled in the back, scooting up to put her face between the bucket seats.

"Don't you wanna solve Kaitlyn's murder now that you know how enamored she was with you?" Maisie asked.

"No." I pulled the door shut and eased my feet out of the shoes. I sighed and wiggled my toes around.

"Win just isn't into solving mysteries," Riya said. "This is always your idea."

Yes. "That's right. I'm not into dedicating any part of my life to solving mysteries, especially the murder kind."

"She'd be into it if it was about that murder cookbook mystery," Maisie said.

"What murder cookbook?" Riya asked.

"Oh! I forgot to tell you, Maisie," I said. I shifted in my seat to face her. "Madeline Markham wasn't murdered. And she sent the wrong book to my grandma. My grandfather still had the book she'd given Grandma Kay."

"Who got your grandmother's book?" Maisie asked.

"What cookbook!" Riya said.

"You didn't tell Riya about the cookbook?" Maisie asked.

"No." I glanced at Riya with sorry eyes. "I felt so bad about even thinking my grandmother had anything to do with what was inside that cookbook that I tried to push it out of my mind."

"Well, somebody could tell me now!" Riya said.

I looked at Maisie. "I don't know who got the one intended for my grandmother."

"Maybe they had something to do with Kaitlyn's murder?" Maisie said, raising her eyebrows. "You remember what it said. Killer Sundae."

"It wasn't a sundae that killed her."

"Oh!" Maisie yelped and bounced up and down in the back seat. "There's Shannon!" She pointed, her arm extending through the seats toward the windshield. "Ooo! Ooo! Riya, you have to follow her."

"Where is she going?" Riya asked.

"I. Don't. Know. But wait until she takes off," Maisie instructed. "We can't let her see us."

"She can't help but to see us," I said. "Who could miss us in this red sports car?"

"We can just stay a few car lengths behind her," Maisie said.

"I'm not going anywhere," Riya said defiantly. She crossed her arms. "Not until someone fills me in on this cookbook that Mrs. Crewse had that killed Kaitlyn."

I frowned. "No one said anything like that. My grandmother, or the cookbook for that matter, had nothing to do with Kaitlyn."

"Ooo! Ooo! She's taking off," Maisie squealed from the back. She reached to the front and shook the steering wheel. "We have to go. Go! Go!"

"I don't think we should follow her," I said. "I should get back to work."

"Now!" Maisie shouted. "We have to go now! She's leaving!"

"I want to know about the cookbook," Riya said. "Like I said, I'm not going anywhere until you guys fill me in. You're always leaving me out."

"*Oy vey iz mir!*" Maisie squawked, her voice so high it could have shattered glass. "You two are killing me. *Oy!* I'm dead!"

Riya and I both turned to look between the bucket seats and into the back. Maisie had ripped her veil off and had slumped back onto the seat. She was shaking her legs so hard, it made the entire car move—the only dead person I'd ever seen do that. She'd placed one hand across her forehead, and her eyes had rolled back in her head. Her mouth was moving but nothing was coming out.

"Did she just speak in Yiddish?" Riya turned to face me, our foreheads almost touching.

"I think so," I said, looking at Riya. "She must be pretty upset."

"We should probably do what she wants," Riya said, turning to start the car.

"We should," I agreed with a nod and turned to face forward. "Definitely follow Shannon."

"I'm on it," she said and pulled off.

"I'll tell you about the cookbook on the way."

MAISIE RECOVERED FAIRLY quickly after we got going. The first we heard from her after her near-death experience was not to get too close.

"We're good. She won't notice us," Riya said, then glanced up in her rearview mirror. "You good, too?"

I had filled in Riya on the cookbook, but declined to talk much about it.

"At least tell me what the woman died from," she said.

"I don't know," I said. "But PopPop said it wasn't murder."

"He's not a doctor, you know," Riya said. "Some things—some poisons—resemble things like heart attacks."

I closed my eyes and shook my head. "I don't want to think about it."

"You really should find out what happened to the book your grandmother was supposed to get," our backseat zombie said.

"I know what happened to it," I said. "Whoever had it gave it to the Around the Corner Bookshop. Probably because they knew that Madeline Markham and my grandmother had both passed."

"Yeah, but you don't know *who* that 'whoever' was," Maisie said.

"I don't think that makes a difference," I said.

"It might," Maisie said.

Riya nodded. "It could."

"Let's change the subject," I said. "Because Shannon just pulled up into the parking lot of that building. And according to Maisie's dying wishes, that is what we're here for. To see what she does."

"Did we just follow her home?" Riya asked, looking up at the building Shannon had disappeared into. "All this to find out where she lives?"

"She doesn't live there," Maisie said.

"How do you know?" we both asked.

"Because no one lives in a downtown loft with a toddler."

We both turned to look out of our side windows. We had driven all the way downtown. We'd been so engrossed in conversation, I hadn't realized how far we'd gone. We were near the heart of downtown on West Third, two streets over from the Flats.

Daytime downtown was all about business. The Flats had been redeveloped for nightlife. At a lower elevation than the surrounding city, the area was on the Cuyahoga River where steel- and sawmills used to reside. Now known for edgy bars, comedy shows and outdoor nightlife at the waterfront, where marinas dotted the shore and water taxis offered ferry service from one side of the bank to the other.

Neither area was conducive to family living.

"Plus," Maisie said, taking opera glasses out of her purse and leaning between the seats, "Shannon lives in Cleveland Heights."

"How do you know that?" I asked.

"I asked her," Maisie said.

"She's just probably visiting someone here," I said.

"Like her boyfriend," Riya said.

"She doesn't have a boyfriend," Maisie said.

"This might have been a waste of time," Riya said.

"We needed to find out what she was up to," Maisie said. "If she was the killer."

"We're not going to find that out here, sitting and watching a building she's gone into. We can't even tell what she's doing." Riya shook her head.

"We need evidence she was the killer," Maisie said. "The best way to get it is to follow her movements."

"I don't know, Maisie," Riya said. "If you wanted to know if she killed Kaitlyn, you should have asked her that, too."

"I did," Maisie said.

"No you didn't," I said, surprised.

"Yes, I did."

"What did she say, Maisie?" Riya asked.

"She said she'd never admit to anything."

chapter TWENTY-FOUR

Other than the funeral, the day before had turned out to be a waste. Maisie wanted to sit out in front of the apartment building until Shannon came out, which was four hours later. She came out with her little boy in her arms, crossed the street to a restaurant, then went right back in with a bag of food. Who knew what happened after that or if Shannon even lived in Cleveland Heights.

I got back home, changed clothes and went back up to the store. My mother was still there and wanted me to give her a play-by-play of what happened at the funeral and afterward.

What was I supposed to say? I mean, what happens at a funeral?

I just used Maisie's line she'd taken from her grandmother. "Kaitlyn looked nice. Just like herself," I said.

"Oh, that's good," my mother said.

I guess she knew what that meant.

I spent the rest of the evening making ice cream, went home, watched a little television and turned in early.

When I woke up the next morning, I went through my regular routine. Keeping my mind off all mischief, including Maisie, who called my phone twice before six a.m.

I had the day planned. I had decided I wouldn't even think of the things Maisie wanted to talk about.

"Are you going to do it today?" my PopPop asked after I'd stopped by for my morning visit.

"Yes, I am," I said, a smile beaming across my face. "And I can't wait."

"I'm real proud of you, little girl. You've taken this family into the future with a bang!"

He was talking about us participating in Walnut Wednesday. Another first for the Crewse Family Food Truck.

Downtown Cleveland, filled with its many offices and businesses, hosted a food truck convoy every Wednesday in a centrally located plaza on Walnut Street. Trucks of all varieties convened for lunch traffic, and today all those hungry, curious people were getting the chance to have ice cream.

I looked up at the sky and already saw the sun peeking through. It was going to be a beautiful and warm fall day.

Because so many people around the area visited the falls behind our store and came out to the Harvest Time Festival, Crewse Creamery had a good following. Clevelanders knew about us. And now, they wouldn't have to travel to Chagrin Falls to taste our delectable wares. We, for the first time in our history, were going to come to them.

Until I'd hired Nevel Ray Quincy, I hadn't been sure if I was going to be able to go to Walnut Wednesday. I hadn't had the manpower to take off all day without finagling the schedules I'd already made up for the week and scheduling extra time on duty due to the Festival.

But now I did. I just needed to get his name on my permit and we were good to go. First things first, though, I had to open up the ice cream parlor.

I didn't have much to do. To help with all the stress and anxiety I'd been feeling, I'd scrubbed and cleaned in the store and on the truck until everything shined. And I'd made enough ice cream to last for a couple of days.

But standing in the middle of the kitchen with nothing to do, I decided to make another batch of chocolate and vanilla for the food truck. I made quick work of that, and it was only seven thirty, so I sat down at the computer and pulled out my phone. I wanted to post to social media some of the photos from the Festival and let people know we'd be on Walnut today.

First thing I saw when I went on Instagram was a picture of Kaitlyn. She was standing by the balloons, a smile on her face. I chuckled at that. She must have been ready to go on camera. It was the only time she looked friendly.

As I stared at the phone, I saw a message pop up. It was from a number that wasn't in my contact list.

I've got pics of ur food truck.

Who are you?

Grey Wolf.

?

Cameraman for Channel 6. Gary. We met at the Festival.

Oh. Okay.

Saw your IG page. Thought u'd like pics I have. Professional images.

Professional pictures of the truck would be a good idea. But what did he want? What was the catch?

How much? I texted back.

Nothing.

Free?

Professional courtesy.

Mmmm . . . That would be really nice of him. I could use them on my social media page.

Okay. That would be nice. Thank you.

U want 2 pick up?

Where?

News station. Downtown. West 6th.

I thought about that. I'd be down that way today, and it wasn't often I got downtown. Heck, it wasn't often I left Chagrin Falls.

Okay. When??

Anytime.

Today okay??

Yep.

2:30?

See u then.

Well, that worked out good, I thought, clicking out of my Instagram page. I put the phone facedown on the desk. Before the ice cream parlor had reopened, I had put ice cream samples on my friend's food truck when we were gearing up for the reopening. I'd found out that the lunch crowd started around ten thirty and ended around two. I figured I'd let Quincy serve the stragglers and ready the truck to come back to Chagrin Falls while I walked over to the news station.

My phone beeped with another message from Gary.

Heard u r an amateur sleuth.

I didn't know why he brought that up. I texted an emoji that expressed that.

Come up with anything on Kaitlyn's murder??

Well. Now there was a reputation I didn't want to have. That I was going around trying to solve murders. I figured I should make that clear to him.

Lol. Really not. Just purveyor of ice cream.

He texted back a smiley face.

I hope he did find it funny. I didn't want anyone to take it seriously that that was a "thing" with me.

Where did he even get that from? That I was an amateur sleuth? Even when I made a concentrated effort to get away from murder and drama, it seemed I couldn't. It found me.

Wilhelmina and my mother were going to run the store for the first half of the day. I told her we should be back by four. It was Candy's day off. She'd worked so hard helping me during the Harvest Time Festival, spending time next to Bobby and me. Maisie was still off the schedule—covered with blisters, she was good per her to attend funerals and do stakeouts, but per me, she wasn't ready to come back to the ice cream parlor.

I pulled the truck up to the front of the store. Quincy and I carried the trays of ice cream out, one at a time, and my mother stood and waved at me when we left like we were taking a long trip and wouldn't be back soon if at all.

I watched her in my rearview mirror as I turned the corner and she was still standing there.

She was such a mother.

We made it downtown by nine thirty. Early enough to get the perfect parking spot. At least I hoped we'd get one good spot. It had been the third time I'd been down this way in the last couple of days. But when I'd come that way with Riya, it had been dark, and when we followed Shannon, we'd been lost in conversation.

Today, I felt like I had landed in Oz.

There was a crystal chandelier in the middle of Euclid Avenue in Playhouse Square. A huge-screen television on a building on Fourteenth Street. Although technically, Quincy and I agreed, it was a jumbotron. I'd seen them all the time in New York, but I never thought of Cleveland as matching up, and I guess I was wrong. I felt like a tourist and was in awe.

We stopped at City Hall on Sixth and Lakeside so I could update my permit, adding Quincy's name as Occupant. A weird term for someone who was just working on the truck. But I made sure I did everything needed to comply.

I parked right in front at a meter and hoped my big truck wouldn't be too much of an intrusion. I climbed the steps to the doors of City Hall. Built in 1916, it abutted Lake Erie. It was made of stone and, today, designated a neoclassic historic landmark. The marble and columned framed rotunda hosted weddings, rallies and funerals.

I had to show my ID and pass through a metal detector to get inside. Permits were inside Room 121. And for the first time I noticed that the Bureau of Vital Statistics was also in that room. It was where a person would go to get birth and death certificates.

Death certificates.

What had Quincy said about death certificates?

They were public record . . .

I could get Madeline Markham's death certificate and find out exactly what she'd died from.

Find out if it was poison-laced blueberry pie.

The entire time I stood in line for the permit and while they were updating my certificate, I couldn't help but to keep glancing over my shoulder at the death certificate counter.

"Ms. Crewse. Ms. Crewse." The woman was trying to get my attention.

"Oh sorry," I said.

"It's okay. I zone out all the time," she said. "Thinking about a sandy beach in Puerto Vallarta." She nodded to a picture hanging on the wall by a desk. "One day, when I have nothing to do with my days, I'll be there."

I chuckled. It was a better thought than the one I was having. All that was on my mind was murder.

I paid her, took my certificate and walked out into the rotunda, but then I couldn't get any farther than that. My feet just wouldn't move toward the exit.

"I don't want to know," I told myself.

But that was the only part that denied it. Every other part of me wanted to know.

"Sorry, PopPop. Grandma Kay," I muttered as I did an about-face and marched up to the counter.

"Hi," I said to the woman behind it. She had on a city keycard with her picture and the name "Frankie" on it. "I wanted to get a death certificate."

"Fill out this form," Frankie said and slid it over to me. She pointed to the large desk-like wooden counters in the middle of the room. "Bring it back here. Certified certificates are twenty-five dollars, uncertified copies are five dollars each."

She turned from me and continued whatever it was she'd been doing before I walked up.

I took the green sheet of paper over to the desk and read over it. It called for information I didn't know. Like birthdate and date of death.

"What was I thinking?" I muttered. "How am I supposed to get this information?" I glanced back over at Frankie. She wasn't paying any attention to me. I could just throw the sheet of paper in the little wastebasket they had on either end of the stand and go. I looked down at my legs. "Because we don't have the answers to the questions," I announced to them. "So we have to leave."

I don't know if they heard me or not, but just as I picked up the paper to toss, O popped into my mind.

I hadn't seen him since the Festival, which was probably a good thing. But something he'd told me was sending electric jolts through me.

Most anything you want to know about a person can be found online . . .

He'd taught me that when Maisie and I were trying to solve the first murder and didn't know anything about the victim.

I whipped out my phone and put in my question: *When did Madeline Markham die.* I hesitated and added, *in Ohio.*

And scrolling down the links provided, I found what I needed. *Find a Grave.*

There I found a picture of her tombstone. There were fresh-cut flowers in the picture, but who knew when this satellite image had been taken? But using my fingers to stretch the image, I could see that the brown-stained stone had an etching of an open book on the front, and carved on the inside were the dates of her birth and death.

A chill ran down my spine.

"I'd thought you'd gotten lost in there," Quincy said when I got back to the food truck. "You were in there forever."

"I didn't take that long," I said, setting down my knapsack with Ms. Markham's death certificate placed neatly inside. "First there were people in line in front of me, and then they asked me a couple questions that I had to search the answers to." I smiled. "But we're good to go now."

"I can't wait," Quincy said as we pulled onto Walnut Street. "I have always wanted to do this. Be part of a food truck convoy."

"I know, right?" I said, smiling from ear to ear. "I can't wait either. Where should we park?"

"I was just thinking the same thing. I wish I'd known about this last week, I would have come and scoped out the street to see where we'd get the most action."

I chuckled. I thought Quincy might be more excited than I was.

"I'll park here. This time," I said. The street so far had only a few trucks. We were early, and unlike other trucks, we didn't have to prepare any food. Everything we had to sell was already made. "You can keep an eye out for the premium spot for next week."

"We're coming back next week?" he asked, grinning.

"If the weather holds up," I said.

After we'd opened our window, we had stragglers coming by buying ice cream. More than a few asked if we were the same Crewse Creamery that was in Chagrin Falls. I started thinking that I'd take the truck back out to the artist who did the design on the outside and have him add our village's name on it somewhere. And maybe Ohio, too. Who knows, we might take her out of town one day.

"Hi, Soror."

It was Denise Swanson, my mother's friend and our sorority sister, standing at the serving window with a big grin on her face.

"Your mom told me you were bringing the truck down today," she said. "I couldn't resist stopping by."

"I'm glad you did." I rested my arms across the counter to be more eye level with her. "We've seen a few familiar faces, but yours is like family. Good to have family around when you start something new."

"Yes. It is." Her eyes beamed back at me. "And it seems like you're not the only one to make your first appearance after the Festival here at Walnut Wednesdays."

"No?" I leaned forward to peek up and down the row of food trucks.

"I just saw Java Joe's truck. They got a new one for the Festival, too." She held up a small cup she was holding. "I guess this idea of mobile food is all the rage."

"I hadn't seen them at the Festival," I admitted. "I should have made coffee-flavored ice cream. Give them a run for their money." I chuckled.

Java Joe's was a big-time, nationwide coffee shop. Supposedly high quality. Definitely high prices. Its shops boasted nooks and Wi-Fi, overstuffed chairs and delicate pastries, and a multitude of coffee and tea blends and drinks.

It had been my friend Rory's brand of choice when she visited from New York. She was totally unimpressed with the Juniper Tree, Chagrin Falls' local coffee shop.

Java Joe's sat in every community across the country, and now, I guess, they were going mobile.

"No one can make ice cream better than Crewse Creamery," she said. "You've got nothing to worry about. I may not have ever seen a coffee or ice cream food truck here before, but what you offer, you just can't pick up on every corner. Quality over quantity."

"Thank you," I said. Crewse Creamery would never have a store spread out in every state. I knew she was trying to motivate me like all good teachers do. "Now, you want ice cream?"

"Of course I do!" she said and tossed her coffee cup in the trash.

Once lunchtime rolled around, though, those stragglers turned into a never-ending line that kept Quincy and me so busy, I thought we might run out of ice cream. So busy that I didn't hear the side door of the truck open and Bobby come in. I didn't know until he tapped me on my shoulder and asked if we needed help.

"Oh my goodness!" I glared at him. "Bobby!"

"You know you've been awfully jumpy lately," he said. "You should drink some tea or change the people you're hanging out with."

"That person would be you," I said. "Did you get my message?"

"The one with you yelling at me?" he asked.

"Yes. That one," I said.

"Nope. Didn't get it." He grinned and pushed up his sleeves. "I came to scoop up ice cream. You want help or not?"

"We want help," Quincy said.

Bobby looked toward the serving window. "It looks like you need it," he said. "Good thing I came." Then he looked at the dipping case. "Are we going to have enough ice cream?"

"I don't know." I was just blowing out a breath. "I've never underestimated before."

"Let's hope you keep up your streak," Bobby said. He grabbed an apron off the rack and the three of us got to work.

It was another hour or so before the line slowed down enough that one of us could sit down. As the boss, I chose me. My feet were still sore from wearing those heels the day before.

"I bet we made ten thousand dollars," Quincy said.

"I wish," I said, chuckling. "I didn't have that much ice cream to sell."

"I was kidding," he said. "But based on how many customers we served every three minutes, the time it takes to serve and process payment, times the cost of the most common ice cream requested—cone versus sundae—within an error margin of plus or minus two, I could give you a more accurate amount."

I looked at him, then at Bobby. We both laughed.

"I just bet you could," Bobby said.

"I'm going to take a porta-potty break," I said and headed out of the door before anyone could protest.

On the way back, I spotted the Java Joe's food truck and just couldn't resist stopping to take a look.

The smell of freshly roasted coffee was like a bubble hovering over the truck that engulfed you when you got close. The truck was a shiny brown—the color of coffee beans and of the background of their logo. In pear green were the words "Java Joe's" and a silhouette of the waxy double leaf of the coffee plant. They had folding chairs and tables scattered about in front, inviting people to hang around and have more.

They even had food-truck-specific swag different from what I'd seen in their store—corrugated cardboard sleeves with a circular stamp that said, *Have Coffee Will Travel.* Refillable travel mugs and a board announcing the Spot Java Joe's contest, awarding a free Java Joe specialty drink.

I needed swag...

Maybe even some new packaging. Different for the truck than what we had in the store...

As I headed back up the two steps to my truck, I felt my phone buzz in my pocket. I stopped and pulled it out.

I realized I'd probably missed a lot of calls in the frenzy of all the customers. I looked down at the screen.

This one was from Gary Woodruff. The cameraman. I didn't recognize the number, but once I clicked on the notification, I saw the previous conversation we'd had.

U still stopping by?? he asked.

I'd forgotten all about going over to the news station. I glanced at my watch. Two thirty-five. Stepping back into the truck, I found Bobby and Quincy doing busywork. There was one customer reading the chalkboard menu hanging on the side of the truck and none at the window. They would be fine without me.

Omw. I texted back.

We were only about four blocks from where Gary worked. I

figured I had plenty of time to make it over there and back before it was time to pack up to leave at three forty-five. And I doubted that we'd have many more customers. Surely not enough that the two of them couldn't handle it.

I mean, how long could it take to pick up pictures?

chapter

TWENTY-SIX

When I walked through the glass front doors of WSKM Channel 6, the chair behind the receptionist desk was empty.

The interior was all white—white laminate walls, white marble floors, a white desk. The only color was the large-screen television on the back wall, which showed clips of the news and the station's orange-and-white logo.

I did a 360-degree turn and didn't know if I should call out with a "Hello," which I was sure would have echoed throughout.

Lunchtime was over, I knew that for a fact. I had chafed hands from washing them and hanging out in a freezing case until lunch had ended.

So where was everyone? I knew there was always something happening in Cleveland. Maybe they were all out getting a breaking news story?

As long as it wasn't something else happening in Chagrin Falls.

I pulled out my phone, ready to text Gary and find out where he was, when I heard a "Hello."

I turned to see Avery Kendricks, her heels clicking across the shiny floor. Gary had given her some middle name, but for the life of me, I couldn't remember what it was. I glanced up at the TV and there she was, the digital version of the woman coming toward me.

L'Rue.

The caption on the soundless news clip gave her full name. That was it. Avery L'Rue Kendricks. Gary had seemed to mock it when he'd said it to me. She, however, must have been quite proud of it.

Then I remembered he'd also said Avery would have killed to have Kaitlyn's job.

With her being front and center on the big screen, I'd guess she'd gotten the job she'd been coveting. Whether she'd taken Kaitlyn out to get it was another story. One I didn't plan on chasing after.

I chuckled to myself. Taking Kaitlyn out was something Maisie would have said.

"May I help you?" she said, arriving and standing directly in front of me.

"Yes," I said. "I'm here to see Gary." I suspected I shouldn't use the "Grey Wolf" nickname he'd texted me with. It'd been only Kaitlyn who'd called him that the day they'd all come to the food truck. If she had killed Kaitlyn, I didn't want to remind her of something she disliked.

"Gary?" She smiled coyly, her eyes twinkling. "What do you want with my cameraman?"

My . . . wasn't she possessive.

I remembered, too, that was the same smile she'd greeted him with.

"He asked me to stop by," I said. Not wanting to tell her our conversation. Not that it was a secret or anything.

"I'm sorry about axing the footage of your food truck from the segment."

I scrunched up my face. I knew they didn't use the footage with Kaitlyn. But hadn't she done a new story? Done a do-over or whatever they call it in TV-speak?

"Sorry?" I said.

"Even after refilming the scenes with your food truck, Gary and I decided that it just wouldn't do. Wasn't very clear and it didn't give the full feel of the Festival and what it was about over the last seventy-five years." Avery had a sickly sweet smile plastered on her face.

I didn't know how that could be. Crewse Creamery had been there for all but twenty-one of those seventy-five years. But I was more concerned with the rest of what she said.

"You and Gary decided that?"

If that were true, then why would Gary text me to ask if I wanted pictures? I didn't voice that to her, but I sensed, from what she said next, that Avery knew what was going on inside my head.

"Perhaps you can still see some of the footage," Avery said. "Gary could make stills for you. You know, like photographs, and give you a few. Although I don't know why you'd want them or what use they'd have."

"It would've been nice to see our business and our truck on

film. In the news," I said. "We're a big part of Chagrin Falls, but I will check to see if I can get stills."

She let out a sigh and her eyes fluttered upward as if it took all her energy to deal with me. I hadn't asked to carry on this conversation with her. I'd only wanted directions.

"That was Kaitlyn's story," Avery said, continuing. "Because she was from there. You know, being the Harvest Empress and all."

"Harvest Time Festival Queen," I corrected.

"Hail to the Queen." She did the "queen" wave. "Blah. Blah. Blah."

"I'm just looking for Gary," I said, ready to move on from her.

"I'm the face of WSKM now," she said, unprompted. "I should have been it a long time ago."

I didn't know what prompted that remark.

"I'm guessing that there was a reason that Kaitlyn got the job," I said. I didn't know why I was egging her on. I glanced down at my watch. I still needed to pick up the pictures and hike back over to the food truck.

"It isn't nice to speak ill of the dead," Avery said. "My momma raised me much better than that."

"I'm sure she did."

"I think everyone around here and out there knows." She lifted her arm and pointed a finger, swinging it back and forth. It seemed she was saying everyone out there gaining knowledge through television wires.

But wasn't everything digital now?

"They'll see how good I am. They know it. I know it. And

Gary knew it." She winked at me. "Everything has been righted and is good in the world."

Okay. I didn't know what that meant, but I was ready to go. She had gotten scary and it seemed she didn't want to help me find Gary. I turned to look the way she'd emerged and it didn't seem like there was anyone back that way either.

I probably should just call him . . .

"Gary is in the production studio," she said. Finally. "Going over the footage we shot today. He's very meticulous when it comes to me. Wants to make sure he gets my best angles."

She was going off on another tangent. Although this time I had gotten a location before she veered. Now I just needed direction.

"Is it back there?" I asked. Pointing in the direction she'd come from. "The production studio?"

"Third floor," she said and pointed to the other side of the lobby. "And while you're talking to him, ask him how I got this job." She laughed. "I'd love to see if he'd admit to that." She turned and walked away.

I was glad she was gone. And I had no plans of asking Gary anything about any part of what she'd said.

"Now to find the elevator," I mumbled. I could have asked her, I turned and watched as she clicked her heels through yet another opening, but who knew where that question would have taken her before I got a useful answer. It seemed like even now that Kaitlyn was gone and she had the job, her not having had it in the first place was still eating away at her.

Maybe she is Kaitlyn's murderer. She seems crazy enough to do it.

I shook the thought from my head. There wasn't a reason to do it. I mean, Melissa had told me at the funeral that Kaitlyn had gotten a job at CNN. She would've been leaving Channel 6 soon anyway. No need to kill to get a job you were next in line for.

Was there?

Unless of course she wasn't next in line . . .

That made even less sense. Because if she hadn't been next, she would have had to kill everyone in front of her in line for the job. And no one else had turned up dead.

Although, as she'd prompted, I could ask Gary . . .

I walked in the direction that Avery had pointed. After a walk down a long, narrow hallway and one wrong turn, I found myself in a big office space, full of desks, people and lots of chatter.

Here's where everyone hangs out.

I stood there unnoticed and scanned the room for Gary. The room didn't look like a production studio to me, not that I really knew what one was supposed to look like. There were no television screens like I thought he'd need to view Avery's "angles." Only computer monitors, and as far as I could see, no Gary.

"Can I help you?" a lady barked at me. She was a few rows of desks down from where I stood. She had a messy brown ponytail and wore a silky white blouse. She'd been staring at a screen when she spotted me. It seemed she'd been the only one to notice me, but then everyone turned to look.

"I'm here to see Gary," I said. "Gary Woodruff."

"Hold on," she said. She looked across the room, maybe at where he was supposed to be, then back at me questioningly.

"He's in the production studio," I offered.

"Oh," she mouthed and nodded. She got up and crossed the room. With her ID card she swiped a keypad on a door and disappeared behind it.

All the ones who had taken notice of me when the woman called me out went back to doing whatever it was they were doing before. Without her, no one seemed to care I was standing there.

I waited for what seemed like an eternity. My watch said it had only been four minutes.

Finally, the door she'd gone through opened again, and I expected to see Gary. But it wasn't. She'd come back and, holding the door open, beckoned me over.

"He says you can come to where he is," she said. "Take the elevator to the third floor. Then follow the hallway to the right. Then take a left. It's Room 3A."

"Thanks," I said.

The quiet in the hall on the other side of that door she'd let me through was jarring. Unlike the room I'd just walked through, the hallway seemed desolate and dark. All closed doors. A wall phone–slash–intercom unit placed near the door I'd come out of, a fire alarm and firebox with hose and hatchet on another wall. I found the elevator, and as soon as I pushed the up button, the doors opened. There were four floors and a basement. I pushed three and waited for it to do its thing. When the doors to the elevator opened, there was another dark hallway.

"Make a right. Then a left," I mumbled.

I stayed close to the wall although there was no one else in the hallway with me.

Room 3A was behind a glass wall and I could see Gary. He had several of the televisions mounted on the wall going, and not one of them had any film that contained Avery.

Every screen that was playing had Kaitlyn, front and center.

chapter

TWENTY-SEVEN

The wall inside the production studio that faced the glass wall I was looking through was covered with television screens, filling in the space with at least fifteen monitors. The light in the room was low and Gary sat in the second row of counter-like desks. He'd stare at the screen, then down at the control board in front of him. Turning dials, pulling up files on a keyboard.

I stood and stared at the screens he had up. There were screens filled with a younger Kaitlyn, and some that showed a more seasoned one. Some looked dark and raw. All, though, showed that signature smile.

As I scanned the wall, I noticed a row of monitors, right in the middle, playing a tape taken the day she died. I knew because I remembered what she was wearing.

Had he been doing this all along, even while the woman had come and told him I was there to see him? Didn't she think that odd? I did.

I glanced back down the hallway from where I'd come and remembered seeing the phone intercom by the door.

Maybe she hadn't seen what he'd been up to? Maybe she'd called and announced my arrival.

But then again, I cocked my head to one side and stared at the back of him. He knew I was coming.

Was he doing this for me? Did he think I'd be interested in seeing Kaitlyn?

And what would Avery think?

She'd thought he was looking at her on those screens.

That made me chuckle. Then my eye caught one screen that seemed to be in a loop. Maybe fifteen to twenty seconds long, playing over and over.

In the short clip, Kaitlyn was smiling. Her eyes bright and her cheeks rosy. Her full blond hair was bouncy and full of curls. Her lips were a glossy pink. She had on a pretty lavender-colored puffy winter jacket. After the first few seconds of just her, there came from off camera a snowball. It hit her, she gave a surprised look to the camera before ducking out of camera range, only to return in view with a snowball of her own. Then it would start again.

I smiled at the playful Kaitlyn, one I didn't think I'd ever seen.

Maybe that was the real Kaitlyn Toles. The one who talked about me to her parents. The one who must have filmed in front of the ice cream truck and at my family's ice cream shop because she liked me. Liked the accomplishments I'd made. Even admired that I'd worked in big-city New York.

I liked that Kaitlyn. The one on the screen.

Not that I hadn't liked the real-life one I knew, well, I didn't *dislike* the one I knew, but this one didn't seem to be so . . . snobbish.

I smiled and glanced down at my watch. I needed to hurry and get back. I didn't see an envelope or anything on the narrow counter-like desk Gary sat behind. All that was there was a cup, probably coffee, from Java Joe's. We might have to still go into another office to pick up what I'd come for.

I walked the couple of steps to the door, ready to knock and go in, but noticed a change in lighting coming from the room. I glanced through the glass and once again trained my eyes on the screens mounted on the wall. I was horrified at what I saw.

It was Kaitlyn at the Balloon Glow. Not her talking in front of the camera. Smiling and bouncing around like she had on the other footage. But her lying on the ground. Dead. Playing on all the screens. All at once.

The gas burners gave the film a ruddiness and cast an eeriness over the scene. Macabre. The shots would zoom out and then pull in closer. Different angles. Different filters. The shots of Kaitlyn were contrasted with the camera fanning the crowd at a high speed, making them all a blur.

Then there was that one shoe with the coffee cup lying next to it. Gary seemed to linger on it. His hand on a lever. The cup toppled over, the top had fallen off.

For some reason, even though I'd seen that shoe and coffee cup that night, that cup now gave me pause.

Maybe because I knew now it had the poison in it.

The poison that had killed Kaitlyn.

I shook my head. That wasn't it. But I couldn't say what.

Then the film started moving again. Kaitlyn lying there. The blur of the crowd. The glow from the balloons.

The shoe.

The coffee cup.

Gary had to have taken those shots. He'd been the only one with the camera that night.

Why would he do that? Why was he watching it now?

I felt sick to my stomach. I couldn't look at it anymore. I needed to get out of there. I turned to run and caught Gary's eye. It seemed a smile started to appear on his face and he slowly raised a hand like he was going to wave, until he realized that I'd been watching the same thing he had. He fumbled with the control panel to shut the monitors down, but I'd gotten past the window and was heading back down the hallway.

I'd already seen it. Seen too much.

My heart picked up its pace with every frantic step I made in retreat down that hallway. I slid a shaky hand along the wall to keep my balance.

What was wrong with that man? And why would he put something up like that when he knew I was coming? He couldn't think I wanted to see that.

None of the footage I'd seen even had anything to do with Crewse Creamery.

"Win." I heard Gary call my name. I didn't want to talk to that man. "Win, wait up. I have pictures for you."

I must have taken a wrong turn, because there were no elevators after I rounded the last corner. I was sure I'd come back the same way I came.

It seemed I could hear Gary breathing. I turned, though, and he was nowhere in sight.

I couldn't help but remember what Avery said about him. *He knew I deserved to have the job . . .*

Had he helped her get it? Had he had a hand in what happened to her that night?

I took a turn down another hallway and it was a dead end.

How could I get lost on the floor of a building?

I turned around and went back the way I'd come, hoping I wouldn't run into him.

As I ran down one hallway, I saw 3A lit up over the room.

Oh my God, I thought, *I've come back to where I started. Right where Gary is.*

I turned around to run the other way and saw Gary at the other end of the hall.

"Win!" he called and waved. "Where are you going?"

"Out of here," I mumbled. I took a turn around another bend in the hallway and saw the door to the stairwell.

I felt as if I was going to faint.

I had been caught in a stairwell with a killer before. The doors on each floor were locked from the inside and the only way out was to get to the ground floor.

I was on the third floor. What if I got locked inside the stairwell? What if he caught up to me? Or what if he took the elevator down, he surely knew where it was, and beat me to the first floor?

Oh. My. God. Oh. My. God. Oh. My. God.

I leaned my back against the wall and rested my head. I couldn't think. I didn't have too many choices. I could just stop running and let him kill me there, where, I thought, someone was more than likely to stumble over my lifeless body. Or I could let him kill me in the stairwell, where I might never be found.

Or maybe you can make it down the stairwell and out the door without dying at all.

"Win, why are you running from me?" There he was. Out of breath, his face covered in red splotches. "I have the pictures." He waved a brown envelope in the air.

No, he wasn't going to get me that easily.

"I'm good," I said, deciding it was now or never. I opened the door to the stairwell and ran down the first flight before hearing the door to the third floor slam behind me.

I ran down the next flight and checked the door on the second floor.

Locked.

I knew it. With a trembling hand, I held on to the rail and glanced up to see if he'd come after me. I didn't see him, but I wasn't taking any chances. I flew down the rest of the steps. I closed my eyes and held my breath when I gave a hard turn on the handle to the door on the first floor, praying that it would come open.

The door swung open with ease and I burst out. The sun invaded the space and enveloped me. I could smell the lake air as I released the breath I'd been holding. I felt a release of tension as a drop of perspiration trickled down the side of my face.

The door had led to an exit on the backside of the building, facing the Flats. Without hesitation, I took off running. I rounded the building and headed up the steep incline to the front. I just wanted to get back to my truck. Back to safety.

Turning for the first time to see whether Gary had followed me out, I rounded the building at street level and ran smack into someone with a thud.

"Whoa," he said. He grabbed my arms, holding them tight, and pulled me into him.

I screamed.

chapter

༺ ❧ ༻

TWENTY-EIGHT

Hey," he said. "What's your hurry?"

He, in this case, was Cameron Toffey. Not the Grey Wolf, who I thought had made me his prey. I leaned my head into Cameron's chest and almost sobbed.

I hadn't ever been so happy to see him. Not in the entire time I'd known him.

"I scared you," he said. "Sorry."

All I could do was pant, try to calm my nerves.

"Are you okay?" he asked. "Where are you going?"

"I'm okay," I said, trying to shake off the fear. "I'm okay. I'm okay."

"Breathe," he said. "You shouldn't go jogging uphill. That's a steep hill coming up from the Flats."

"I wasn't jogging," I said. I pulled free of him. "I was . . . Umm." I turned and looked back down from where I'd just come. "I was just . . ."

"What?" he said. "You were just what?"

"Nothing," I said. "What are you doing here?"

"Snooping," he said and chuckled. "But I live right over there." He pointed to a high-rise that was the next street over. I scrunched up my face. I knew that place.

"What are *you* doing here?" he asked before I could remember why the building he'd pointed to seemed familiar to me.

"I don't know." The words just came out without me thinking about them.

I'd had a purpose when I got there—picking up the pictures. But now I felt like Avery. I didn't know why I even wanted them.

"You don't know?" he said, ducking his head to look into my eyes.

"I mean, yeah, I know." He raised his eyebrows like he was waiting for an answer. I huffed. "I came to get pictures."

"Pictures?" he asked.

"Yeah, from Gary Woodruff. You know, one of the cameramen."

"The creepy cameraman," he said.

I chuckled. "I think now I'd agree with that. He said he had pictures of my food truck and of the ice cream parlor."

Cameron looked down at my hands. "Where are they?"

I shook my head, my eyes fluttering. "I just wanted to get out of there," I said. "Everyone I ran into in there was creepy."

"My word," he said and laughed. "Who else did you see?"

"Avery Kendricks," I said.

"Avery *L'Rue* Kendricks," he corrected.

"Exactly."

"I know you don't want to get involved with this. This figuring out who did this and all," he said. His words hesitant, he lowered his head, looked intently at his hands as he rubbed them together. "But I have my suspicions. I think I may know what happened. Who did it. That's why I'm, you know, *lurking* around." He looked back at the news station.

I followed his gaze. "You think someone who works there killed Kaitlyn?"

"I do. I hate suspecting people, you know, but solving this thing is eating away at me." His eyes met mine. "I know. I know. Before you even say it. I should just let the cops do their job. But I can't let it go."

I mentally shook my head. He was just like Maisie. Only Cameron did have a good reason to want to catch the killer. He'd just lost the person he'd planned to spend the rest of his life with.

"I'm beginning to think it might be someone in there, too," I said.

"You do?" he said, a smile lighting up his face. "What a relief. I don't want to seem like some crazed, brokenhearted conspiracy theorist, you know?"

I laughed. Yep. He was like Maisie.

"Who are you thinking did it?" he asked.

"Right now I'm thinking Gary. The Grey Wolf. And maybe Avery was in on it with him."

"Avery?" He scrunched his nose. "I never thought of her, but you're right on the money with Gary. That's who I think did it. I wouldn't put anything past that dude. And what's up with that nickname?"

That made me think about him chasing me down the hallway again. I glanced at the front door of the news station we were standing in front of. "I have to go," I said.

"Go?" He looked around behind him like he was trying to

figure out where it was I was headed. "I didn't mean to upset you with my theories," he said, turning back to me. "I know you didn't want to get involved with it. But o-okay." He nodded his understanding. "Where'd you park? I'll walk you to your car."

"I'm parked on Walnut Street."

"Really?" He looked toward St. Clair, the street I'd need to go down to get there. "Isn't today Wednesday? They reserve that street for the food trucks . . . Oh," he said, realizing why I was parked there. "Okay. You've got your food truck out today." I nodded. "C'mon. I'll walk with you."

"Okay," I said. Figured I'd feel better with company.

"Do you want to know why I think it's Gary?" Cameron asked as we crossed the street and headed back to Walnut.

"No," I said.

"Because he was the one that picked up the truck from the mechanic's shop."

I felt like I was with Maisie. He was going to tell me his theory whether I wanted to hear about it or not.

"And?" I said.

"Oh, you don't know," he said. "She was killed with anti-freeze."

I did know, I just hadn't ever told *him* I knew.

"And how do you know?" I asked.

"Why wouldn't I know?" he asked.

"I just thought the police weren't telling anyone," I said.

"Yeah. At first they didn't. But you . . ." He hung his head and cleared his throat. "It was on her, you know, death certificate." I saw him bite down on his bottom lip. I knew he was trying to keep tears at bay. "The funeral home had to have a copy of it."

I nodded my response instead of commenting. Kaitlyn's death was hard on me, I knew how it made him feel.

"Anyway," he said, trying to regain his composure. "So. Yeah. They put it in her coffee. The poison has a sweet taste, so I've learned. Kaitlyn put so much sugar in her coffee, I always wondered how come she was so picky about the dark roast blend she had to have."

"Couldn't taste the coffee?"

He shook his head. "Not for all the sugar she put in it."

"And that's why she didn't know . . ." My voice trailed off. The thought of it made me sad.

"And I never could understand how she only wanted Java Joe's."

"She did?" I knew for a fact that Java Joe's had a cult-like following. People loved their coffee.

"Yes! But how did that matter when you can only taste the sugar?" He smiled, it seemed, remembering her.

"I have a friend like that. She lives in New York and she swears by Java Joe's."

"Gary, or the Grey Wolf as he liked to be called, had the opportunity to do it," Cameron said. "He always was the one to stop by Java Joe's to get her coffee. I don't know why the police haven't zoomed in on that yet."

I shrugged. I didn't know what the police were doing, other than noting how clean my truck was. I hadn't seen Detective Beverly since he'd stopped by the truck to talk to me about the day Kaitlyn died.

"And I don't know if you noticed," Cameron said, "Gary had this mega crush on her."

Figures, I thought. The way he was playing her life—and death—on the monitors in the production studio.

"Avery likes him, I think," I said. "Her eyes get all twinkly when she talks to him."

"Really?" he said. I saw a smirk cross his face. "That's why you mentioned her. You said they were in it together?"

I held up my hands. "I said *maybe*. I don't really know. I don't want to know."

"Hear me out, though," he said. "Because if it's true. That Gary killed her. I'm not saying Avery. Just Gary. That would really be messed up."

"You're telling me," I said.

"Kaitlyn really trusted him. Let him in on her personal life. Talked to him about things."

"Really?" I said. "Then that would be messed up. Someone she let into her life like that."

"Right." He put his hands out in front of him. "And not only messed up because Kaitlyn is dead." He shook his hands like he was shaking away what he'd said. "I mean, it is because she is, but then it would mean that it's my fault. He did it because of me."

"How would it be your fault?" I asked.

"Because he did it because he couldn't have her. We were getting married and every day he'd have to look at her and know she was coming home to me."

"Oh," I said.

"Like a couple of nights before . . . you know . . . before she . . ."
I nodded.

"We had dinner. At my place." He gathered his thoughts and his emotions and got back on beat with his story. "A little Italian food." He leaned toward me, a smile crooked on his face. "Family recipe I cooked myself." He nodded. "A little wine. A little . . ." He started blushing. "Well, you know. But no sooner had we started to wind down than her phone starts going off."

"Gary?" I asked, figuring that was where the story had to be going.

"Gary," he confirmed. "Like he couldn't be away from her for more than five minutes."

"It wouldn't have been long before he wouldn't have seen her anymore, though," I said. "He was working himself up for nothing."

"Why do you say that?"

"Because she—well, I guess the two of you—were moving to New York."

"New York?" He frowned.

"Kaitlyn's new job at CNN."

He stopped and looked at me with a blank stare. I could see his chest heaving under his shirt.

"What?" I said, holding out my hands.

"Nothing. Nothing." He started walking again. "I just didn't know that had gotten out. She wasn't telling people about it yet."

"Oh. Yeah. She probably wasn't. I don't think Avery even knew. Melissa told me." I shrugged. "I guess it didn't matter that it's out now. Because . . ."

"Yeah. Because she's not here anymore." He swiped a finger at the side of his eye. I hoped he wasn't going to start crying. "It's just that I can't even picture my life anymore. You know? She made me want to have a family. Kids. Wife. Picket fence." He laughed, and it seemed to ward off the tears. "All I see in my future now is a big black hole."

"So you think that Gary got the antifreeze from the mechanic shop?" I didn't know why I asked that question. I'd been rebelling against trying to figure out anything about what happened to Kaitlyn.

"Yep. I do," he said, nodding.

"Spirelli's." We said the name at the same time.

"I just saw Mike Spirelli," I said. "He saw me coming off my truck and came over to take a look at it."

I didn't mention the part about him wanting to fill it up with antifreeze.

"What did he say?" Cameron asked.

"That I need to have it winterized."

"Are you going to do that?" he asked.

"Probably. We're going to store it once the weather turns cold. Don't want any pipes or anything bursting." I shrugged. "I might go tomorrow before the store opens."

"I was thinking about stopping over there, too," he said.

"Seeing how you're feeling about all of this, that's probably not a good idea," I said.

"No." He looked at me, his eyes glazed over. "I'll be fine. You know I just wanted to take a look."

"I don't know." I'm sure he could hear the skepticism in my voice.

He gave a firm nod as if to let me know his mind was made up. "You want to go with me and check out the place? Take your truck at the same time? It would be a good cover."

Just then my phone buzzed. I pulled it out of my back jeans pocket and swiped the screen and gasped.

Wat happened to u??

It was a text from Gary. I clicked the phone off, my hand visibly shaking.

"You okay?" Cameron asked and nodded toward my phone.

"Oh." I shook the phone in the air. "Bobby," I lied. I slid it back into my pocket and swallowed hard. "Yep." I put my hands in my pockets. "Asking where I was. Saying he was going to leave me."

"He's on the food truck?"

"Yeah."

"I've got to run up to Cleveland Heights, if you need a ride," he offered. "I can take you home."

"Cleveland Heights is a long way from Chagrin Falls," I said. "That would be out of your way."

He shrugged. "I don't mind. Anything to put off helping my step-grandfather."

I raised an eyebrow. "You don't want to help?"

He chuckled. "Of course I do." He shook his head, seemingly indicating I didn't understand. "He's moving and he has so much stuff in that house. They were such hoarders and he doesn't want me to throw anything away." He laughed. "It is an uphill battle trying to clear that place."

I laughed. "I can imagine. But I'll be fine. Bobby will *not* leave me." I squinted, looking down the street where the truck was parked. "He better not."

Just then I saw the truck pull around the corner.

"Here he comes now," I said.

"Okay. Good." He looked down at me and smiled. "I'll head back to my loft. Thanks for listening to me and my conspiracy theories."

"No problem," I said, smiling back. He turned and started jogging back the way we'd come. "Have fun with your grandfather."

He turned, jogging backward, and said, "My *step*-grandfather."

I chuckled to myself. He'd do anything to get out of helping his *step*-grandfather, I said it like he had, if he was willing to take me all the way out to Chagrin Falls and he only had to go to Cleveland Heights.

Cleveland Heights . . .

Wasn't that where Maisie said Shannon lived?

His loft . . .

He was going to "his loft." That's why that building looked familiar. I slapped my thigh. "That was where we'd followed Shannon to after the funeral," I muttered and shook my head in disgust as I climbed up in the truck. "That girl just won't give up."

S o you were face-to-face with the killer?" Maisie asked. "In close quarters, an arm's length away from the clutches of a cold-blooded murderer?"

We were at Riya's house. In her kitchen, to be exact. She and Maisie had met me at the truck when we pulled up. They were bearers of bad news. They told me about a broken water main, closing all restaurants and public restrooms in the village, including Crewse Creamery. I knew my mother and PopPop had taken care of everything and probably hadn't wanted to worry me while I was working the truck. I'd have to call them later and see if there was anything else I needed to do.

"So it's dinner at Riya's," Maisie had said, pulling me off the truck. She'd toned down her costume today, wearing wrist-length white gloves, a straw sun hat and none of the pink lotion on her face.

"How'd you know when I'd be here?" I'd asked.

"Bobby called your grandfather," Maisie said. "Told him how

the day went and that you had disappeared for more than an hour."

I didn't mind going to Riya's after finding out what Bobby-the-Tattletale had said. After what I'd gone through with Gary, the topic of our current conversation, I would have choked my brother if I were anywhere in close proximity to him.

It was my turn to tell the *real* events of the day. I got them up to speed on what I'd gone through, why I'd been gone for that hour, maybe longer, and how much Gary had frightened me, although upon the retelling of my story, the whole thing didn't seem as frightening as when I was going through it.

"I wasn't in his clutches," I said to Maisie. "And now that I think back on it, I'm not so sure that he was 'chasing' me." I sniffed and hunched my shoulders. "He just wanted to give me pictures. I think I just got caught up in the moment."

"What a moment to be caught in," Riya said. "Is that what that Avery person was talking about when she said ask Gary how she got the job? That he'd killed Kaitlyn?"

I raised an eyebrow. "He's murdering people and telling others about it?" I shook my head. "I don't think so. And if he did, why wouldn't she go and tell the police?"

"Because she's grateful," Maisie said, her voice low as she relayed her theory. "Without him and his murderous adventures, she'd still be low person on the totem pole. That's why we need to get cracking on this." It sounded as if she was giving her rallying cry. "You guys ready to solve this murder?"

"I am," Riya said. "I want in on some of the fun. Plus, we get to work with Liam, right?"

"Who is Liam?" Maisie asked.

"Detective Beverly," I answered.

"He is so cute!" Riya went over to the refrigerator and grabbed a carton of eggs. "I can only do scrambled."

"We know," we said in unison.

"There is no working with the detective," Maisie said.

"Believe me, Riya, solving a murder is not fun. And Liam Beverly is not all that cute." I sighed. "I don't want in on it," I said as per my usual. "But you guys could hook up with Cameron. He's got this whole thing figured out."

I didn't want to tell them about my realization that Shannon had been visiting Cameron in that high-rise loft we'd staked out. It would just get me in deeper. I didn't want to discuss murder.

And there was still something nagging at me about what I'd seen on that video that I couldn't pinpoint. I guess I couldn't share with them something I didn't know anyway.

"He doesn't know what he's doing," Maisie said.

"Oh, like you do," I said.

"This ain't my first rodeo," she countered. "I've done this a time or two."

Laughter erupted from me and Riya. She almost dropped her eggs and I nearly fell out of my chair.

"Okay, Miss Cowgirl," Riya said, trying to check her amusement. "If Cameron's wrong, what you got?" She cracked a couple of eggs in a bowl and came over to the table, whipping them around with a fork.

"I didn't say he was wrong," Maisie said. "Only he didn't know what he was doing." She looked in her book bag and pulled out a notebook. "You have to be methodical."

I was still laughing at the rodeo comment when Riya gave me a look that tickled me even more before she went over to the stove.

"We have to list our suspects," Maisie said. She looked over at me, her pen poised to write hovering over the legal pad.

"Remember. I'm not in this," I said.

"Aww. C'mon, Win," Riya said. "You talked whodunit with Cameron and we're your besties."

"I didn't *talk* anything with him. I listened."

"He's just clinging to Win because he misses Kaitlyn," Maisie surmised. "And it's nice." She turned to me. "That you're being nice to him." She turned to Riya. "But don't worry," Maisie said. "She'll come around and work with me. Us. She always does."

"I can hear you," I said. "And hearing you discuss me while I'm listening will just make me more resistant to your enticements."

The sizzling butter for Riya's eggs was starting to smell good. I could hear my stomach growling, and with the look Maisie gave me, she could, too. She was betting that hunger was going to help wear me down.

The kitchen was not our usual meeting place when we wanted to discuss murder, although we always did it over food. Our hangout was a special booth we'd designated as ours since second grade at the Village Dragon Chinese Restaurant. But it was Jewish high holidays. Rivkah had shut it down for two weeks, unrelated to the break in the water main. Maisie guessed the water problem had to do with the overcrowding of the streets and facilities during the Festival.

"I think we should have Michael Spirelli on the list for sure,"

Riya said, ignoring me not wanting in on the planning. "He had the means and the opportunity. He's got the murder weapon there at his shop."

"Yeah, but he didn't have Kaitlyn there," Maisie said.

"You don't know that," Riya said. "When they got the flat, Kaitlyn might have been there, the one making arrangements to have it repaired. The one with the expense account and credit card." She spoke over her shoulder as she stirred the eggs. "Then she left her camera guy there to finish up and walked over to River Park. Alone. To wait. All the time sipping on the laced coffee. She had coffee when you saw her, right, Win?"

"Right," I said.

"Ethylene glycol takes a few hours to work."

"It does?" Maisie asked.

Riya nodded. "Plus"—she turned off the fire under her skillet and turned to us—"it wouldn't be the first time Michael Spirelli has been suspected of murder."

"What!" Maisie and I said in unison.

Riya raised an all-knowing eyebrow. She grabbed a plate out of the cabinet and sat it in the middle of the table.

"No!" I said. "I don't believe it."

"Believe it," she said. She brought the skillet over to the table and slid the scrambled eggs onto the plate. "Serve yourselves. Bacon's coming up next."

"Who cares about bacon? We're waiting on the part about murder and our friendly neighborhood mechanic," Maisie said. "Not what else is on the menu."

I cared. I realized I was starving. I hopped out of my seat and grabbed three plates out of the cabinet and set them on the table, then grabbed forks from the drawer.

"He used to live in Toledo," Riya said matter-of-factly. "I think he went to college there or something. But he got into some trouble and was charged with murder."

"That is the vaguest answer I've ever heard," I said. I scraped eggs onto my plate. "Did that really happen?"

Riya shrugged. "My uncle told me."

"Which uncle?" Maisie and I queried at nearly the same time.

Riya came from a huge family. Her Italian side of the family was just as large as her Indian side, with still more relatives across the water in their respective countries. Then she called family friends—no blood relation—aunty and uncle. I'd venture to guess she had somewhere near a million uncles.

"I don't remember which one," Riya said. She was standing at the sink rinsing out her skillet. "I just remember one saying he wouldn't let a killer work on his car."

"Maybe he was talking about a car killer," Maisie suggested. "Like he didn't do a good job on cars."

Riya shrugged. "Whatever he meant, you guys are always re-searching stuff, look it up." She put the skillet back on the stove, turned the fire back up and went to the fridge.

"Do you only have the one skillet?" I asked, my mouth full. "Are we getting served one thing at a time? I'm starving."

"We're talking murder," Maisie said. "Not about filling your stomach. You only get food if you join in."

I stopped. Fork midway to mouth. Hadn't she noticed I was already stuffing my face? And who put her in charge of the food?

"Okay," came out the muffled response, mouth chock-full of food. "I'll talk murder."

"Good. I'll put Michael Spirelli on my list and we'll look up this murder story later," Maisie said, and started scrawling across her pad.

"Murderer or not. Opportunity and means or not. Mike Spirelli didn't have a motive," I said, chomping down on the wad of food in my cheek.

"Told you she'd join in," Maisie said to Riya.

"She might have joined the conversation, but she isn't basing what she said on known facts." Riya was flipping the bacon she'd put into her single skillet. "We don't know for sure he didn't have a motive," Riya said. "Maybe he and Kaitlyn had a past."

"He's like fifty," Maisie said.

"It doesn't have to be that kind of past," Riya said. "Something else to research." She waggled her eyebrows. "Never know what it might be."

"Who else?" I said, moving the conversation and hopefully the food on.

"I think we, of course, should include Shannon Holske. Avery Kendricks"—Maisie was writing as she spoke—"and the Grey Wolf, real name Gary Woodruff." She tapped her pencil by each name, counting. "That's four."

"Who is Avery Kendricks and what did she do?" Riya said.

"I just told you about her," I said. "She works at Channel 6. She kept me hanging out in the lobby with her with all of her insinuations."

"Oh yeah." Riya nodded. "They all have motives?"

"Avery Kendricks because she wanted Kaitlyn's job," Maisie

said. "Shannon Holske because she wanted Kaitlyn's life and her man."

"Gary 'Grey Wolf' Woodruff because he wanted Kaitlyn. And couldn't have her," I added. "And he gets my vote."

"We're not voting yet," Maisie said.

"Just letting you know for when we start," I said, eyeing the bacon Riya was draining on a paper towel.

"I don't think we should exclude Amelia Hargrove and the Dixby sisters off this list," Maisie said. She started writing again.

"What?" Riya said. "How did the three of them get into the murder mix?"

"Because of the mall fiasco," I said. "Need I remind you it was Kaitlyn who came up with that name?"

"Wait," Riya said. "That was why Zeke Reynolds got murdered. Not Kaitlyn. How does that put the three of them in on this one?"

"Because maybe they were still upset with her," I said.

"That makes no sense," Riya said, bringing over the plate of bacon. "They didn't kill when there was a chance they might lose their store. Their livelihood. Why would they kill just because Kaitlyn made a big deal of it on the news?"

"And because the killer cookbook was bought from Amelia's bookstore," Maisie said, completely ignoring Riya's logic.

"Oh!" I said, stuffing the rest of my slice of bacon into my mouth. "I didn't tell you." I swiped my hands down the legs of my jeans, grabbed my knapsack and pulled out the death certificate. "Madeline Markham wasn't murdered." I handed the paper to Maisie and looked at Riya. "Unless you can make a murder look like cancer."

"Let me see that," Riya said and had to tug the certificate from Maisie's tight fingers. I watched as her eyes scanned the document. "Cause of death: Laryngopharyngeal cancer. Manner of death: Natural."

"Cancer is not natural," Maisie said, standing up and taking the certificate back from Riya before plopping back down in her seat.

"Manner of death is the determination of how the disease or injury led to death. Death is a natural consequence of cancer."

"Not all people that have cancer die from it," Maisie said, like she could out-medical-talk Riya.

"Then manner of death on their death certificates will have something else listed," Riya said and went back over to the refrigerator. "I have strawberries and blueberries."

"What a morbid conversation," I said. "And then to throw fruit into the mix."

"This says Madeline's information was given by her granddaughter, Thomasina Bowers," Maisie said, looking back down at the paper. "We can ask her."

"We already know how Ms. Markham died," I said. "And we can't ask her granddaughter anything, we don't know where she is."

"She could be dead, too," Riya said.

"No," Maisie said, shaking her head. "We need to ask her who got the other book. The one you got from the bookstore that had the killer recipes."

"Why would we want to do that?" Riya asked.

"Riya. C'mon," Maisie said. "Isn't it obvious?"

chapter

THIRTY

Maisie would have made the perfect murderer. She'd get away with it because no one would ever make sense of her logic.

"You think the recipe book has something to do with Kaitlyn?" Riya asked. It was easy to see that Maisie had gotten her attention.

"No," Maisie said and frowned.

"I thought you told me before that it did," I said. I even thought that's what she meant by saying it was obvious.

"We need to find out about the recipe book to keep Win on board," Maisie declared. "She, for some reason, has an aversion to being an amateur sleuth. I just meant it as a way to keep Win in the loop."

"Aversion?" I squawked. "Uh, how about almost getting killed? Twice. Three times if you count my run-in with Gary today."

"There's a reason. The killer was chasing her," Riya added. "Almost in his clutches." Her words singsongy.

"Not funny," I said.

"You just said that your encounter with Gary wasn't as bad as you originally thought, and he didn't ever try to kill you," Maisie said.

"Is that what it takes to get your attention, Maisie?" I said. "I have to be almost killed?"

"Well, maybe not *almost*, but *close* to it," Maisie said.

"I don't see a difference," Riya concluded. "Almost. Close. Dead is dead."

"You didn't want to help find the murderer long before someone tried to make you their next victim," Maisie said.

"In Win's defense . . ." Riya said.

"I second what Riya is saying," I said.

"Second what?" Maisie said. She grabbed her book bag and pulled out her phone. "Riya didn't even say anything." She slid the death certificate that now sat in the middle of the table over to herself. "I'm going to see if I can find the granddaughter." She pulled up her keypad and started typing. "Thom-a-si-na," Maisie sounded out the word as she entered it into her phone. "Bow-ers."

"You should probably put a location in." I nodded at Maisie. "Although, as I said, we don't know where she is."

"Google will find her," Maisie said. "Dead or alive."

"Anyone want toast?" Riya asked.

"I've never been served breakfast one food at a time," I said, shaking my head.

"It's not breakfast," Riya said. "It's brinner. And that can come in courses or *à la carte*."

"Brinner? Did you just make that up?"

"Breakfast for dinner," Maisie said without looking up from

her phone. "Aaann-dah, I found her!" She turned her phone around, although I couldn't make out anything on it since she turned it back so quickly. "Looks like she lives in Beachwood." She looked at us and smiled. "And guess what else?"

"What?" Riya asked.

"She's an author."

"I hope not of cookbooks," I said.

"She's having an Author Talk at the South Euclid Lyndhurst Library." Maisie smiled, pleased with herself, and she ignored my comment. "Guess when?"

"Is working with Maisie to find the murderer always a game of forty questions?" Riya asked.

"When?" I asked, playing Maisie's game, because as Riya would soon learn, yes, it was.

"Thursday."

"Tomorrow Thursday?" I asked.

"Yep. And we're going."

Maisie had my evening planned for me, and the Cleveland Water Department had dictated my day.

Still no water at the ice cream parlor.

I slept in late, well, until six thirty, not that I knew what the morning would bring. But the shop had been closed most of the day before and I knew I had enough ice cream. And after my spurious run, I needed to calm my nerves. It seemed as of late, I'd been so jittery.

I padded around my upstairs apartment, not sure what to do. I rarely had lazy mornings. Running my family's ice cream shop always kept my daily schedule full.

After eating a toasted bagel and a cup of plain yogurt with strawberries and blueberries, the only thing in my refrigerator, I drank the corner of orange juice left in the bottle. Throwing the bottle away, I thought of how my mother would have fussed at me for leaving that small amount of juice in the fridge in the first place. Glad she wasn't there to see it.

I washed up my dishes, got dressed and headed out. My first stop, as usual, was PopPop's house.

"You think you'll be able to open today?" he asked as he let me in. I hadn't seen him at the store the day before. Maisie and Riya had kidnapped me from the truck and taken me right to Riya's kitchen.

"I hope so," I said. "But I've got good news about the ice cream parlor."

"Oh yeah?" he said, coming out from the refrigerator with a carton of eggs in his hand.

"Yeah." I held my hands in front of me. Not sure why I'd gotten nervous about telling him. "We got an offer to be part of an ice cream crawl."

"You trying to move the store?" He cracked his eggs in a bowl, added a little salt and pepper and started whisking them with a fork.

"What?" I scrunched up my nose and giggled. "No, it's a—"

He held up a hand. "I know what it is. Bobby told me all about it."

"Of course he did," I said and plopped down in one of the kitchen chairs. "With all the stuff going on, I just hadn't . . ." I looked at PopPop. "I mean, I was going to tell you. I wanted to tell you." I tilted my head. "To be the one."

"It's okay," he said. "I'm just as happy about it with you telling me as when Bobby told me. He didn't ruin the feeling, just maybe the surprise."

"It's good for business," I said, unsure if he approved of me signing us up for something without asking him first.

"With you at the helm, we're going to be a household name, huh?" A smile curled up his lips.

"Aren't we already?" I teased.

"Not nationally, but I don't doubt that might soon be coming."

"Maybe even globally," I said.

"If anyone can get us there, you can, little girl."

He offered me some of his scrambled eggs as he sat down at the kitchen table.

"Just ate," I told him.

"Then let me finish up my eggs and we can go."

"Go?" I said, looking up at him.

"I want to check on the store. You may have given it a face-lift, but its bones are old. Don't know if that water main break caused any problems."

PopPop grabbed a short-brimmed straw hat off a coatrack and a gallon of bottled water from the floor near the door, then held it open for me. "Plus, I need to check on the water for our tenant."

Our tenant was Rivkah. She lived in an apartment over the ice cream shop. She'd been there for as long as I could remember.

Rivkah had started out being my Grandma Kay's friend. I wasn't sure when she and my PopPop had become close. I always say that there were only two things that made my grumpy grandfather smile—me and Rivkah.

I knew why I made him smile. His only granddaughter, I had spent my early days up under my grandmother and him. But like Bobby had questioned, I didn't know what was up with PopPop and Rivkah.

"Our tenant?" I said and chuckled.

"That's what she is," he said.

"Sometimes it looks like it might be more."

"More?" he said and frowned. "Seems like that to who?"

I didn't throw Bobby under the bus like he'd done to me. I shrugged. "I don't know, just seems like sometimes you two have more than a landlord-tenant relationship."

"We're friends," he said.

"More than friends?"

He chuckled and tugged down on his hat.

"Sometimes, when you reach a certain age, and want to hold on to certain memories. Certain times in your life. You gravitate to others and from there grows an appreciation—a mutual appreciation for the other's company." He looked at me, trying to see if I understood what he was saying. "She was good friends with your grandmother."

"I know," I said, my voice getting squeaky with the words. I didn't want to put my grandfather in an uncomfortable position.

"Sometimes it's hard to figure out your feelings for someone and you tend to ignore them or even deny them."

"PopPop," I said, "whatever you're feeling, it's okay."

"I'm talking about you," he said.

"Me?"

"O came by the store looking for you."

"Yeah?" I wasn't sure what PopPop was getting at.

"He's always around looking for you."

Now he was putting me in an uncomfortable position.

"Soooo . . ." I stuffed my hands in my jeans and changed the subject. "You think the break in the water main might have caused some permanent problems with our pipes?"

PopPop chuckled and shook his head.

‗ ‗ ‗ ‗ ‗ ‗

ONCE WE GOT to the store, PopPop checked the pipes and then went upstairs to check on Rivkah. Her store wasn't open and he offered to walk over with her to check the pipes there, too.

I wasn't sure what pipe checking included—he just seemed to peek under the sinks, walk the length of the basement and the perimeter of the building. But it seemed to satisfy him.

He and Rivkah had left and I was turning off the lights in the kitchen, ready to lock up, when there was a knock on the front window.

The same knock that had come nearly every morning since Kaitlyn died. I knew without looking who it was.

"Are you stalking me?" I asked after unlocking the front door and pulling it open.

"Stalking." Cameron placed his hand over his heart. "I would never do that."

"Then how did you know I was here?"

He looked around and back at me. "You're always here. Making ice cream . . ." His eyes strayed toward the kitchen. "Serving customers."

"We're not open," I said.

"I know. You don't open till eleven. I came by to go over to Spirelli's like we talked about yesterday."

I rolled my eyes. "We didn't talk about that yesterday."

"Yes we did," he said, frowning. "You're going to get your truck winterized and I'm going to snoop. So get a move on"—he glanced down at his watch—"gotta get you back in time to make ice cream and open up at eleven."

"You sure do know a lot about what I do."

"You're kind of boring, Win. And predictable." He smirked. "Always have been."

"Well, not today," I said. "We're not opening because the village's got water main problems. I only came down to check on everything."

"Oh good," Cameron said. He licked his lips and tugged on his bottom lip. He slapped his hands together and then started rubbing them back and forth. "We'll be able to do some investigating."

"No!" I held up my hands. "No investigating."

"Why not?"

"Cameron." It came out in exasperation. "What do you want? Why do you keep coming here every day?"

"Because I want you to help me."

"Help you do what?"

"Prove that Gary killed Kaitlyn."

"Oh Lord." I let my head roll back and my shoulders slump.

He was just like Maisie indeed. She'd always zone in on one suspect and cling to them. Most times her suspect wouldn't have any connection to the murder.

At least I tended to agree with Cameron's choice.

"I'm not helping you do that," I said. "I have a business to run."

"Not today," he said. "Remember, the water main? And you need to see about your truck, right?" He turned around and looked out the window. "Looks like it might turn cold."

I looked out the window. There were blue skies, no clouds and the early-morning sun coming up over the horizon was bright.

I looked back at Cameron, too confused to formulate an answer.

"Where'd you park the truck?" he asked.

Like Maisie, there was no changing his mind.

"I did say I was going to take my truck." I felt myself relenting to his eager request.

"Of course you have to take your truck," he said. "You wouldn't want the lines to freeze up. I'm sure you just dropped a pretty dime on that masterpiece."

He was so much like Maisie.

"I don't even know if his mechanic's shop is open this early." I glanced up at the clock.

"It's open," he said. "Opened at seven."

"How do you know that?"

"I pay attention." He opened the front door and made a sweeping motion for me to go out. "Plus, I have a murder to solve. Can't be caught sleeping on the job."

All I could do was shake my head.

I didn't go with him out the front door. I had to shut it behind him, lock it and head back into the kitchen to go out the side door. It was the way we always went in and out when the store wasn't opened yet. I used it most times even if we were open.

But that was the only thing I didn't do that he'd asked. I dutifully got the truck from where it was parked on River Street and drove it over to Spirelli's Garage to have it winterized.

Yeah. I couldn't believe it either. But the man was suffering. I could see it in his eyes. And even though the situations were different—I had tried to keep my father from being accused of murder, he was trying to figure out who the murderer was—I understood how he felt.

Cameron, leaving his Charger parked in front of our store, walked with me over to River Street and hopped in the truck with me and talked nonstop on how we could "play" it. He acted as if we were conducting a sting operation.

"You keep him distracted," he said.

"And what are you going to do?" I asked.

"I'm going to case the place."

"*Case?*" I chuckled. "Have you talked to Maisie lately?"

"Maisie Solomon?" he asked. I nodded. "No, why?"

"Just wondering," I said. "Just wondering."

THIRTY-TWO

Spirelli's Garage was on Bell Street, just around the corner and down the street from the ice cream parlor. It was a small, square brick building with four parking spaces in front. Painted white on the outside, it had two bays on the inside and a huge parking area in the back that was always filled with cars in varying degrees of being dismantled. A long, rectangular dumpster for scrap metal and two square ones for trash lined the back boundary.

Today, however, there was a small river running in front of it.

"What is going on here?" Cameron asked.

Water was gushing from a fire hydrant just beyond the drive, and there were men in hard hats and vests with yellow reflector strips and a big hole in the concrete near the curb.

"Repairing the water main?" I said, my answer more of a question than a statement.

"How are we supposed to get in there?" he asked. A scowl on his face.

Looked like he hadn't been paying *enough* attention to what was going on. He probably should have cased the joint before he decided we needed to come.

"Looks like we can still get in the door." I pointed to a large, flat sheet of wood that acted as a bridge from the street to the sidewalk in front of the garage. "I can go in. Walk in. But I can't drive the truck in."

"What's our cover if we don't take the truck in?" he asked.

I wanted to remind him that this was all his idea.

"Okay. Okay." He licked his lips. "You go in the front. Across the homemade bridge. Just act natural, Win," Cameron instructed. "Tell him the truck is across the street."

"How else would I act?" I said. "I'm just going in to talk to him about my truck and I'm sure he'll see where I had to put the truck." I looked at him. "And just what are you planning on doing?"

"I'm going to go around back."

"You've got a lot of witnesses," I said and nodded toward the workers. "If you're planning on some kind of stealth mission."

"Shoot!" he said, visibly distressed by the inconvenience the water main problem was having on his planned sleuthing endeavors. "I'll figure it out. I'll just figure it out."

"Okay," I said and looked at him questioningly.

"Okay," he said and nothing else.

"Okay," I repeated. "I'm going in."

"Roger that," he said and cracked his door. "We'll rendezvous back here in fifteen. Try to keep him busy at least that long."

I opened my door and chuckled. I didn't know how he thought I had enough to say to Michael Spirelli that we could talk for fifteen minutes. Or that that would be enough time for him to search the place.

And exactly what he was looking for and what he was going to do with it if he did find it was a whole different matter entirely.

I decided not to think about it. I needed to get my truck winterized and Cameron could, as far as I was concerned, do whatever he wanted to while he was there.

I just hoped he had sense enough to be careful and not to disturb anything if he did find something crucial to the investigation.

I walked gingerly over the makeshift bridge and into the front of the shop. It was cold inside, the air-conditioning unit must have been cranked up high.

I rang the bell on the desk and Michael Spirelli came stepping out of the back, wiping his greasy hands on an even greasier rag.

"Hi, Win," he said.

"Hi, Mike," I said. "I came by to have you winterize my truck."

"Oh," he said. His eyes drifted out through the front window of the building. "Sorry about the inconvenience."

"No problem," I said. "Just didn't know if you could still do it?"

"Sure I can," he said. He laid the rag on top of the counter and pulled out an invoice. "They told me that they'd turn the hydrant off in about an hour. Stop the flow of water."

"They'll have it fixed by then?" I asked. "We'll have water again?"

"Not sure about that. They had to flush something in the

pipe they're working on there." He pointed. "Seems like it's the infrastructure. The city is checking the pipes."

Their way of checking the pipes was so different than the way my grandfather checked them. They had dug a huge hole and gone underground. PopPop hadn't even cast his eyes ground level.

"So what do you want me to do with my truck?" I asked.

"You can just leave it there." He scrawled something on the top of the paper. "Sign here and then come back this evening. Say after six. Leave the keys in the glove compartment."

"What time are you closing?" I asked.

"Not 'til around eight. I'm waiting for a part to come from Youngstown that I need for a car that I promised the owner I'd have ready by tomorrow. I'll get to yours while I wait."

"Okay," I said. I signed the paper. "See you at six."

"Sounds good," he said. "See you then."

He disappeared back into the bay area and left me standing there. I glanced at my watch. I knew I couldn't have been in there more than five minutes.

I was supposed to keep Mike busy for fifteen.

I leaned forward and tried to peer into the back. I hoped Mike didn't catch Cameron back there snooping.

I was going to have to walk to wherever I was going from here. Instead of riding with me, Cameron should have followed me in his car.

I didn't mind walking, I didn't know what Cameron would think about that. Or what he was going to say about me waiting for him out in plain sight.

I looked around. There was really nowhere for me to hide. I

was starting to feel afraid. Scared. Apprehensive. Like I was the one sneaking around.

I decided to wait for him in the truck.

I pulled open the truck door and was scared out of my wits.

Cameron leaned over and in a strained whisper told me to, "Get in!"

"Oh. My. Goodness." I put my hand over my heart. "What is wrong with you?"

"We have to get out of here," he said, looking around like someone might be watching us.

"Well, we can't leave in the truck."

"Why?" he shrieked.

"I brought it to be winterized, remember? I have to leave it for them to do that."

"Oh." He sat up straight. He had a look that said he hadn't thought about that. "Well, how are we going to leave from here?"

"Walk?" I said. It came out like a question although there was no other answer to his question.

"Oh no! We can't. Someone will see us."

"What did you do, Cameron?"

"Nothing!"

I gave him a look.

"Really. I didn't. But I was sneaking around and I may have, like, climbed up onto the dumpster in the back."

"Why would you do that?"

"I was looking for evidence!"

"What evidence?"

"I don't know. Find out when was the last time he bought

antifreeze." He shrugged. "Something—anything that would connect Gary to Kaitlyn's murder."

"Did you find anything?" I asked.

"No," he said. "Nothing."

"Then there is nothing to hide from."

"Maybe not for you," he said. "But I was the one snooping."

I shook my head. "Well, I'm going home." I raised my eyebrows.

"My car is at your shop."

"I can walk back to the shop with you," I offered.

He thought about that for a moment. "Nah. Might be better for the two of us not to be seen together."

"Might I remind you, I didn't do anything the least bit sneaky."

"Yeah. Nothing but aid and abet my intrusion into an open, official police investigation, which is probably just as bad."

I hadn't thought about it that way.

chapter

⤳∽◉∾⤴

THIRTY-THREE

It took nearly twenty minutes to get to the South Euclid Lyndhurst Library and another five to find a parking spot.

We were going to talk to Madeline Markham's granddaughter. My day had been long. It was the first time since I'd come back home and taken over the shop that I had a day filled with nothing to do.

Michael Spirelli called close to four thirty to announce he hadn't gotten to my truck and there was still a moat, courtesy of the Village of Chagrin Falls, surrounding his property. He was sure I'd be fine to stop by the next morning to get it.

By the time five o'clock rolled around, Maisie was already on the phone, trying to coordinate pickup times with Riya for our field trip to the library.

"There must be a lot of people going to this author event," I said after we'd driven around a couple of minutes and were still not finding anywhere to park.

"I think people are parking here for the Notre Dame College

game," Riya said, pulling into a spot that had just become vacant. She pointed over her shoulder at the college campus across the street.

We piled out of the car and entered the building through the sliding glass doors, the cookbook nestled in my knapsack. I had hopes that its presence would jar Thomasina's memory.

"We're looking for the author event with Thomasina Bowers," Maisie said as we stopped at the front desk. Her blisters had healed well enough where she just looked like she had a bad case of acne.

"It's nearly over," the clerk said, glancing up at the clock on the wall. "It's through those doors. Room 162."

The author's presentation, whatever that consisted of, was over by the time we quietly slid into the room. There were a few people milling around the table and Thomasina Bowers was signing books from a stack that was in front of her.

"Hi," a woman said, approaching us. She wore earrings that dangled and black wire rim glasses. "You here for the author event?"

"Looks like we're late," I said apologetically.

"Oh no." She smiled and brushed her hand over her short black hair, which had a streak of gray. "Still time to speak to her."

"Actually, we wanted to ask her a question about a book her grandmother wrote."

"*Recipes of Chagrin Falls?*" the librarian asked.

"Yes," I said. "I'm surprised you know it."

"I'm a librarian," she said, smiling. "I know about books."

"Show her the book," Maisie prompted, then stepped in front of me. "Hi"—she stuck out her hand—"I'm Maisie, and these are my friends Riya and Win."

"I'm Beth McCuen," she said, shaking Maisie's hand. "And I'll be happy to look at your book. What are you trying to find out?"

"Who the writer sent this copy to," Riya said.

I dug inside my knapsack and handed her the book. "That's it"—I nodded at it as she took it—"but I'm sure you couldn't tell us that."

"No," she said and pursed her lips with a half smile. She took the book and looked it over. She opened it and ran a finger down the copyright page and the table of contents. She closed it, turned it over and checked the paper edges. "I can tell you that it used to be a library book."

"It did?" Maisie and I said in unison.

"How do you know that?" I asked.

"Here." She pointed to the top of the book. There were faded words stamped onto the edge. "CCPL Mayfield. That stands for Cuyahoga County Public Library, Mayfield branch."

"Oh," we all said in some form. Resting on the silence to figure out what to say next. That information didn't help much.

Maisie broke the silence with her question. "But there's an inscription on the inside," she said. "Library books don't have inscriptions in them, do they?"

"Sure, if they're donated, they might. But it's very, um, rare." She nodded. "We still catalog them and put them on the shelf."

The three of us looked at each other.

That meant that anyone in the entire circulating area of the county library could have had the book.

That definitely wasn't helpful.

"Then how did it get to the Around the Corner Bookshop?" Riya asked. "If it belonged to the library?"

"Well, I don't know that. But we don't use this designation anymore," Librarian Beth said, running her finger over the stamp. "This book probably circulated in the nineties." Her face lit up with an idea. "We have a book sale room." She shrugged. "Books that people aren't checking out can end up there."

"So," I said, tilting my head and putting all of it together. "This book came to the library, Mayfield branch, that's the one in Mayfield Heights?" Beth nodded, adjusting the cotton scarf she had double looped around her neck. "It got old. Too old to circulate. The library sold it at the book sale."

"Then someone bought it and donated it to the bookshop in Chagrin Falls," Maisie added.

"Mystery solved," Riya concluded.

"It was probably whoever got the copy from the library who added their own version of recipes," I said. "And I already know, knew, that my grandmother didn't put the killer recipes in it."

"Killer recipes?" Beth asked. That piqued the librarian's interest.

Maisie took the book out of Beth McCuen's hand and flipped it open. She pointed to one of the pages that had the inserted ingredients.

Librarian Beth made her lips tight, snorted out a breath and nodded, her earrings bobbling back and forth. "I've seen this before and it's probably why we canceled the book. No one wants to see books with highlighting. Writing. I don't."

"I know that book."

Thomasina Bowers walked up and pointed at the book. I hadn't noticed, but it seemed while we were talking, the few people who had been in the room had left.

"Hi! Ms. Bowers, I'm Maisie." Maisie stuck out her hand again, all smiles, like she'd known the woman for years. She was enjoying our little foray out of Chagrin Falls. As she pumped her hand, she introduced us to the author as well.

Thomasina Bowers looked to be in her late forties or early fifties. I hadn't imagined her that old. If her grandmother had been my grandmother's friend, I thought she might have been closer to my age.

Her blond hair was thinning and she had fat ankles and fingers, the several silver-colored rings she wore made the skin around them poke out. She smelled fresh and lemony and reminded me of the lemon-lime sorbet I'd made a few days earlier for the Festival.

Riya and I nodded and said, "Hello."

"May I?" Ms. Bowers reached out a hand for the book. "What are you three doing with this?"

"I found it in a bookstore," I said. "In Chagrin Falls."

She lifted an eyebrow.

"We wanted to see if you remembered who the book was sent to," Maisie said.

"Ahh," she said. She opened the front cover. I saw her lips move as she silently read over the inscription. "It finally surfaced."

"Kaylene Crewse was my grandmother," I said.

"Oh, you're Win Crewse!" She smiled. "I remember your grandmother talking about you. Isn't it ironic that you were the one who found the book that was originally intended for her!" I smiled. I hadn't thought about it that way. At least since I'd found out what had been scrawled inside. "Miss Kaylene was a wonderful friend to my grandmother."

"Do you remember who you sent her book to?" Maisie asked. "Do you know which one of the contributors got Mrs. Crewse's book?"

"No," she said and chuckled. "I didn't remember back then." She sighed. "I surely can't remember now." She rubbed the top of the book with her hand. "I was only about eighteen and was in a hurry in helping my grandmother. I wanted to get it over with. Do the things I thought were important. Not paying attention, I put the wrong book in the wrong envelope."

"My grandfather told me," I said.

She nodded. "There were only about seven I had to send out. You would think I could get that right." A faraway look told me her attention had been taken from us and to a memory. "Then my grandmother took sick right after that." Her words were slow and thoughtful. "Didn't take long for her to pass." She tugged at the side of her eye. "I regretted so much after that not getting it right. The books. To the people she wanted to have it. To have each one of her friends have one signed by her. She was so proud of that book."

"Are you trying to solve the mystery of the erroneously mailed book?" Beth asked and looked at us, amusement in her eyes.

"Sort of," I said.

"Why are you trying to find out who got your grandmother's book?" she asked.

"No reason in particular," I said. I couldn't very well say that I wanted to prove that my grandmother hadn't put the killer recipes in.

And that made me realize I was doing it again. Looking into

something I didn't believe—that my grandmother had something to do with the scribblings inside. I shouldn't have let Maisie get me going about the book again. "In fact," I said and reached for the book, "we should just be going. It was good to meet you." I smiled at her, an outward display that I was okay, but inside I was feeling that same shame I'd felt the day PopPop found out what I was doing.

I saw out of the side of my periphery Maisie's face. Her eyes were wide and her mouth had started to drop open. I'd have to explain to her that finding out about the book was not going to work to goad me into finding out who murdered Kaitlyn. I didn't want any part of it.

"Thank you for your time," I said, ready to leave.

"What about asking which book your grandmother returned?" Beth asked.

"That I remember," Thomasina said, jumping in, a bright smile appearing on her face. "It was George Draper's."

"George Draper?" Beth said. "I know him. If it's the same one. He worked at the Mayfield branch with me. I do remember he lived in Chagrin Falls until his wife died."

"I'll bet that's the same one," Thomasina said. "Gave my grandmother one of the recipes, but I couldn't tell you which one."

"Did she give credit to the people who gave recipes?" Riya asked.

"No," Maisie said, shaking her hand knowingly. "Win has scrutinized that book from cover to cover."

I frowned. That was something I wasn't proud of.

"Let me see that book," Beth said. She opened it up and

scanned the table of contents. She tapped her finger on the page. "I bet this is it." She held the book open and turned it around to us like we were in a kindergarten class and she was sharing a picture book with us. "Lasagna. He always bragged that he made a killer lasagna."

chapter

THIRTY-FOUR

We'd evidently been going about it the wrong way.

If Thomasina Bowers had checked each book as she put it in the envelope, she wouldn't have sent out her grandmother's books to the wrong people.

But that didn't matter anymore.

"We have a name now," Maisie said as she climbed into the back seat of Riya's car. "We could go and talk to him."

"We can't," I said. "There's no reason to."

"He might not have killed Kaitlyn," Maisie offered, "but maybe he killed someone." She'd pushed her face between the seats. "Why else put poisonous additions to the recipes?"

"The 'killer' lasagna recipe didn't have any poison added to it, remember?" I shook my head. "You just want to go around finding murdered people, don't you?"

"It's a mystery," Riya said, nodding, "as to who scrawled, with murderous intent, I may add, the additions to the recipes."

"I don't care who did it," I said. "Not anymore. I hurt my

grandfather's feelings when I tried comparing Grandma Kay's handwriting to the scribbles in the book." I blew out a breath. "And I feel just as bad now. I shouldn't have even come here. He can't ever know I did."

Maisie huffed. She squeezed a shoulder through the gap and turned to me. "Okay, Win. No more book snooping. No telling your PopPop about coming here. But you gotta still help with the current investigation, right?"

"Current investigation?" I repeated, then shot a look at Riya. We started laughing. "Maisie"—I shook my head and gave hers a push—"get away from me. We do not have an *investigation* of any kind going on here. But I'm in."

I couldn't keep getting roped into learning about who killed Kaitlyn and not help Maisie.

"I've been thinking," Maisie said, squeezing through a little more. "We should find out the lowdown on Michael Spirelli. What went down in Toledo. You know. How did he get tangled up in a murder rap?"

"Maisie," Riya said, "you have to stop talking like you're in a 1940s gumshoe novel."

"So about that," I said, moving away from Maisie and pushing my back against the door. "I actually went to Mike's garage this morning."

"Michael Spirelli's garage!" Maisie squawked. "Why would you go there without us?"

"I hadn't planned on going—" I started apologetically.

"Then why did you go?" Maisie interrupted.

"Because Cameron came around and I had told him yesterday I was going to take the truck in—"

"Wait!" she said and yanked an arm through the seat. I was afraid she was going to try to wiggle her body all the way through. "You went with Cameron?"

I scrunched my face. I knew she was going to let me have it after finding out that.

"I didn't mean to," I said, squinting my eyes, telling her I shared the pain she felt because of my wrongdoing.

"Oh," she said sarcastically. "You went with him by accident?"

"I didn't mean by accident." There was no way of getting out of this one. "No one can go with someone by accident . . ." I mumbled.

"If you and Cameron figure this out before I do," Maisie said, her lips tight. "Ooo. I am going to be so mad." She took the one hand that was on the front side of the bucket seats and started scratching. First her nose. Next her cheek and then up to her forehead.

"We didn't find out anything," I assured her.

"You're making me itch!" she said and unwedged herself from between the seats, slumping back. "I just can't believe you did that!"

Riya glanced at me. "If she starts speaking in another language again, you're on your own."

"Thanks," I said.

I really did feel bad. I only went to get the truck winterized, but I could have not let Cameron talk me into him going along. I could have gone with Maisie.

"Sorry," I said, peeking through the seats. "I still have to go back and pick up the truck." I had hope in my voice, hoping it would be contagious, that she'd be happy with the opportunity to question him.

"When?" she said, leaning forward.

"Tomorrow. You wanna come with me?"

"Did you find out anything when you were there?"

"No. I didn't really ask. But we can get a head start on what to question him about." I pulled out my phone. "Let's see what Google has on him."

"No need to google him," Riya said. "I found out what happened with him."

"You did?" I asked.

"Yep." She glanced at me, then Maisie. "I asked my uncle."

"I thought you couldn't remember which uncle had said something to you about him," Maisie said, putting her head back through the seats.

"I couldn't. I just asked the first one I ran into, he told me to ask my father because he was the one who took his Cadillacs downtown to be serviced instead of around the corner to Spirelli's Garage."

"Did you ask your father?" Riya nodded. "What did he say?" I asked.

"He said that he doesn't take them downtown, he takes them to the dealership on Chagrin."

I rolled my eyes. "Not about his Cadillac, about Mike Spirelli's murder involvement."

"He didn't know."

Maisie slapped her hand on her forehead.

"But my mother overheard the conversation."

"This is beginning to resemble a conversation with Maisie," I said and looked over at Riya. "Convoluted."

"It's a murder investigation," she said. "I'm just trying to keep good notes."

"Are you going to tell us what happened or just about your family tree?" Maisie asked.

"It was a hazing incident," Riya said.

"Hazing?" I said. "As in fraternity pranks and the likes?"

"Exactly."

"So he and his fraternity brothers killed a pledge?" Maisie asked.

"A pledge died. They found the cause to be a myocardial infarction secondary to hazing."

"That's what your mother said?" I asked. "It sounds like you injected your own conclusion into that with all that doctor talk."

"It may not be what she said word for word," Riya said.

"Did Michael Spirelli go to jail?" I asked.

"No. He was in the fraternity but he wasn't there that night. But that didn't come out until later. No one would talk at first, so they took everyone down to the police station. Booked all of them for murder."

"Did that really happen?" Maisie asked. "Your mother told you all of that? How did she know?"

"My aunty told her."

I chuckled.

"But I knew what that meant. Story could have gotten twisted a hundred times. So I checked it out. Found a newspaper article. It didn't mention Spirelli's name, but it did mention the incident and Toledo."

"Riya," Maisie said, "you should have told me. We are supposed to be doing this together."

"I was trying to be a fact finder. Didn't know I'd run into my uncle."

"I found out a fact, too," I said. "I may have forgotten to mention."

"What?" Maisie seemed exasperated with us.

"I know who Shannon was going into that apartment to see."

"What apartment?" Riya asked.

"The one we followed her to?" Maisie surmised.

"Yes," I said. "The one we followed her to and sat outside of for ten hours."

Maisie smirked. "It was only four hours," she said.

"Felt like ten."

"Spill it. Who was she going to see?" Maisie asked.

"Cameron."

"Cameron," Maisie repeated and got a thoughtful look on her face. "She went to the funeral and he didn't. Then afterwards she goes over to his house? What was that all about?"

"Yep." I nodded. "She went there and I don't know what that was all about."

She looked at me. "So what? He was her babysitter?"

I hunched my shoulders. "I don't know. I just said I didn't know what it was all about. But it sure looks like he was the babysitter."

"It's not babysitting if it's your own child, is it?" Riya asked.

"He told me," I said, "in a roundabout way, that he didn't have any children."

"Why is he hanging out with Shannon, then?" Maisie asked. "Doesn't make sense."

"Or is it why is Shannon hanging around with Cameron?" I turned her question around.

"We need to figure this out," Maisie said. "Find out if Shannon's son is Cameron's son and what Kaitlyn knew and what she had to say about all of it."

"Because if Kaitlyn did know and she and Cameron were still going to get married," Riya said, a smile on her face like she'd just eaten the canary, "that would give Shannon all the motive she needed to make sure that Kaitlyn was out of the picture. For good."

chapter

THIRTY-FIVE

Shannon was looking like a viable candidate for murder. Even to me. But I still was placing my money on Gary. They hadn't seen that wall of screens he had played over and over.

Maisie, on the other hand, never mentioned him, and even when I told her how he'd frightened me and how he watched those death scenes, she never gave him a second thought.

But for now I was going to keep my theory to myself.

"So I think Shannon should get priority," Maisie said, squeezing her body through the seats a little farther.

"Priority what?" I said.

"On our list to investigate." She held up a hand. "And before you say it, we do have a list of people to investigate."

"How are we going to investigate her?" Riya asked. "We've already sat in front of an apartment building and didn't find out anything."

"We found out that Cameron babysat for her," Maisie said.

"We found that out because of subsequent snooping by Win." Riya, stopping at a red light, glanced back at Maisie.

"I wasn't snooping," I said. "It's just that Cameron volunteers a lot of information."

"You should have asked him if Shannon killed Kaitlyn," Maisie said.

"I already told you, he thinks it was Gary," I said. "And like you, he narrows in on one person and sticks with them."

"He might know something about her and just hasn't put it together with Kaitlyn's murder," Maisie said.

"I've never even heard him mention Shannon's name." I shook my head. "He thinks it's Gary."

"I agree with Maisie. Maybe he just doesn't see the clues because of his history with Shannon," Riya said. "She was trying to get in where she didn't fit in, just like she always has. He didn't see this time how far she'd go to get what she wanted."

I chuckled. "Riya. You agreeing with Maisie now?"

She grimaced.

"The first thing we need to find out is if that's Cameron's baby," Maisie said, ignoring my comment and Riya's reaction.

"How do we do that?" Riya asked.

I knew how, but I didn't want to volunteer the answer because Maisie wouldn't stop until we got one.

"Why does your face look like that, Win?" Maisie asked.

"No reason," I said, trying to hold back my guilty chuckle.

"You know how to find out?" she asked.

I nodded. "I do. The Bureau of Vital Statistics at City Hall."

Maisie snapped her fingers. "Where you got the death certificate."

"Yep," I said. "There."

"That is such a good idea!" Maisie said.

"Don't you have to know the baby's name to get a birth certificate?" Riya asked.

"Don't you know the baby's name, Win?" Maisie asked. "Didn't Shannon tell you?"

I frowned.

"She had to say his name the day you saw the two of them?"

I had to stop and think about that one. Squinting my eyes, I started slowly shaking my head back and forth. I couldn't remember if Shannon had said his name or not.

"Think, Win," Maisie said.

I closed one eye. "I am. Trying to, at least. But I'm not remembering one. I remember it was a boy . . ."

"What's his name?" Maisie asked a little forcefully.

"I. Can't. Remember!" I said. "I'm not even sure she said it."

"Go through the alphabet," Maisie said.

"What?"

"Start with A and see if a name that starts with that letter pops into your head."

"That's not going to work," I said.

"Then go to B," Maisie said. "And do it again."

"Maisie, you can't go through the entire alphabet," Riya said.

"It's the way you do it. It's a mnemonic device."

"I know what it is, Maisie," Riya said. "But I'm sure that if Shannon did mention the name, it was too trivial for Win to remember even with your memory-jogging trick."

"Win, what about D?" Maisie asked. "Did it start with a D?"

"You skipped C," Riya said. "If you're going to do it, you can't skip letters." She sucked her tongue. "Plus, you're going through the letters too fast."

"I thought you said it wasn't going to work," Maisie said. "Now you're telling me how to do it."

"Well, it won't work if you skip letters. Go back to C. Ask Win if it started with C."

"Win, was it an E—"

"Ronnie! It was Ronnie," I said. I closed my eyes, bracing against the backlash. "I think."

"You think?" Maisie squawked.

"I'm sure," I said, although I wasn't. But I'd say anything to get the two of them to stop throwing letters of the alphabet at me. "She called him Ronnie."

"Well, that doesn't help," Riya said. She threw a glance at Maisie. I was sure she was trying to hurl her into a meltdown.

"Why doesn't that help?" Maisie asked, slapping her hand down on the seat.

"Because Ronnie is a nickname," Riya said.

"Short for Ronald," Maisie said knowingly.

"But maybe, if Cameron is the father as Shannon claims, it could be a nickname for that. Cam-er-*ron*. Ron. Ronnie. Or some form of Ronnie could be his middle name."

"You do have to have the correct name to get a birth certificate," I said.

"And we don't know what his last name is either," Riya said. "Holske? Toffey? Or if Cameron really isn't the father, maybe 'Ronnie' has his real father's last name."

"Okay. I guess we should forget that idea," Maisie said.

"What about the white pages?" Riya said.

"The white pages?" I frowned, then I knew what she meant. "White pages dot com?"

"Right. Sometimes they list members of the household. You can find the name that way, maybe."

Maisie pulled out her phone. "I doubt if they'd list a toddler," she said, leaning back in her seat, "but I'll check. I remember she said she lived in Cleveland Heights . . ." Her voice trailed off as she did her search. Maisie's silence didn't last long. "You have to turn around!" she squawked and sat straight up. "Oh my gosh! I knew she did it!"

"What?" Riya asked, keeping her eyes off the road too long in my opinion to take a look at Maisie and her phone. "What did you find?"

"We *have* to talk to her."

"About what?" I asked.

"Turn around." Maisie belted out the words in song. I guess it was better than doing it in another language.

"Around?" Riya said and glanced at Maisie in the rearview mirror.

"Turn the car around and go to Shannon's."

"Maisie, you have to tell us why," I said.

"Do they list Ronnie as living with her?" Riya asked. "We don't need to see him, just get his name so we can find out who his father is."

"No," Maisie said and sat up to put her face between the seats. "It's more than that." She was breathing hard and heavy. "Better than that."

"What?" I asked again.

"It says that she lives in the same household as a George Draper."

George Draper, according to the white pages link Maisie found, was seventy-seven years old. He lived on Blackmore Road in a household that included Shannon Holske and one Daisy Draper, age seventy-two. There was no mention of Shannon's toddler. But we figured he had to be part of the household. The only way he couldn't was if he didn't live with his mother.

But that all seemed inconsequential with the information we'd just learned.

"This is really all starting to fall together," Riya said.

"How is it coming together?" I asked nervously. Were we close to solving the murder? And if so, were we now heading to the house of a murderer? I had definitely had enough of being in close proximity with people who were prone to taking people's lives.

"You thought that recipe book had nothing to do with the murder," Maisie said, giving me an all-knowing nod. "And look at this revelation." She raised her eyebrow. "Now it just might."

"I don't know." I shook my head. "How is it she lives in the same house with a man that had my grandmother's book?" I asked.

Riya glanced over at me. "Strange coincidence?" Her voice ended the question a few octaves higher.

Maisie pushed herself through the seat enough that she could reach the dashboard. She started punching in numbers on Riya's in-car navigation system.

"What are you doing?" Riya said and swatted at Maisie's hand.

"Putting in the Drapers' address."

"I don't know," I said, "if that's a good idea."

"We need to go and talk to Shannon," Maisie said, still inputting the information.

"We're almost home," I said. I didn't want to get started with the book again. Now we were going to visit a man who'd possibly had my grandmother's book? It couldn't turn out good.

"We can't turn around now," Maisie said.

"Don't tell me you don't want to know why Shannon and the guy who had Grandma Kay's book know each other," Riya asked.

I didn't want to admit to that because that would mean I had to go to his house. Where Shannon was.

I glanced at Riya. She turned on her turn signal and did a U-turn. We were headed back to Cleveland Heights.

BLACKMORE ROAD WAS in the Forest Hills district of Cleveland Heights, a suburb right next door to South Euclid, where we'd just left. It was where the Rockefellers had lived during the early part of the twentieth century. They donated land for a park and homes, some designated historical.

The Draper house was a white colonial with black shutters. There was a cobblestone walkway to the front door. Begonias and impatiens in hues of pink in full bloom and tall, willowy adagio maiden grass with creamy white plumes dotted the nicely manicured lawn.

"What are we going to say to Shannon?" I asked as we walked up the walkway to the house. Not only was I nervous about what we might find out and any danger we might be in, but I felt like we were ganging up on her. All three of us swooping in unannounced to question her about things that anyone would consider personal.

"We're just old high school buddies coming to visit," Riya said.

"Without an invitation?" I asked. "How is it that we know where she lives?"

"She told me she lived in Cleveland Heights," Maisie said.

"Yeah. Well. There's about forty thousand people that live here," I said. "I'd wonder how you pinpointed exactly where I lived if I were Shannon."

"She'll have more to worry about than how we found out where she lives," Maisie said, keeping her eyes focused on the house, "when she's arrested for first-degree murder."

"First-degree murder?" I mouthed to Riya and made a face as Maisie rang the doorbell. "How does she know what degree it is?"

Riya hunched her shoulders.

"It was premeditated," Maisie said, evidently overhearing me. "That's first degree. A capital crime in the State of Ohio."

The door swung open with Maisie's words, and Shannon's face, after the shock of seeing us standing there wore off, looked like she could kill, possibly as Maisie believed, again. This time it would be a triple homicide.

"What are you three doing here?" she asked. She had her blond hair pulled up in a high-top ponytail and she had on a maroon jogging suit and white tennis shoes.

"We came to visit," Maisie said, putting a big, wide fake grin on her face. "We were in the neighborhood."

She stared at us. Her hand gripped on the knob so tightly, her knuckles were turning white. She was ready to slam it in our faces.

"We came because we were worried about you," I said. I pushed in front of Maisie, who was standing front and center. I wasn't in the habit of lying, but I didn't have to feel bad about this one. It was true we were worried, just not in the way she might have thought I meant. We were worried that a killer—her— might be on the loose.

"You were crying so at the funeral," Maisie said, taking up on what I was saying. She sidestepped in front of me. "Are you okay?"

Her face changed. It went from anger to skepticism to sadness. "I was—am—brokenhearted about Kaitlyn."

Maisie slid to the side of her, making Shannon push the door open more. I could see moving boxes scattered throughout the living room. A bookcase half empty and the dining table stacked with crystal glassware and bowls.

"You moving?" I asked.

Shannon turned and looked back into the house.

"No," she said, turning back.

"Where's your son?" Maisie asked. "Ronnie, right?"

"How do you know I have a son?" Shannon asked.

"Is it a secret?" Maisie asked.

She was so pushy.

"I told her," I volunteered. "He's so cute, I must have been gushing over him."

Shannon smiled. "That's my little man."

"What's his father's name?" Maisie asked.

"What?" Shannon's facial expression changed again.

"Do you even know who the father is?" Maisie asked.

"I know exactly who the father of my child is," Shannon said, her irritation with Maisie starting to bubble over.

"What did Kaitlyn say about you having a child with Cameron?" Maisie asked.

"Maisie!" I said. "You shouldn't ask—"

Shannon cut in before I could finish my sentence. "Why don't you ask Cameron that?" She raised an eyebrow and put her hand on her hip. "He'll be home any minute, I'm sure he'd love to hear your questions."

Shannon had directed her question to Maisie. She'd forgotten about Riya and me standing there, although Riya hadn't contributed anything to the conversation. She'd driven us there, to our demise, and didn't offer one tittle of support.

Although she did have black belts in a few forms of martial arts . . .

"Cameron doesn't live here," Maisie said, frowning. "He lives downtown."

"How . . ." She looked at us, red flushing up her face. She

pressed her lips together, and her cheeks filled with so much air, I thought it would come sputtering out at any minute. She drew in a big nostril full of air, balled her fists and said, "I think that you should leave before I have you arrested for trespassing!"

She took a step back inside the door and tried to shut it, but Maisie was in the way. Not budging. Shannon stuck out her hand and gave Maisie a push, but even after nearly two weeks of Maisie being sick and bedridden, Shannon couldn't move her.

"Get. Out," Shannon huffed. She put one foot in front of the other for leverage and moved closer to Maisie. She pushed with the strength of her full body, garnering enough force, she hoped, to relieve Maisie from her stance at her door.

"Maisie," Riya said and yanked her arm. She came tumbling toward me. "We should go."

The door slammed and the three of us turned and stumbled back down the cobblestone walkway.

We'd gotten no information from Shannon to ascertain the identity of her son's father or if she was the one who killed Kaitlyn.

We did find out that it didn't take much more than Maisie's questioning to make her mad.

But after dealing with Maisie's shenanigans during one of her murder investigations, that was understandable.

"We need to find out about this George Draper," Maisie said. She was sitting in the back seat, pushed up against the window. She'd been quiet for most of the ride home.

As per my usual, I questioned Maisie's motivation. "Why?"

"Because he has a murderer living with him."

And as usual, I couldn't follow her logic.

"And with that revelation, what do you think he'll do?" I asked. "Without evidence he can't do any more than what we've done, questioned her."

"Maybe it's not Shannon," Riya offered. "Maybe he's the killer."

Maisie scooted to the middle of the seat, but refrained from sticking her head through. "He was the one who had the book," Maisie said. I could hear the wheels turning in her head. "The book with the killer recipes. And he was the one who has gotten rid of it. Twice. Once at a book sale. Once at the Around the Corner Bookshop."

"But like Michael Spirelli," I said, "he doesn't have a motive."

"He might. We've never talked to him."

"Well, it's not something we can do tonight," I said.

"And I've got work early tomorrow," Riya said as she pulled up in front of my place. "No snooping without me."

"You don't have to worry about me," I said.

"Win," Maisie barked. "You're still helping, right?"

"I just meant I would wait for Riya to get off from work."

I climbed out of the car and up the steps to my apartment, and laid my knapsack on the kitchen counter. I blew out a breath and tried to shake off the day. I needed to put Maisie's murder investigation out of my mind. I had my own worries. Two days' business lost because of a water problem and a new recipe to come up with.

I opened the refrigerator to find something to eat, but as usual, the shelves inside were bare. I had better luck in the freezer. I'd brought home a pint of tin roof and there it sat, all by itself, in the middle of my cold freezer. I stared at it and smiled.

The outside of the carton was light blue with *Crewse Creamery* in a bold yellow cursive font. Like that Java Joe's sleeve I'd seen on their truck, we had our own seal. A darker blue circle with our name around it, along with "EST. 1965."

I didn't need to change anything. What we had at the store

was good enough for the food truck. I didn't need to be like Java Joe's. What we'd always had was good enough. I reached for the carton. Crunchy peanuts and smooth, rich chocolate. That was what I needed. What could be better?

I grabbed a spoon from the drawer, turned the burner on and passed it through it a couple of times, then padded down the hallway to my room. I was going to work on recipes for the ice cream crawl.

I kicked off my shoes and sat cross-legged on my bed. Pulling off the top of the container, I dug the warm spoon down into the creamy frozen concoction and came up with a big bite. I wrapped my mouth around it and felt like all was good in the world in spite of all the things that were going on—until my eyes met that book.

That recipe book.

"Ugh!" I said, and sticking the spoon down into the ice cream, I uncrossed my legs and reached for it. It had spilled out of my knapsack.

"Who are you, George Draper, and why do you and this book keep popping up?"

I held it in my hand and stared at it. I sure wasn't going to be able to push all this murder stuff out of my brain if it was staring right back at me.

Not that I was sure there was a connection between the book and the murder. But just in case . . .

I hopped up, stuffed the book down in my knapsack and grabbed the pint of ice cream.

I might not be able to keep Maisie from being on me about

the murder, but I didn't have to have that book nagging at me. It had caused me enough trouble.

And that made me think about my Grandma Kay. And of course that made me think about Crewse Creamery.

I headed back out the door and got into my car. I wanted to go back down the hill to check on the store. I drove past it. It was dark, the sign on the door still turned to Closed. I did a U-turn and parked out front of the store.

The lanterns on either side of the front door were on. It looked peaceful and ready to serve our customers. I went around to the side and let myself in. Flipping on the kitchen light, I took a look around. I walked over to the sink and turned on the water. It ran clear. I turned the knob off and bent over to peer at the pipes underneath, but unlike my grandfather, clear water and shiny metal pipes meant nothing to me. I couldn't tell if anything was still going on or not.

I walked over to the walk-in freezer, pulled open the door and a swirl of frost enveloped me. I stepped inside and ran my hand along the rims of the pans of ice cream that had been waiting there for nearly two days.

I was going to have to dump those out. Rarely did a batch of ice cream last that long in the store, and I didn't want to serve any that hadn't even been out of the walk-in.

I didn't know what I had in the pantry and freezer. I was going to have to come up with what flavors I wanted to make. That made me remember that I also needed to work on recipes for the ice cream crawl. Something new, never before heard of. Ha! Like that was possible.

I went back out the way I'd come in, locked the door and went around the building to get back in the car.

And there, standing at the front door peering in, was a man. One I didn't recognize.

"Hello," I said, walking up to him.

"Hi," he said and turned to me, and I stopped, unable to say anything.

He was dressed in a suit. A light-colored tan one. An expensive-looking one. He sported a pale pink shirt and a paisley tie. He reminded me of my father, but not in a *fatherly* sort of way. Dark. Short-cropped curly hair and the whitest teeth I'd ever seen, and his nails, like my father's, were nicely manicured.

For some reason, just him standing there made my stomach start to flutter.

"The store is closed," he said, like he hadn't expected that.

"I know," I said, smiling.

Why was I smiling? I had to stop.

"We had a water main break. A few stores did. We did. So . . . you know . . . we—they—had to close."

"Oh," he said. I could hear the disappointment in his voice.

I was still smiling, and it seemed it was all I could do. Words certainly weren't forthcoming.

"Do you have any idea when they'll open up, or maybe how I can get in touch with the owners?" he asked.

"Oh." I shook my speechless, thunderstruck gaze off. "I'm the owner. My family is. We are."

What was wrong with me?

"Are you Bronwyn Crewse?"

"Win. Yes. Bronwyn." I swallowed to try to hold down the butterflies and the stuttering. "But you can call me Win."

I didn't know who he was, or what he wanted, but for some reason I was glad he was there.

How weird is that?

He stuck out a hand. I just looked at it. Then up at him. I couldn't quite process what to do with it.

He thrust it out farther. "I'm Dr. Evan Hayes. With Children's Hospital. I'm the chairman of the planning committee and one of the sponsors for the Ice Cream Crawl next summer."

Take the hand, Win, and shake it.

At least some part of me was paying attention.

"Hi," I said. "I thought you were going to call."

"I was out this way, thought I'd stop by and get a taste of the ice cream and meet the owners."

Again, I was at a loss for words. What should I say? "Thank you"?

"Thank you," I said, and then thought, *What am I thanking him for?*

"Are you alright?" he asked.

"Yes." I had to chuckle. I didn't ever remember a man, or anyone, setting me so off-kilter, especially after just meeting them. "Yes. I'm fine. Just a lot of things going on around here is all." I pointed to the store. "We've been closed for a day and a half, and I was just here checking on things. Hoping it won't be long until we can open again."

"Oh," he said, nodding his head. "Okay." He turned back and looked at the door, then back at me. "Maybe we can do this again?

Meet up?" He tipped his head. "I can taste your ice cream that I've heard so much about, maybe over coffee?"

I was nodding like a bobblehead doll.

"And we can discuss the logistics?" he offered.

"I would lov—like that," I said, stumbling over my words. I closed my eyes momentarily to find my balance. "I'd just been thinking about what we could do here as the anchor store and how I would come up with new flavors for the event."

"Okay then." He held his coffee cup out, sealing the deal. "It's a date."

"Yep," I said, loving that he called it that, but hoping that it hadn't shown on my face.

"Okay," he said again. "I'll give you a call." He pulled out his phone and looked at me.

Thank goodness I remembered my phone number. I really was afraid I wouldn't. I rattled it off, he locked it into his phone and asked me did I want to take his. I was certain that my hands were shaking badly enough that I wouldn't be able to get his number in without hitting the wrong digits a bunch of times and him noticing.

"I'll get it when you call," I said, which I knew wasn't the best thing to say. But he smiled. A nice, big smile. And before he got into his car, he looked back at me and smiled again.

I stood there. Not moving. In front of the shop as if I didn't know which way to go, and I watched him drive away. Once he turned the corner, it seemed that whatever hold he had on me lessened and I realized I had been acting—silly.

What the heck . . .

What in the world were those feelings all about?

chapter

THIRTY-EIGHT

I scrambled over to my car feeling—well, rather embarrassed. Climbing in, still in some kind of daze, I took a moment to scold myself. What had gotten into me?

He was nice looking, yes, and he did remind me of my father, but in a not so fatherly way. But what did that mean? Why did it put me so off-kilter?

"Oh brother!" I said and started the car. "I need to get back on track here. It was just a man. One I'm evidently going to have to work with."

That made my stomach take another tumble.

I pulled off and turned down Bell Street. I'd decided to drive by Michael Spirelli's mechanic's garage. Maybe from there I'd be able to gauge how the repair on the water main was going.

Mike's place was dark. No welcoming outside lighting. My truck was no longer on the street and the moat around his building was all dried up. The turned-off hydrant stood isolated and innocent as if it couldn't have ever been the cause of any trouble.

The workers were gone and the hole was covered by a big metal plate. I didn't know what that all meant, but I was crossing my fingers that it was a good sign.

"Now to get rid of that book."

Ever since the Festival, I'd been jittery, and I didn't know if getting rid of that book would calm me any, but I was happy that I wouldn't have it anymore.

I drove around the corner to the Around the Corner Bookshop and parked. Getting out, I grabbed the book out of my knapsack and headed into the store. I was going to dump it, but I thought I should let Amelia know what was scrawled inside on its pages.

"Hi, Win," Amelia said as I came through the door. She stood behind the large wooden counter. "I was just thinking about you."

"You were?" I said.

"For some reason, you asking me where I got that book from stayed in my mind."

"The book?" I looked down at it and back up at her.

"You know, the recipe book." Then she noticed it in my hand and chuckled. "Do you carry it around with you?"

"No." I held it up as I walked over to the counter. "I was going to throw it away, but I thought I should show you first."

"Why?"

"Because it has all these additions to it." I opened up the book and showed her. "There is enough going on around here lately with murder. I just don't want to have a book with whispers of it scrawled inside, even if it does have an inscription to my grandmother."

"Let me see that," she said. She flipped through the pages. "Oh my. Why didn't I notice that before?" She looked at me. "Sorry, Win. I shouldn't have ever had that out."

"It's okay," I said. "I just don't want it." I squinted my eyes. "And I don't think anyone else should have it either."

"I agree," she said and smiled. "No problem. I'll dispose of it."

"Thanks," I said and turned and headed to the door, but before going out, I turned back. "Amelia, I know you said you don't remember where you got it from, and I know this is so random, but by any chance do you think maybe someone named George Draper brought it in?"

"George?"

She only used his first name. That made me wonder . . . "Do you know George Draper?"

"I do, if we're talking about the same George Draper. And he has donated books in the past."

"So you think it might be him?"

"Honestly, I can't remember, but it is possible. He used to live in Chagrin Falls, so he'd come by here often." She lifted a cup to her lips to drink, but then didn't. "Remember," she said instead. "I mentioned him to you? Told you he owned a diner around here in the sixties?"

"Uhm . . . vaguely," I said.

"Come to think of it, I'm almost sure he was a friend of your grandparents."

Of course he was.

"Maybe you could ask your grandfather. If he doesn't remember him, I'm sure he'll remember the diner." She picked up the cup of coffee and took a sip. I could see it was from Java Joe's, but instead of the cardboard sleeve with the food truck logo on it, it was an orange one, the color of their logo. "I'll tell you," she said, swallowing the coffee, "if it was him who did this to this book, the next time I see him, I'm going to give him a piece of my mind. This is terrible."

But I wasn't paying attention to what she'd said. That coffee cup had triggered a memory. One that might just help solve Kaitlyn Toles' murder.

I needed to go and see Detective Liam Beverly.

THE LAST TIME I'd gone to the Village of Chagrin Falls City Hall to see the detective, I had gone to plead my father's innocence. The good detective had narrowed in on him because he had access to the drug that was used in a suspicious demise and because our family had had a beef with the man who had died.

I had to admit, after listening to Maisie and her crazy ideas, I appreciated Detective Beverly's methodology.

And that's why I was going to see him now. I had information that I thought was a good clue to who the murderer was.

I think it's the first clue I'd ever had, too . . .

Like I'd told Cameron, with me and Maisie's investigations, I hadn't ever really figured out who the murderer was in the first two murders. The answer in the first one fell into our laps when the killer answered the phone. The second one only became clear to me when the killer tried to kill me.

I checked my watch. It was nearly eight p.m.

I hoped he was in his office.

The last time I tried to visit him at the station, he hadn't been there. I'd been so anxious to see him, I'd gotten back in my car to wait and had fallen asleep. All the way to the next morning when he knocked on my window.

I pulled into the parking lot of the redbrick, two-story building. The police department was attached to the side of the complex with its own separate entrance. I got out of the car and walked up to the door hoping that he'd not only be there, but he'd be receptive to what I had to say.

"Hello," I said to the desk officer. "I was wondering if I could speak to Detective Liam Beverly. Is he in?"

"Do you have an appointment?"

"Um, no. Didn't know I needed one."

"What's your name?"

"Bronwyn Crewse."

This man hadn't answered one of my questions. I didn't know if Detective Beverly was even in.

"From Crewse Creamery?"

Another question . . .

"Yes. I'm from Crewse Creamery," I said. "Is he in?"

"Have a seat," he said and nodded toward an empty chair along the wall. "I'll see if he can talk to you."

I guessed that meant he was in.

I took my seat, but didn't have to wait long before Detective Beverly appeared in front of me.

"Hi, Bronwyn," he said. "You wanted to talk to me?"

"Yes." I stood up. "If that's okay."

"Sure," he said. "Is it about my nephew?"

"Nephew?" I frowned. "Oh, Quincy? No. No. Not about him."

"Is he doing okay?"

"Yes," I said, nodding. "I enjoy having him on our team. Fast learner. Works well with the public."

He chuckled. "That sounds like something on a résumé." He pointed back toward the way he'd come with his thumb. "You want to go back to my office, or can you tell me what you need here?"

"Your office, if that's okay," I said.

"No problem," he said, stepping aside to allow me to go first.

"I'll follow you," I said.

"Okay." He smiled. "You know, you just caught me. I'll be leaving in about five, ten minutes. Going out with your friend."

"My friend?" I asked.

"O."

"Oh," I said and smiled.

"You know, Morrison." He looked at me questioningly.

"I know who you meant," I said. "I said 'oh' like O-H."

"Oh," he said and chuckled. "You and he are pretty close, huh?"

I didn't know what he was fishing for, but his line was going to come up empty asking me anything about that. Then it made me wonder what O had said to him about me. About us. I knew the two of them were close friends. They'd known each other for years. I was sure Detective Beverly talked to him about cases. I didn't know, though, what else they talked about.

"I came to ask *you* a question," I said instead.

"Okay." He gestured to a chair by his desk. "Shoot."

"How is the investigation into Kaitlyn Toles' murder going?"

He looked at me sideways. "I can't tell you anything about that. Why, do you want to confess to it?"

"Confess! No." I shook my head and closed my eyes. "No. I don't." I blew out a breath and looked at him. "I think I might have something that might help."

"Let's hear it," he said.

"Java Joe's," I said and paused. I wanted to relay my observations to him clearly. I blew out another breath before I started. "They have different sleeves for their—"

"What is a sleeve?"

"The cardboard thing that goes around a to-go coffee cup. To enable you to hold it and not burn your hand."

He nodded his understanding. "Go on."

"So Java Joe's has different sleeves for their cups that are sold on their food truck and the ones they have in their brick-and-mortar stores."

He nodded for me to keep going.

"I saw the one for their food truck at Walnut Wednesday. You know what that is?" I asked.

"I do," he said.

"It has a circular stamp on it and the words 'food truck.' I've been to enough Java Joe's, especially when I lived in New York, to know that one is new. Unique."

"Okay," he said.

"They have several different ones for their stores," I said. "I'm sure you've seen them."

"I have," he said. "They are orange and green like their logo."

"Right," I said, and then nothing else.

"Do you have a point?" he asked.

"Kaitlyn," I said.

He waited for me to say something else. But all of a sudden

what I had to say didn't seem to be that big of a deal and I wondered if I should even be here telling him.

"Go ahead," he said.

"Kaitlyn," I said. I was here now, may as well tell him what I'd come to say. "When she was at the food truck, the sleeve on her coffee cup was from the store. A brick-and-mortar store. But the one she had when she, um, died, was from their food truck. It had the brown cardboard one with the logo stamped on it."

"What are you saying?" he asked, his voice serious, but there seemed to be a gleam in his eye. I didn't know if it was amusement or intrigue.

"That whoever gave Kaitlyn the coffee laced with ethylene glycol got it from the food truck and not a store. I think." I swallowed. "And although I think I may know who did it, according to where that truck was parked, there may be video caught on a nearby surveillance camera. Like the one at the bank." I shrugged. "You know, if it was parked in the triangle."

"Interesting," he said. "But now I have a couple of questions of my own." He leaned in to me. "Do you mind?"

"No," I said, although I was thinking I probably would regret that answer.

"How is it that you know what Kaitlyn ingested?"

My eyes shot up to the ceiling. I hoped something up there might help me come up with an answer. It didn't. I surely couldn't tell him that his nephew told me. Cameron had told me, too, and while he hadn't sworn me to secrecy like the eponymous Quincy had, it probably wouldn't look good for me to let the detective know the cat was out of the bag.

"My second question," he said, saving me, I prayed, from

having to answer the first one, "is why do you think you have information—enough information—to feel you can form an opinion as to who killed Ms. Toles?"

I looked at him. He looked back. I was waiting for him to ask his third question and let me off the hook in answering the second one.

"Seems to me, Ms. Crewse, we should have conducted this conversation in a locked interrogation room. Perhaps with me having"—he slid a yellow legal pad over toward me—"something for you to jot your confession down on."

chapter

❧

THIRTY-NINE

I figured that wouldn't go well.

I walked aimlessly out of the police station with my head down. Detective Beverly had never told me not to meddle in his investigation. At least not in those exact words. He'd even asked me to let him know if I came across information that might help (Maisie took that request to a whole new level). But today, I offered up information showing I'd been sticking my nose into his murder investigation. Something he *did not* like. At all.

I hadn't thought about how bad that would look.

I at least hope he listened to what I had to say.

He didn't ask before he put me out, though, who I thought the murderer was.

I would have offered that information, too. Without hesitation.

Contrary to Maisie's conclusion, I sided with Cameron. My money was on Gary. Especially after seeing those coffee cups and knowing that he was the one who would get her coffee every day. Cameron said Gary knew exactly how she liked it.

"Oops!" someone said.

"Sorry," I said, looking up. I'd bumped into someone, not paying attention to where I was going.

When I looked up, I saw that it was O.

"You ran into me on purpose," I said and smacked him on his chest.

"You've got your head down. Why aren't you watching where you're going?" he asked. He looked over my shoulder at the police station and back at me. "You okay?"

"Yeah," I said and added a smile to prove it. "I was just thinking."

"A penny for your thoughts."

That made me laugh. "You said that the first time I met you."

"I did?" he said. "And did you tell me your thoughts?"

"No," I said. "But I didn't know you then."

"You know me now."

I blew out a breath. "I was in there telling Detective Beverly evidence I've gathered about Kaitlyn Toles' murder."

"Evidence you gathered?" He leaned back to look at me, a grin on his face.

I chuckled. "Yeah, that kinda did sound like it would come out of Maisie and not me."

"What did he think about it?" He nodded. "Your evidence."

"He thought, after he found out what it was, that I might be a good suspect."

"Oh!" He chuckled. "So I guess that didn't go over too well then, huh?"

"Nope," I said. "Not well at all."

He looked at me, into my eyes. "I've missed you," he said. I didn't say anything. I didn't know what to say. Or even that I wanted to say anything. "You know . . ." He tried to fill my silence with hurried words. "Miss seeing you at the ice cream shop."

"Fingers and ice cream scoops crossed that we'll be open soon. Maybe even tomorrow." I held up my hands, showing middle fingers hooked over the pointers of each hand.

"I've stopped by every day to check."

"O," I said, shaking my head. "It hasn't been that long. Only one full day. A half a day that first day."

"I know," he said. He hung his head and looked at a loss for words.

Since I'd met him, he'd been to the ice cream parlor nearly every day. He'd hang out with PopPop and play backgammon or sit in the booth by himself grading papers or preparing a presentation. Never talking much, he'd catch my eye every now and then and offer up a smile.

"I know what you mean, though," I said. "Seems like forever."

"It does," he said. "At least to me."

"Me too." I smiled. "Hey. I heard you were hanging out with the good detective tonight," I said.

"I am," he said. "And if he tries to pin anything on you, I'll tell him I'm your alibi."

"Ahhh!" I said, my eyes getting wide. "You *are* my alibi!"

"Yep. I am. We were together that afternoon. Together at the Balloon Glow."

"We sure were," I said. "Ha! With you on my side, I feel much better now."

He stared at me for a moment, then said, "I guess I better get going."

"Okay," I said. "See you later."

I watched him as he walked away and went inside the police station. Then I looked down at my stomach and placed my hand on it.

Nope. No butterflies.

It didn't matter. I had no time for men or murder.

THE RINGING OF the phone at three forty-five a.m. startled me. I shot straight up, jumped out of my sleep and scrambled out of bed to get my phone. I checked the screen and saw a picture of my PopPop. That made me worried about what a call so early could mean.

"We've got the okay to reopen up the ice cream parlor," he said. "No time to sleep. Time to get up."

Even if I'd known the shop was scheduled to open, I wouldn't have been up that early. But of course, I didn't say that to him. I was raised that you didn't talk back to your elders, and as Pop-Pop would remind me, he'd always be my elder. It didn't matter anyway, I thought as I pulled the cover back, I had ice cream to make.

I showered and dressed with one eye open. I grabbed my knapsack and headed to PopPop's house. It was an hour earlier than my usual morning visit, but after his three o'clock call, I knew he'd be up.

"Morning, little girl," he said, pulling open the door. "I cooked you up a couple of eggs and I've got coffee going."

"I'm not hungry," I yawned.

"Gotta eat something." He picked up a plate he had sitting on the counter and put eggs on it. "I'm sure it's going to be a busy day."

"It is. I have to pick up the food truck and store it, and I'm going to have to make all new ice cream."

"Sounds about right when it comes to the ice cream," he said, putting the plate down in front of me. "Don't think we've ever served ice cream that has sat in the freezer for two days."

"And we won't today either." I smiled up at him and he handed me a fork and a paper towel.

"I can help you get that truck parked if you need me to."

"Okay," I said. "I'll have to check the schedule to see who's coming in today."

"You probably should get them on the phone. Let them know that the store's reopening."

"You're right," I said. "I can't wait to get the store all stocked up again and flip that Closed sign to Open."

"Me too." PopPop went back over to the stove, filled his plate and poured himself a cup of coffee before coming to sit down across from me at the kitchen table.

"What did you do with your day off?" he asked. "Don't get many of those."

I almost choked on my eggs.

He held his forkful of scrambled eggs up to his mouth but didn't eat them.

I really didn't want to say what I'd done, but I couldn't think of a way not to answer that question.

"Riya, Maisie and I went to the South Euclid Lyndhurst Library."

"The Chagrin Falls branch didn't have what you were looking for?"

"We went to a book signing."

"Was it for an author I would know?" he asked.

"Thomasina Bowers," I said.

"That name sounds familiar, what book did she write?"

That stumped me. My eyes rolled up, I was trying to think. "Ummm . . ." I couldn't believe it, I realized I didn't know the name of her book. When Maisie found her, she hadn't said what it was. I didn't notice it at the event at the South Euclid Lyndhurst Library and I never thought to ask anyone about it.

I wasn't going to get out of this one.

"She's Madeline Markham's granddaughter."

I flinched as the words came out. I didn't want PopPop upset with me again.

He nodded, seemingly unfazed, and took a sip of his coffee. "And what did you find out?"

"That the book with all the scrawling in it and Grandma Kay's inscription probably belonged to a man named George Draper."

"George," he said and took another sip of his coffee. "Is that who had it?"

"You know George Draper?" I asked.

"Lasagna." He set his coffee cup down on the table. "He wrote the lasagna recipe."

"You do know George Draper."

"Now I understand why the book inscribed to your grandmother never showed up."

"You do?"

"He lost his wife right before Madeline died. He was a wreck. Sad and depressed. He wouldn't open the mail. Didn't clean his house. Wouldn't eat. His daughter came and got him. Probably saved his life."

"He lives in Cleveland Heights with . . ."

I thought about it. Shannon couldn't be his daughter. She was the same age as I was. And the other member of the household, at least according to the internet, was a woman who was in her seventies.

But I wasn't as concerned about that.

"I wasn't checking up on . . ." I lowered my eyes. I didn't want to do this again with my grandfather. I'd made him sad about this book thing once. That was enough. "We were just wondering who would write the killer . . ." I didn't even say "killer recipes." I didn't want to finish the explanation.

"It's fine," he said.

"We think it might have to do with Kaitlyn's murder," I said, still trying to explain whether I wanted to or not.

"You don't think George did it, do you?" He wiped his mouth on a paper towel.

"No!" I sat up straight in my chair. "We don't think he did it. We've never even met him."

I didn't want to mention that Maisie thought it was one of his relatives. Maybe the daughter of his daughter. The one who'd come and got him.

But then I thought, if Shannon was his granddaughter, and they had all lived in Cleveland Heights, how did she go to school in Chagrin Falls?

"Good." My grandfather brought me out of my reverie. "Because George is a good man. He wouldn't hurt anyone, let alone kill them. Been through a lot. Heard he lost his daughter, too."

"The one that came and got him?"

"Yeah."

"Awww," I said. Then I remembered the Daisy that lived in the household per whitepages.com. She was his age. Same last name. "Did he get married again?"

He nodded. "He did. But it still hurts to lose a wife and a child, no matter how old they are or if things turn out for good."

"I know," I said.

"Come to think of it, she was your mother's sorority sister. A member of Alpha Kappa Alpha."

"Who?"

"His daughter." He closed his eyes. "Let me think—what was her name . . ."

"Wait." I scrunched up my face. "His daughter was an AKA?" That didn't compute.

"Oh. I forgot that would've made her your sister, too, huh?"

"Soror," I said thoughtfully. "We call sorority sisters sorors." I cocked my head to the side. "George Draper is black?"

"He was last time I checked," PopPop said. He stood up, picked up his plate and grabbed mine, taking them over to the sink. "Now, I think we need to get cracking."

"We?"

"I'm going in with you," he said, rolling up his sleeves. He rinsed off the dishes. "Make sure everything is okay. The water's running like it's supposed to."

"Okay," I said. I got his coffee cup and took it over. "You want me to put this in a thermos?"

"That'll be nice," he said. "Top it off with what's left in the pot. I'll put more milk and sugar in it down at the parlor." He put the dishes in the drainboard and shook the water off his hands. "Just let me grab my hat and newspaper and I'll be ready."

"I'll wait right here," I said.

chapter

FORTY

PopPop and I got down to Crewse Creamery, and after checking the water and flushing the toilet, he once again rolled up his sleeves, this time after donning an apron.

"I'll leave you to the fancy stuff," he said, going over to the refrigerator. "I'll make the staples."

"You're making ice cream, PopPop?"

"You don't think I can?"

PopPop hadn't made one tray of ice cream since I'd reopened the ice cream parlor, but he'd been a full-time employee during the more than half century we'd been in business. I had no doubt he could do it.

"You could probably run circles around me," I said. I thought about what I had in the pantry and fridge. What would have kept over our two-day hiatus and what wouldn't have. Nuts and kiwi had long shelf lives and I had picked some of both up the week before the Festival. "I'll make smashed toffee and pralines," I said, remembering I had some toffee candy, "kiwi sorbet and . . ."

"How about you make some carrot cake ice cream?" PopPop said.

"I don't know if I've made that before," I said. "I do remember Grandma Kay making it."

"It's delicious. Gotta be sure to get the carrots done right." He glanced up at me. "The recipe for it is probably in her tin. You got it here?"

I swiped my hands on my apron. "I do," I said. "I'm not sure I have carrots." I was already thinking of the ingredients I needed. I found Grandma Kay's recipe box and riffled through it. "Found it!" I studied the card. It was a carrot cake ice cream with a cream cheese frosting swirl. It had all kinds of written additions, but I was able to figure out the last iteration of it. "I'm not sure if I have carrots," I said again.

I looked up at PopPop and he was looking at me expectantly. "I'm making it," I said and headed over to the fridge.

"I didn't see any carrots in there," he said before I even got to it. "I'll run out and get you some when I finish with my batches."

"What'chya making?" I said, swinging open the refrigerator door.

"French vanilla. Chocolate. Black cherry."

"Mmmm . . . black cherry. Yummy." I was impressed. "We have cherries?"

"I picked some up yesterday. Put them in the fridge."

I looked down and there was a brown bag tucked neatly in a corner.

"You had this all planned, huh?"

"I'm always prepared."

"You need me to get you the recipe card for it?"

"Nope." He tapped his index finger on his temple. "I got it all right here."

We worked for a couple of hours in silence, PopPop almost keeping up with me. He was showing off his culinary skills. I made my first two batches but I needed the carrots to make my last one. PopPop said he'd go to the store. He was working on halving the cherries. I grabbed a butcher knife and went over to help him. Almost done with the bag, there came a knock on the front window.

"Who in the world . . ." PopPop laid down his knife.

I rolled my eyes. I knew exactly who it was. "Cameron," I said and headed toward the front of the store.

"Who?" he said and followed me.

"Cameron Toffey."

"Oh," he said.

I flipped on the lights to the front of the store and unlocked the door. "Cameron," I said, making sure I showed exasperation in my voice. "I have to open the store today."

"How you doing, young man?" PopPop stuck out his hand. "Win and I were just talking about your grandfather. How is he?"

"He's fine, sir," Cameron said and smiled pleasantly.

"Sorry to hear about your grandmother. My Kaylene used to say that she didn't have a green thumb, she had ten green fingers."

Cameron chuckled. "We all miss her a lot."

"Okay. Since we were interrupted," PopPop said. "I'm gonna get Rivkah and go with her to check out her restaurant. First, though, I'll stop and get you some carrots." He looked at me. "You need anything else?"

"Nope. I'm good," I said.

"Nice seeing you again," PopPop said. He turned around and went back into the kitchen, untying his apron and pulling it over his head.

"I didn't know you knew my grandfather," I said, surprised.

"Everyone in Chagrin Falls knows your grandfather," Cameron said. "He was the one who ran the ice cream parlor. Every kid wanted to be his best friend."

I laughed. "I guess that's true."

"Rivkah? Isn't that Mrs. Solomon, who owns the Village Dragon?"

"Yep."

"They dating?"

"I don't know what they're doing. My grandfather says at a certain age you just enjoy the company of others."

"Yeah. I guess that's what happened to my grandmother," he said. "Loneliness. But it worked out okay."

"Is that how you ended up with a 'step'-grandfather?"

He laughed. "Exactly." Then shook his head. "But I just stopped by for any updates."

"Funny you should ask that," I said. "I just went and talked to Detective Beverly last night."

"The detective on the case?" he asked.

"Yeah. I figured out that the cup that Kaitlyn drank out of . . ."

Then it hit me.

Just like that.

I realized I again was all alone with a murderer.

I knew it for a fact this time.

"Is Daisy Draper your grandmother?" I asked.

"Yeah. Do you remember her? She moved from Chagrin Falls after she remarried."

I didn't hear much after he said, "Yeah." Nerves were starting to bubble up in my stomach and I could feel a ball of tension in my head. It started throbbing.

I looked back into the kitchen through the plexiglass window at the door where PopPop had just gone through, wishing he'd turn around and come back.

But turning back, my eyes landing on Cameron, everything about Kaitlyn's murder became crystal clear.

I realized Bobby's concern made me see the truth. Him vocally upset about a possible relationship between our grandfather and Rivkah Solomon. A pairing that Candy had said when she saw them together at the Festival was "perfect."

A relationship my grandfather said was easy to see was nothing more than a genuine appreciation for the other person.

A *mutual* appreciation . . .

Cameron even agreed that his grandmother had gotten lonely. He didn't say anything about love.

But there had been no love or mutual *anything* between Kaitlyn and Cameron. Not from what I'd seen. And not one of two people so in love that they were set to spend their lives together.

Candy had called the two of them together "toxic."

I knew now, Cameron was standing in front of me telling me lies. That was what he'd been telling me since the day Kaitlyn died. Lies.

All lies.

"Why are you looking at me like that?" Cameron asked. A grin appeared on his face. But it wasn't the one he'd usually shared with me. It was sinister. His head turned to one side, he was walking around like I was his prey.

He wasn't going to marry Kaitlyn. No, take that back, *she* wasn't going to marry *him*.

He hadn't known she'd gotten the job and was moving to New York.

How could they have been dating and he not know that?

He was still seeing Shannon. She went to his apartment after the funeral and it seemed that he was the babysitter. To the son they shared. Now that I knew who Daisy was, I understood she was a fixture in his grandfather's home. *Step*-grandfather. And how could he be waiting for Kaitlyn to start his family like he'd told me on Walnut Wednesday? He already had a son.

And Kaitlyn's sister, Melissa, and even her parents, didn't seem too keen on him. I couldn't imagine Kaitlyn going against her parents and marrying him. Not after all the things I'd learned about her.

"I'm not looking at you any certain way," I said. I lowered my eyes and stepped back from him. I knew my eyes would betray me. They would tell him that I knew. I knew that he'd killed Kaitlyn.

It was why he'd been coming around me. Wanting me to help him figure out who did it. After him thinking I'd solved the other Chagrin Falls murders, he was afraid I would figure it out.

"You know, don't you?"

"No." I shook my head. "I don't know anything," I said. My mouth had gotten so dry, I could hardly get the words out.

"I thought you told me you wouldn't be able to figure out who the murderer was. You didn't know before. Remember you said that? You said that you only knew because they told you." He leaned his head to the side. "Did you lie to me?"

I shook my head vigorously. "I haven't figured this one out either."

"Then why do you look so nervous?"

I swallowed. "I don't. I'm not nervous."

"You do." He narrowed his eyes and stared at me. He circled around the floor, not once letting his eyes stray from me. "I thought you believed it was Gary."

"I did," I said.

"But what? Not now? You don't think so now?"

"I d-d . . . do."

"Listen, you can't get the words out, can you? You were never good at lying."

"I went to tell Detective Beverly that I thought it was Gary," I admitted. Hoping it would convince him. "Last night."

"Did you tell him?"

"H-he thought maybe I was a better suspect."

Cameron laughed. "So did I. Or at least someone in your family. Whenever your trash gets picked up, if it hasn't already, they'll find a bottle of antifreeze sitting right alongside the receptacle."

"What?" I snorted out the word. I was so nervous, I could hear myself breathing.

He shrugged. "That's why I needed your help going over to Spirelli's Garage. I needed to get that container. Figured planting it at your place would be better. Now, to make sure you aren't able to convince anyone of anything different, you know what's gotta happen, right?"

How did I keep getting myself into these situations?

I thought about that sleeve on Kaitlyn's cup. I'd touched it when she was at the truck. My fingerprints were on it. But that wasn't the cup with the poison in it. That cup was the one lying at her feet. The one with the sleeve from Java Joe's food truck. I was sure of that.

I'd lived in New York nearly five years, and never got mugged or assaulted. Not even a prank phone call with heavy breathing. I come home, according to Wikipedia, to one of the safest cities in the nation and I run into three murderers who all want to kill me, too.

Why was this happening to me!

Then I remembered that Kaitlyn had shoved one of the coffee cups into my mother's hand. Had it been the one from Java Joe's food truck? The one with the poison in it?

An antifreeze bottle in our trash. My fingerprints as well as my mother's all over the cups.

That couldn't be good . . .

"Hey! I'm talking to you." He stepped toward me, and I leaped back at least three steps.

"I hear you," I said. "I'm listening."

"Then answer me," he said.

"Um . . . I—I . . ." I looked at him. "I don't know what you asked me." I felt the tears streaming down my face. "I'm sorry."

"I said"—his lips were tight and he spoke through clenched teeth—"I'm going to have to keep you from talking."

"Keep me from talking?" I couldn't even process his words. "Talking about what?"

"Don't play with me, Win."

My eyes went down to his hands. No gun. No knife. No weapon like what the other two who'd tried to kill me had had.

But I had a knife. Back on the prep table in the kitchen. The one I'd been using to help PopPop halve the cherries. The knife he'd been using was there, too.

I glanced to the back. If only I could get to them. To one of them.

"My PopPop's coming right back," I said.

Cameron shook his head. "I heard him say where he was going. He won't be right back."

"Wha-what are you going to do? Poison me, too?" I asked.

He held out his hand. "Do I have anything here to poison you with?" He shook his head. "Don't be ridiculous. But I do think you're going to have to come with me."

I glanced out of the window. It was still dark out. The street was quiet, and I knew if I went out that door with Cameron, no one was going to see me.

"I'm not going anywhere with you," I said with all the bravado I could muster. "You'll have to kill . . ." I swallowed. "Do whatever it is you're going to do to me here."

"Win," he said, talking to me like I was a defiant child. He tilted his head to the side. "I don't think you can stop me from doing what I want."

"I am sure going to try," I said. I'd made up my mind that this was probably the day I was going to die. But I wasn't going down without a fight. "Don't think it'll be easy for you, Cameron."

He smiled at me. "You always did think you could beat me."

"Hey! You've got the sign switched to Closed, but with all the lights on and the door unlocked, people are going to think you're open." O came in the door. Talking over the bell jangling, he seemed to be announcing himself.

My eyes welled up with tears, and this time I did feel butterflies. Him walking in made all the tension that had consumed me leave. I didn't know if O had a weapon, or any martial arts skills like Riya, but his presence made me know it was going to be okay. It changed my mind. I wasn't going down. Not by Cameron's hands.

"Well, look at this," Cameron said. A cocky smile on his face. "Now I'm going to have to kill the both of you."

Evidently, O's appearance hadn't changed Cameron's mind . . .

chapter

FORTY-ONE

The bell over the door jingled again.

This time it was Detective Beverly with two police officers.

He stood next to O and gave him a nod. "I got this," he said. "Thanks."

O nodded and took a step back.

"I didn't do it," I said, tears streaming down my face, spittle coming out with my words. "I thought it was Gary who'd killed Kaitlyn." I was sobbing. "You know, the cameraman. But it wasn't. It was Cameron."

"It's okay, Win," O said. "That's why he's here."

I looked at O and back at the detective. "You know? You know it's Cameron?"

Detective Beverly put his hands on his hips, revealing the gun holstered on the one side. "We were beginning to think it was," he said, not taking his eyes off Cameron. "The evidence has started pointing his way. That video you told me to check on the Java Joe's truck helped." He nodded a smile at me. "But it looks like you put all the pieces together before we did."

"Not all of them," I said. "I didn't think it was Cameron. At least not then."

Cameron put up his hands. "Listen, man, I don't know what you're talking about," Cameron said. "I called it right at the Balloon Glow. Win did it. And if I were you, and wanted to solve this thing, I'd take a look outside by her trash. I saw it there, not sure if Win or her grandfather has gotten rid of it since, but it was a container of antifreeze. Probably the same that killed my fiancée."

"She wasn't your fiancée," I said, my shoulders shaking now from my tears. "She didn't want you. That's why you killed her."

"Whoa!" Cameron said and looked at Detective Beverly. "She's talking crazy. She always had a thing against me. Since high school. But this is . . ." He shook his head. "Far-fetched even for her."

"We'll see about that, Cameron, although I do tend to trust Win when it comes to catching the killer," the good detective said.

"You can trust me," I said, sniffing back my tears of fear. "You can watch Gary's video. And talk to Cameron's grandfather. He'll probably know something, too. He's the one who had the book."

"He's my *step*-grandfather," Cameron said, right before he took off running to the back of our store.

He didn't get far. There were police officers standing by the side door, who caught him before he could get anywhere.

It seemed that on their boys' night out, Detective Beverly and O had discussed the Chagrin Falls police investigation into

Kaitlyn Toles' murder and a list of suspects. They'd discussed how, statistically, more than 50 percent of the women murdered in the United States are killed by intimate partners or *ex*-partners, but they were still simmering over that idea.

And O, coming by early, saved my life. He had stopped by, so he said, because he wanted to check to see if we were opening. Said he'd heard that the water main was fixed. How he was "stopping" by when he didn't live or work anywhere near the store gave everyone more fodder to tease me about him.

But thank goodness he had. And it was a good thing he'd recognized Cameron's car from the day we'd seen him drive recklessly wanting to park it during the Festival. After that, coupled with the conversation about significant others being the murderer, he thought I might need some help.

Unfortunately, the amateur, me, figured it out first. Who would have thought? Well, okay. Maisie would have thought that, and she was going to be upset that she missed the whole "revealing the murderer" scene. And it seemed that was why Gary, the Grey Wolf, wanted to know if I had found out anything about the murder yet. He wanted to work on solving it, too. He worried about her getting hold of a cup with poison in it because it had always been his job to ensure she got her Java Joe's fix. He figured there must've been some sort of switcheroo going on. That was why he'd been looking at the footage of Kaitlyn when I visited the news station. He thought he might have captured on camera when that happened and who did it.

He didn't call himself the Grey Wolf for nothing.

And lucky for Detective Beverly's investigation, Java Joe's food truck had been parked close to the bank's ATM. The ATM that Cameron had gotten cash out of so as not to leave a trail, and the one that caught him buying the coffee with the food truck sleeve.

Cameron told the police that he'd planned on pinning it on me. Getting a hot fudge sundae, which he knew she loved, from our store and adding the poison, but she had beat him to it and gotten the ice cream herself. So he'd gotten the antifreeze from his grandfa—well, *step*-grandfather's garage. He'd tried to pass it off as coming from Spirelli's, but changed his mind, for whatever reason. The day I "helped" him snoop at Mike Spirelli's garage, he stashed it in the back of my food truck. But since I was leaving the truck there to be serviced, he had to bring it to our store. That's why he'd kept a close watch on me, trying to help push his narrative of me being the culprit.

Because of her sweet tooth and the spoonfuls of table sugar she piled into every cup, Kaitlyn never knew the syrupy taste was ethylene glycol and not sucrose.

The detective, being the professional sleuth that he was (as opposed to Maisie and me and our amateurish antics, which always seemed to put me in the line of fire), found out that Mr. Draper had kept a container of antifreeze in his garage, as he told the police officer, "For at least five years."

Cameron was the author of the additions to the cookbook. It was after making the lasagna from the *Recipes of Chagrin Falls* cookbook by Madeline Markham, and serving it to Kaitlyn with some red wine and a proposal, which she promptly declined. And that was why the lasagna recipe was the only one without any changes. Cameron, who threw the recipe book away, according to Mr. Draper, didn't anticipate that he'd take it out of the trash, hoarder that he was, and donate it to the Around the Corner Bookshop.

Life went back to normal at the ice cream parlor. Maisie's blisters healed, and although she came back to work, she decided to keep Felice at home with her. Over much objection by me. And my bout with the butterflies just didn't seem to end. While O was hanging around, his presence reminding me of just how grateful I'd been to him for coming in and saving me from Cameron, Dr. Evan Hayes called and asked me out to dinner.

I was sure it was to talk business, but the butterflies in my stomach had a different idea about it.

Acknowledgments

I thank my God for seeing me through this last year, seeing the other side of it and the ability to persevere. My mother for shaping me into the person that I am and showing me what it means to be family.

Chagrin Falls, Ohio, is a wonderful little village that I am happy to live near. I want to thank all the wonderful people there, the great neighbors and community, for giving me such an awesome backdrop for my story. (So sorry for having all my murders happen there!)

As always, I can't thank enough my online and in-person writing community. I couldn't make it without you. Thank you for your inspiration, critique and help in making it all happen. Writing is not a solitary endeavor. You need a writing family, and I have the best one a writer could ask for.

And of course I want to say thank you to my team at Penguin

Berkley. They are so patient with me when it's time for decisions and deadlines and are always supportive. Thank you, Jess and Miranda. And to my cover artist, Vi-An Nguyen, you rock! My covers are so awesome. I get so much love over them! Thank you! And the rest of the team—thank you.

Crewse Creamery

⤸⤷

ICE CREAM RECIPES

For these recipes, you don't need an ice cream machine. But if you do use one, be sure to follow the manufacturer's instructions. And if you don't have one, remember to use whipped cream to create a better texture. It'll take a little longer for your mixture to freeze properly, but it'll be fine. Just check on it every couple of hours and give it a good stir.

Here are a few other tips before you get started:

TIP #1: When it comes to the milk you add, embrace the fat content. Low-fat products don't freeze as well, don't taste as good and give the ice cream an icy texture. Always use heavy cream, whole milk or half-and-half.

TIP #2: If you use an ice cream maker, never pour your warm (or even room-temperature) base into your ice cream machine. A base that isn't chilled prior to going into your ice cream maker won't freeze. The colder, the better!

TIP #3: Don't overfill your ice cream machine. Remember, liquids expand as they freeze, and if your machine is filled to the top, it will end up spilling over the sides. Fill it no more than three-quarters of the way full.

TIP #4: Don't over churn your ice cream. The ice cream will start to freeze as it churns in your machine, but it won't freeze to the right consistency. Churning too much will cause your ice cream to have an icy texture. Churn just enough until the mixture is thick, about the consistency of soft serve, before transferring it to the freezer.

Aloysius and Kaylene's Favorite Pralines and Cream Ice Cream

❧

Pralines

½ cup brown sugar

¼ cup granulated sugar

¼ cup heavy cream

2 tablespoons butter

Salt, to taste

1 cup pecans

Caramel sauce

1 cup granulated sugar

¼ cup water

½ cup heavy cream

6 tablespoons unsalted butter

1 teaspoon vanilla

Pinch of salt

Small glass jar with lid

Ice cream

1¼ cups milk

2 teaspoons vanilla extract

1 cup granulated sugar

Pinch of salt

2 cups heavy cream

To make the pralines, combine brown sugar, granulated sugar, cream, butter and salt in a skillet over medium heat. Bring to a boil and continue to boil for three to four minutes to start caramelization. Use a wooden spoon to stir in the pecans until they are coated. Remove from heat. Keep stirring until the candy coating cools. Spoon onto a parchment-lined baking sheet to cool completely.

To make the caramel sauce, combine sugar and water in a medium-sized saucepan over medium heat. Stir until the sugar dissolves and continue cooking without stirring until mixture turns amber colored, eight to twelve minutes. Slowly mix in cream and continue simmering until mixture is smooth, two to three minutes. Then add in butter, vanilla and salt. Set aside to cool. Pour into glass jar to cool completely and thicken.

To make the ice cream, combine milk, vanilla and sugar in a medium saucepan over medium heat. Stir occasionally until the sugar completely dissolves. Take off heat and add salt. Allow to steep and cool. Whisk in cream. Cover with plastic wrap and place in fridge about two hours, until completely chilled. Using an ice cream maker, add the chilled ice cream base and churn according to the manufacturer's instructions. Once the mixture has thickened, add the pralines and about ¼ cup of caramel sauce. Continue churning until well mixed. Place in a freezer-proof container and freeze for at least two hours.

Enjoy!

Riya's Disapproving Blood Orange Sherbet

❧

2 cups blood orange juice, strained (about 10 blood oranges)

1 cup sugar

Juice of 1 lemon (about ¼ cup)

¼ teaspoon salt

1 tablespoon blood orange zest

¾ cups heavy cream, chilled

Combine the blood orange juice, sugar, lemon juice, salt and zest. Whisk until smooth. Chill about two hours in the refrigerator, then add cream. Pour mixture into an ice cream maker and churn according to manufacturer's instructions. Place in a freezer-proof container and freeze for at least three hours.

Enjoy!

Kaitlyn Toles' Mocha Fudge Ice Cream

1 cup whole milk

⅔ cups sugar

1 teaspoon vanilla extract

1½ cups half-and-half

3 tablespoons instant coffee

1 teaspoon unsweetened cocoa powder

2 cups heavy cream

4 ounces dark chocolate, coarsely chopped

Combine milk and sugar in a medium saucepan over medium heat. Stir occasionally until the sugar completely dissolves. Add vanilla, half-and-half, coffee and cocoa. Stir until combined. Remove from heat and whisk in cream. Let cool. Cover with plastic wrap and place in the fridge for about two hours, until completely chilled. Using an ice cream maker, add the chilled ice cream base and churn according to the manufacturer's instructions. Once mixture thickens, add chocolate. Place in a freezer-proof container and freeze for at least two hours.

Enjoy!

Read on for an excerpt from the first installment of
Abby Collette's delectable Books & Biscuits Mystery Series

Body and Soul Food

Available now!

He put his foot in those greens."

Reef stopped and looked at me. Hand hovering midway between bowl and open mouth. A forkful of collards dangling. Juice dripping. His eyes went from mine to Koby's flip-flop-clad feet to the dark, limp greens in front of him. "You mean like they do with grapes?" Scraping his teeth across the surface of his tongue, he stuck it out and scrunched up his face. "Ugh! Is that how you make 'em?"

A bright, sun-filled afternoon, we were out back of our soon-to-be bookstore and café. We'd put out three umbrellaed wooden tables with our logo in the bricked alleyway and scattered brightly colored potted plants around.

"No." Koby pursed his lips and shook his head at me. "That's not how I make them. She just learned that term," he said, and chuckled. "It's just a saying, Reef. You know. You say it about the person who cooked something that's really good."

"So you didn't actually *stick* your feet in 'em?" Not moving his head although talking to Koby, Reef rolled his eyes my way.

"Nope." Koby was sitting on one of the benches with the head of his yellow Labrador retriever, Remy, resting on his lap. "Not literally." He grinned and scratched Remy's head and around his torn ear. "My feet"—he held up a hand like he was swearing—"at no time during the cooking of those collard greens were anywhere near them."

Satisfied, Reef slurped the greens from his fork and covered his mouthful of food with his fist. "Man! These are good." He smacked his lips before shoveling in more, letting everyone in earshot know how much he liked them.

"You've mentioned that with each mouthful," I said, and laughed.

"Because they are." He chewed while he talked. The grin on his face matched the one Koby was wearing. "Even if you did try to sabotage my enjoyment." He narrowed his eyes at me. "Bad sister."

Koby laughed. "Don't call my sister bad."

"Koby," Reef said, swallowing his food, his laugh almost causing him to choke. "You know Keaton's my girl." He winked at me. "But what I don't get is why haven't you ever made these for me before?"

"I'm not in the habit of cooking for you, Reef."

"Well, you should, bro. Even if you need to stick your feet in them. I mean, even the juice is good."

"Guess what the juice is called," I said.

Reef looked down in his bowl and swirled the brownish-green liquid around. "Okay, I'll bite. What is it called, Keaton?"

"Pot liquor," I said.

Reef mouthed the words as he sat on the picnic bench next to my brother. "Didn't you cook 'em in water? I thought you said you put them in a pot of water. You know I don't drink anymore."

"I did cook them in water," Koby said. "It's just another word that Keaton's learned. You'd think as a librarian, her vocabulary would be broader."

Reef laughed.

"Gotcha," I said. As much as Reef teased me, it was fun to get him.

"Koby Hill and Keaton Rutledge." Reef held up his plastic bowl and winked at me. "Here's to your new venture together. If all the food is as good as what I've sampled so far, it is definitely going to be a success." He turned up his bowl and downed the juice.

Koby Hill was my twin brother. Fraternal. Of course. But there's a story to why we have different last names. One that tends to tug on the heartstrings of whomever we tell.

Born July 2, twenty-five years ago. As far as we know, the only two children of one Morie Hill, age twenty-two.

And as it was to be our fate, on July 3, two years later, we were separated after having our last birthday together the day before. Abandoned, maybe orphaned, I was soon adopted. Koby wasn't. That's how he still got to keep our biological mother's last name. Or our father's. We weren't sure about that either because we knew nothing about him. Yet.

Koby had grown up in foster care. I didn't find out about him until he showed up at my door, a DNA kit in hand. "Just to make sure," he'd said. But standing there looking at each other, neither one of us had any doubt. We knew right then that there was an incontrovertible bond between us. And the resemblance was obvious. We had no idea whom we looked like, but we definitely looked like each other. Light skin, full lips, big eyes and long lashes. He was taller than me by nearly a half a foot, one of our few differences. Our hair was sandy brown, and it had Koby questioning if we were biracial. Then his DNA came back, knocking that idea down. According to our countries of origin, we were Black.

We found each other shortly after my dad died. Koby's appearance in my life was just what I needed to pull me through my grief.

My father had left me a little nest egg, and with Koby's help, we found my house in Timber Lake after I landed the library job. That was when I first found out that my twin brother was a phenomenal chef. He'd come over and hang out, cook me food and borrow from my bookshelf as if it were part of the county's library system.

It was a late-fall evening, over a big bowl of creamy, cheesy grits with big juicy blackened shrimp, that I found out about his dream. I had told him he should open a restaurant.

"You could clean up!" I said. "Everyone would come and eat your food."

"I've been thinking about doing that. With you," he'd said. "Ever since I was thirteen. That's when I first went to Mama Zola's, and she let me hang out in the kitchen with her."

"Doing it with me?" I placed an open palm on my chest. "You didn't know me when you were thirteen. How did you think you would have a business with me?"

"I knew I would find you."

"And did you think I would be able to help you cook? Because I can't cook."

"You wouldn't cook."

"What would I do?"

That was when he pulled out a tattered folded picture from his wallet. He must have found it in a magazine. The color had started to rub off.

"It's a bookstore and café." He gently passed the picture over to me. "A soul food café."

"A bookstore café?"

"No. A bookstore *and* a café. One business, two sides. You would run the bookstore. Which is perfect for you. I would run the restaurant."

I stared down at the picture. An archway separated the two sides, but books were everywhere. "And did you know at thirteen I was going to be a librarian?"

"I *learned* to cook, but my love of books was innate." He touched his heart. "I was sure you'd have that same love, too."

And he was right. My love of books came from deep inside. Going to the library was one of my first memories.

Koby had had a clear vision for Books & Biscuits. It had been his idea in the first place. And even though I had just started my first job as a librarian, it didn't take much for him to talk me into it. I could hear my father, who, at the time, hadn't too long before become my guardian angel, telling me to go ahead, spread my wings, because he knew I was ready to take on the world.

Koby had known about me all along, and after that conversation, I found that once he learned about me, he'd made plans for our lives to be spent together. Sure, he didn't know my name, but he knew I was somewhere out there.

That was thanks to Reef Jeffries. The man who'd been stopping by to help us get our new soul food and book café up and running. Yep, I decided to partner with my brother to fulfill the dream he had for the two of us. The money my dad had left helped us to do that.

But anyone who stopped by while we were getting the bookstore and café up and running would have thought that Reef was in on the deal. He was always dropping by, and usually, like now, it ended with him eating up whatever Koby was working on in the kitchen.

Six years older than us, Reef had remembered that when Koby came to the group home, he hadn't come alone. A sister had been with him. Koby decided to find me. Starting at thirteen, he tracked down people who might have known us, dug through county records that might have documented our hazy history and googled whatever information he'd come up with to find any links that might lead him to me. And thanks to all his sleuthing, eventually, somehow, he did.

Unfortunately, the only branches popping up on that genealogy website after I got my results back for us were the ones that linked us to each other. That was enough for me. But not Koby.

Koby wanted to find our biological mother. I didn't care about it. About her. I figured I just had two mothers. One I knew. One I didn't. I couldn't imagine my life any different or any better by knowing about the one who'd given birth to us. The one who'd given us away. I had Imogene Rutledge. The best mother anyone could ask for. Adoptive or otherwise. I didn't have any need to find out more. But for Koby, Morie Hill was the only mother he'd ever had, and he needed to know what had happened to her.

A beeping sound interrupted my thoughts.

"What's the alarm for?" It had gotten Koby's attention, too, but he needed to know what it was about.

"Man, mind your business." Reef laughed. He pulled his cell phone out of his pocket and silenced the alarm.

"You got an appointment?" Koby raised his eyebrows. "Maybe you need a reminder not to eat up all our food? I'm all for that." Koby was enjoying ribbing his friend.

"Always trying to be a detective," Reef said. Shaking his head, he stuffed the phone back in his pocket.

"You hiding something?"

"It's a reminder to take my pill. You know, my vitamin. I am so absentminded lately that I forgot to bring the vitamins with me," Reef said. He dismissed the alarm and dug into his pocket. He pulled out a red-and-white round peppermint candy and popped it into his mouth. He was always sucking on those minty hard candies. "Now you know all my flaws. I stopped drinking. I'm taking vitamins. My short-term memory is shot. But I'm trying to be healthier."

"Koby, come and see what I've done."

Our attention was drawn away from Koby and Reef's banter to the back door. Georgie was standing in it. Our only employee so far, she'd come to report her progress in the kitchen.

Georgie Tsai had pale skin and black hair, and her entire left arm and right lower leg were covered in colorful tattoos. Green. Red. Blue. Her body said more than she did.

After she'd worked for us for a few weeks, I wasn't sure she'd work out, and I was ready to let her go. Her nose was always stuck in the books we'd ordered when she should have been placing them on the refurbished bookshelves we'd painted white. I didn't want to have the headache she was sure to cause after we opened. But my softhearted brother took her hand, literally, led her to the kitchen and put her to work. "We've already hired her," he said to me later. "She's counting on us, just like we're counting on her. How about if we give her another chance?"

Koby had Georgie learning recipes, helping him pick out plates and flatware, painting walls, setting up tables and putting up groceries. She hadn't missed a beat with him.

"Something to show me?" Koby said, standing up. He walked over to the door. "Okay. Let's see what you've done." He placed a hand on her shoulder and turned her around. "Lead the way." Remy followed right behind him. Koby stopped and patted Remy on the head. "You know you can't come in the kitchen." He held out a hand for him to sniff. "Stay." He lowered his hand and Remy sat. "You stay here. Okay?"

I followed. I hadn't been given any commands to the contrary. Plus, butterflies took flight in my belly whenever I was alone with Reef. But I was doing my best to calm all the nerves because I liked him hanging around.

Inside, I looked at the stack of boxes and books scattered everywhere and let out a huff. I needed to get to work.

The bookstore and the eatery were separated by a wide, curved archway. Each of us in charge of one side. My side was the bookstore. I had books to shelve and cozy little corners and nooks to fashion for browsing and reading. Koby had the kitchen and café seating area.

Our first tasting party and the official opening were fast approaching, and I wasn't ready. I had grand ideas that took a lot longer to execute than it did for Koby to put up groceries and set up the tables and chairs. His motto was to keep it simple. I could learn a thing or two from him.

The new furniture I'd ordered was still covered in plastic. The new wood floor was covered in drop cloths because we still needed to finish painting the walls and crown molding I had added to create ambience.

"I'm going to head out," Reef said. He'd come in behind me, thrown his disposable plastic bowl into the big trash can we kept in the middle of the room. He brushed his hands together, then stuck them down in the pockets of his blue jeans. Walking over to me, his eyes locked with mine. He came and stood right next to me, brushing his bare arm against me. I could feel his warm breath on my face and smell peppermint when he turned to talk to me.

"Tell Koby," he said, "if he needs me to try any more dishes you guys are thinking of adding to the menu, to call me." Then he leaned in closer. "But *you* can call me anytime. For anything."

I wasn't able to speak until he had moved away from me. And then I wasn't sure if my voice was even audible.

He stood at the door. Hand on knob and a grin on his face.

"I—I thought you were going to help me . . ." I cleared my throat. "You know, finish unpacking books," I said, and gestured to the stacked boxes.

"I thought you were going to come hear me play my sax. I'm going to be at the Hemlock Jazz Club Friday."

"The one on Lake Street?"

"Yup." He smiled. Tilting his head, he gave me another wink. "But don't bring your brother when you come. I don't want him coming and messing up us having a good time."

"I don't . . . I don't know if . . ." Blushing, I lowered my head, lifting my eyes, looking toward the kitchen to make sure Koby hadn't heard him. He didn't like Reef flirting with me. He'd just started doing it, or maybe I just started noticing it.

But I didn't mind it at all.

"Okay." I finally stopped stumbling over my words and gave him an answer. I wondered, did he consider this meetup a *date* . . .

"Good. I'll come pick you up. Friday," he said, and nodded to confirm before he flipped the lock and left.

Swinging my eyes away from the door, I caught sight of a man out of the corner of my eye. Bent over one of the low book-cases, he stood up, three or four books in his hand he'd evidently taken from the ones I'd already shelved. He placed them on top of a pile of books I'd just taken out of a box. He looked surprised to see me.

I felt the same way about him. *Where had he come from?*

"Who are you?" I asked. I wasn't frightened. I always felt safe when my brother was around.

"Pete."

Pete had on a trench coat, and when he raised a hand up to cover the cough that erupted when he told me his name, I saw he was holding a Totes umbrella. Unusual for these parts. Timber Lake hadn't seen anything but blue skies for the last week and a half, not a drop of rain in sight. But I guess it was always good to be prepared.

Everything about Pete was odd. From his lopsided haircut to

his ruddy complexion, Hello Kitty book bag hanging off one shoulder, to the misbuttoned blue shirt he wore underneath his open coat.

Cocking my head to the side, I blew out a breath. "Pete," I said, making my voice even and calm. "We're not open yet." I waved my hand around. "Not for another week. Maybe you can come back then?" I let my eyes rest on the books he'd put down.

"I'm here for a job," he said. "To help get everything, you know, in order and then afterward, too."

"A job?" I hadn't listed anywhere that we were hiring. I shook my head, trying to understand. "How did you get in?" I asked. Which, in hindsight, should have been my first question. I knew the double front doors had been locked. We'd just finished painting them and cleaning the windowpane inserts with Windex and newspaper that morning. No one had been in or out. At least not through that door.

"The girl with the tattoos." Pete gestured with his head toward the front door. "She let me in."

"Georgie?" I frowned. She hadn't said one word to us about anyone else coming here.

"I don't know her name."

"So who is this?" Koby was standing in the archway. He was drying his hands with a red-and-white-checkered tea towel. He smiled at the stranger.

"I'm Pete." The man said his name again for Koby.

"You got a last name, Pete?" Koby asked.

"Only if I'm getting hired."

At that, an impromptu interview with Pete commenced with everyone still standing in the middle of the floor. Koby did all the talking, including me only at the end to ask if I had something to add. Twenty minutes after I'd found him loitering in our yet-to-be-open bookshop café, Pete, last name Howers, was hired and helping me put books on the shelves.

My brother was always picking up strays, like that rescue dog that he took everywhere with him. He said that's what we were—strays—and that I should be more flexible about helping out others like us find their place in this world, especially seeing that someone had been kind enough to give me a home.

Wall Street Journal bestselling author ABBY COLLETTE loves a good mystery. She was born and raised in Cleveland, and it's a mystery even to her why she hasn't yet moved to a warmer place. As Abby Collette, she is the author of the Ice Cream Parlor Mystery series, about a millennial MBA-holding granddaughter running a family-owned ice cream shop in Chagrin Falls, Ohio, and the Books & Biscuits Mystery series, starring a set of fraternal twins who reunite and open a bookstore and soul food café. Writing as Abby L. Vandiver, she is the author of the Logan Dickerson Mysteries, featuring a second-generation archaeologist and a nonagenarian, as well as the Romaine Wilder Mysteries, pairing an East Texas medical examiner and her feisty, funeral-home-owning auntie as sleuths. Abby spends her time writing, facilitating writing workshops at local libraries and hanging out with her grandchildren, each of whom is her favorite.

CONNECT ONLINE

AbbyCollette.com
 AuthorAbbyL.Vandiver
 AbbyLVandiver
 AbbyVandiver

Ready to find
your next great read?

Let us help.

Visit prh.com/nextread